GETTING EVEN

OTHER BOOKS AND AUDIOBOOKS

BY CLAIR M. POULSON

I'll Find You
Relentless
Lost and Found
Conflict of Interest
Runaway
Cover Up
Mirror Image
Blind Side
Evidence
Don't Cry Wolf
Dead Wrong
Deadline
Vengeance
Hunted
Switchback
Accidental Private Eye
Framed
Checking Out
In Plain Sight
Falling
Murder at TopHouse
Portrait of Lies
Silent Sting
Outlawered
Deadly Inheritance
The Search
Suspect
Short Investigations
Watch Your Back
Fool's Deadly Gold
Pitfall
Kingfisher

GETTING EVEN

A SUSPENSE NOVEL

CLAIR M. POULSON

Covenant Communications, Inc.

Cover image: *Silhouette of Modern Man Running in Woods* © Magdalena Russocka, Trevillion Images.

Cover design by Kimberly Kay © 2020 by Covenant Communications, Inc.

Published by Covenant Communications, Inc.
American Fork, Utah

Printed in the United States of America
First Printing: February 2021

28 27 26 25 24 23 22 21 10 9 8 7 6 5 4 3 2 1

ISBN 978-1-52441-430-6

CHAPTER ONE

Emil Eifler's short and skinny stature did him no favors in that moment as the full force of Devonte's threat hit him. Devonte Grillo was extremely angry. "It's not my problem how you collect from your clients," he said, glaring at Emil. "But it is your problem how and when you pay *me*. I don't know why I let you have stuff on credit, but it isn't happening anymore. I only did it because you begged me, if you recall. Well, begging won't help now. And there's one more thing: I think you're skimming off some of what you owe me." He stepped closer and shoved a finger at Emil's face. "Nobody steals from me."

Devonte was six feet tall and stocky with large muscles. His black hair was combed straight back from his forehead, and his narrow face held a neatly trimmed beard and moustache. If one could see his heart, it must also have been black. He was a dangerous man. He took his business seriously, and when a small-time drug pusher like Emil did not pay after being granted a special favor, or skimmed some of the proceeds, Devonte would breathe out threats, and he meant every word.

"I haven't skimmed anything. I promise you that. I'm an honest businessman," Emil said.

Devonte snorted. "You're also a liar."

"I'll get you the money in a couple days," Emil said, his whole body trembling. "I've got some guys who owe me, and I'll get the money from them right away."

Devonte stared at him, threat pouring from his eyes. "If you want to give credit, that's up to you, but you will not use that as an excuse to not pay me on time. You're an idiot. Pay tonight, and I want to see some extra to make up for what you've been stealing. Go get the money and get everything paid to me tonight. You get no more product until you pay and then only if you have the cash."

"But I need it today. I have guys who depend on it or they get angry," Emil begged. "Let me have some up front one more time, and I won't ask again. I'll be able to pay you if you do."

"Your customers won't be as angry as me," Devonte said. "Tonight, Emil. Pay up and bring extra cash if you need more product. I'll let you know where to meet me with the money."

"I'll get the money," Emil promised even as he wondered how he would. His problem was that he not only sold drugs to a number of people in the Carbon County area, but he personally used some of what he'd gotten from Devonte. Emil knew that it was stupid to be using the stuff he was supposed to be selling, but he was hooked, and his habit caused him to make stupid mistakes. He was a serious addict as well as a pusher. He was sober now but also scared. He had to find a way to make enough from his customers to pay for his own habit. The solution was simple: he would raise his prices to his customers to cover what he was using for himself. Yes, that's what he'd do. He could see no other way.

Devonte gave him one last but very long threatening look as these thoughts raced through Emil's mind. Then Devonte climbed into his silver Mercedes and pulled away. Emil got in his rusty Volkswagen Beetle and sat there shaking so badly he couldn't get the key in the ignition. Sweat poured from his forehead and stung his eyes, blurring his vision. He'd messed up. He had to do something or Devonte would do more than threaten him.

As he sat there, the fear slowly turned to anger. He wiped his eyes with the back of his hands and then pulled a small pistol from the jockey box, checked to make sure it was loaded, and stuffed it inside his belt. His hands were steadier now, and he shoved the key in the ignition and started the car. If Devonte could threaten, then he could threaten too. That's exactly what he would do. Desperate times called for desperate measures, and this was a desperate time.

His first stop was at the rundown apartment in Price where Lucas Soto and his pregnant young girlfriend lived. Lucas sent his girlfriend, Nattie Shrader, to the bedroom while he talked to Emil.

"Where's my heroin?" Lucas asked before Emil had a chance to remind him that he owed him money. "You told me you would get me some more, and I've been waiting for you to call so I could come pick it up. I'm almost out."

"There isn't any for you to pick up. You get no more until you pay up," Emil said, puffing out his chest to look bigger and tougher than his short, skinny frame seemed to proclaim. "I need the dough right now, or you will suffer the consequences."

Lucas's eyes narrowed. "Are you threatening me?"

"Just stating a fact," Emil said. "You pay up, and I might find some more for you. And bear in mind that I will need interest on what you owe me." *Interest.* Emil didn't know why he hadn't thought about that before. Charging his customers interest would cover what he was using himself.

"My girlfriend is pregnant. She had to go to the doctor, and it took all our money. I'll have a welfare check next week. I'll pay you then," Lucas said.

Emil glared at him for a moment. He'd never threatened one of his customers before, but he had no choice now. Devonte was a dangerous man, and Emil feared he would do what he'd threatened if Emil didn't find a way to appease him very soon. Slowly, but with as much menace as he could muster, Emil pulled his little pistol out and pointed it at Lucas Soto's chest. "I'll be back in a couple hours. You find the money—borrow it, steal it, whatever it takes, but you have it when I come back later. And I'll need a hundred dollars for interest on top of the rest."

"What if I don't?" Lucas asked with fear in his eyes.

"If you don't, your girlfriend will have to raise your baby all by herself," Emil said, trying to look as dangerous to Lucas as Devonte had to him.

For a moment, Lucas glared at him. Then, mustering some courage, he said, "You better not even think of it. I have a gun too, you know."

"Don't you threaten me! I'll be back," Emil said, waving the pistol at Lucas. "Don't disappoint me."

With that, Emil tromped angrily from the apartment, being careful not to slip on the ice on the sidewalk, and got in his car. He then drove his ancient VW Beetle to a house in Price where another of his errant customers lived. It was a rundown house badly in need of a paint job and a new front door. Weeds grew everywhere, even between the cracks in the sidewalk. The living room window had a large crack in it, which had been patched with gray duct tape.

Emil made sure his pistol was tucked out of sight when he headed up the cracked, icy sidewalk and pounded on the disintegrating door. A skinny woman with sallow skin and straggly hair opened the door, but she had to put her shoulder against it to keep it from falling inward as only the bottom hinge was still attached. Emil knew she was the wife of Bryan Bayle, a customer who owed him well over a thousand dollars. He was angry at himself for letting Bryan get in debt so steep, but he transferred the anger to Bryan as he stepped inside without being asked, knowing Mrs. Bayle couldn't slam the broken door if she tried.

He asked for Bryan, fighting to keep his anger in check, and she turned without a word to search for him. She had to make her way between stacks of empty takeout cartons, dozens of beer cans and bottles, and other trash. Ashtrays were overflowing with cigarette butts. The place smelled like a sewer, maybe slightly worse. And it was cold. The sagging, busted door couldn't help but let in cold air.

Bryan came in, his pants sagging, a large belly protruding from above the waistline. It looked like his wife must have rousted him from his bed because he swayed as if half asleep. Of course, Emil knew from experience that it could simply be a bad hangover.

"Got my weed?" Bryan asked. "You didn't have to deliver it. I'd have come over if you'd called. I appreciate it, but I'll have to owe you again. Ain't got no cash right now."

Bryan walked with a waddle. His hair must not have seen a good washing for a very long time, and his beard was filled with scraps of food. A disgusting mess.

"No marijuana today, man," Emil said. "You know I don't make deliveries."

Before he could go on, Bryan said, "Then I guess I'll have some meth since you're here."

"Bryan, you ain't getting nothing today," Emil said with gritted teeth. "I came to collect what you owe me plus about a hundred in interest." Emil really liked that interest idea.

"I already said I ain't got it," Bryan said. "And you didn't say nothing about interest before. I don't know what's got into you, but sit down if you can find a spot. Just shove those magazines off that chair. I got a couple joints left. We'll have one together."

Emil had not anticipated that, but even though he had a little in his car and a little more at home, he said, "Sure, we can do that, but this ain't going away."

So in what seemed like companionable silence, the two men smoked their joints. When they were done, Bryan said, "I need more now that we've smoked these two joints. Can you have some for me to pick up tomorrow?"

"Bryan, I have to pay my supplier today. You understand, I'm sure. I'm like any other businessman. I can't buy more to sell to you until I pay my supplier off." Again he thought about not only the pot but also the small amounts of meth, heroin, and cocaine he had in his car with still a little more at home. He didn't want to sell any of it because he was going to need it for himself. If he could collect interest, he wouldn't have to sell it. Bryan wasn't getting anything else until he gave Emil some money, and that was simply the end of it.

"Your problem ain't my problem," Bryan said, raising his massive bulk from the sagging chair he'd been seated in.

Emil also stood. "Actually, it is your problem. You pay me. I pay my supplier. Then I can get more weed for you and maybe a little meth."

"You'll have to come back. I don't get a check for another week. My woman and I gotta survive until then," Bryan said. "It's cold in here, and if we don't pay the power bill soon, they'll shut off my electricity, and we'll freeze to death. So you see, I got problems too. But it was nice of you to come by."

Emil pulled his gun out and waved it in the direction of his errant customer, whose eyes suddenly widened in fear. "You don't understand. I gotta have money now. Today! You don't want me to have to use this, do you?" he asked with a sneer. "Cause I will if I have to."

"You just pulled a gun on me!" Bryan thundered, his round face red with fear and sudden rage. "Ain't nobody pulls no gun on me and lives to tell about it."

"I just did," Emil said. "And while you think about that, also think about what you have that you could give me that I could pawn. Maybe something that will get you even on your bill along with a little interest."

"I thought we were pals. We just smoked weed together. Now you go all crazy on me. Well, I got news for you, Emil: I ain't got nothing you can have," Bryan said. "So just get out of here before I take that gun away from you and shove it down your throat."

Just then his skinny wife entered the filthy room. "What's all the shouting about?" she demanded. Then her eyes grew wide. "A gun! You gonna shoot us?"

"No, Belle, he ain't gonna shoot us. He's just losing his mind. He thinks we gotta pay him right now, or he won't give us more of what we need."

Belle's eyes narrowed. "You always get what we need. What's the matter with you?"

"He says he can't get no more until we pay him," Bryan explained, all the while keeping his eyes on Emil's pistol.

"That's right. He needs money, so I need money. You need to pay me today," Emil said.

"I explained that we ain't got nothing to pay him with right now," Bryan told his wife.

Emil waved the gun at Belle. "Get me your jewelry, all of it."

"So you're robbing us now?" Belle said, her skinny body trembling as she hugged a threadbare jacket around her.

"Get what you got and give it to me. I ain't robbing nobody. I'm just collecting what you owe me," Emil said. "So get moving, both of you."

Nobody moved. But after a moment of throwing daggers from their eyes, Belle finally said, "I ain't got much, but I'll go get what we got. Then you gotta leave us alone."

She started to move away, but Emil said, "Both of you go, and I'll follow you. You try to pull a fast one, and somebody gets it." He waved the gun to make his point.

"We'll call the cops," Belle said.

"No, we won't," Bryan countered. "We don't need no cops coming around. Let's get your jewelry. You never wear it anyway."

"The jewelry probably ain't enough," Emil said. "I want anything else of value that you have."

He followed them into a bedroom. At least it had a bed in it, but Emil could barely see it for all the junk. Belle opened a drawer to a dresser once she'd plowed her way through the mess to get to it. Emil watched both of them while she dug around in the drawer. She quickly pulled out a dented metal jewelry box.

"Open it," Emil ordered.

She did, and it did in fact contain some necklaces, rings, bracelets, and earrings. He took it all and shoved it in his pockets without once letting the gun stray from pointing at one of them. "Okay, now let's see what else you have," Emil said. "I bet you got guns somewhere in this mess."

"I ain't got none," Bryan said. "If I did, I would use it on you."

"I don't believe you. Everybody's got guns. Where do you keep them?" Emil asked. He was shaking now in a mixture of fear and anger. He wasn't used to having to threaten people, but he also feared threats directed at him. He hadn't considered Bryan as a dangerous man, but the look in his eye made him think that perhaps he was.

Bryan looked at his wife. She was shaking with fear.

"Take the jewelry," he said. "If that ain't enough, then we'll talk some more."

"Talking's done," Emil said as he waved the pistol at them. "Show me some guns."

"I ought to kill you right now," Bryan said.

"I got the gun. Show me where yours are or I'll have to use it. And when you show me, you ain't to touch them," Emil said.

Without another word, but glaring threateningly, the pair led him to another room, one just as messy. In it was a gun case with the glass broken out of the door. There were two rifles that Emil could see, but he wondered if there might be a pistol or two in the drawer below the rifles. "I knew you had guns. I'll take them. And if I can't get enough out of them and the jewelry, I'll be back, so be thinking what else you have or go borrow some money. I need the entire thousand plus a hundred for interest *today*. I'll be back after I hawk these things. I need to pay my man tonight."

Bryan pushed toward the gun cabinet.

"No you don't, Bryan," Emil said. "You two stay over there." He pointed past a twin bed piled high with junk. "I told you that you wouldn't touch the guns. I'll get them."

He took the rifles out one at a time and checked them. They were both unloaded. Then he opened the drawer and found two pistols. One was a revolver, a .357 magnum. The other was a 9mm semiautomatic. Both were loaded. He shoved them inside the waistband of his pants using only one hand so he could continue to threaten with the pistol in the other.

He hoped these were all the guns Bryan had, but he had no way of knowing for sure. He didn't want to leave Bryan with a way to carry out his threat if he decided to. "Where are your other guns? I know you got more."

A look passed between Bryan and Belle. She looked very scared, and Emil was sure the look Bryan gave her was a warning to keep her mouth shut. He could see fading bruises on her face and suddenly realized she was afraid of her husband. "I want the rest of your guns," he repeated.

Belle responded then, after another threatening look from Bryan. "He doesn't have any more," she said in a shaky voice.

He didn't believe her, but he wasn't going to search the whole house. "Belle, you get the rifles," Emil said. "You're going to carry them to my car and put them in the back seat. You stay close to her, Bryan. Any funny moves, and I'll plug both of you."

Emil then forced them to go out ahead of him. He kept his pistol out of sight once they stepped onto the sidewalk in case there were snoopy neighbors. They all walked slowly because of the dangerous patches of ice on the ground. Once the guns were in his car, Emil said, "I'll be back this afternoon if I need more than this. I'll give you credit toward your debt from exactly what these pawn for."

"Hey, you owe me for a joint," Bryan suddenly said. "You smoked one of mine."

"You gave that to me, but sure, I'll take it off what you owe me," Emil said magnanimously. "But from now on, you pay me up front for what you want from me, so I won't have to collect interest." What he didn't say was that he would charge more to make up for the interest because he wasn't going to go without the stuff he needed for himself.

Bryan gave him a look that could kill. "You just made a dangerous enemy, Emil. Don't come back trying to sell me more. What you took from us just now is worth more than we owe you, even with interest. And I won't be going to your house no more either. We'll get our stuff from someone who ain't crazy."

Emil sent them back inside, and then he got in his car and drove off. He stopped a few blocks later, shaking like a leaf. He'd never had to resort to threats before, and he didn't like it. Despite that, he thought about going back to Lucas's place to force him and his nice-looking young girlfriend to give him something he could pawn. It was the only way he could think of to get the money together to pay Devonte.

Suddenly a worrisome thought hit him. Bryan probably had guns in his car. He should have looked because he'd just made an enemy out of the guy. He cursed his bad luck.

He decided to drive back into Price and shake Lucas down for guns and jewelry. Within a few minutes, he was parked in front of Lucas's house. Now or never.

"Hey, man, what're you doing back here? We ain't had time to get no money for you," Lucas said when he came to the door.

"I came to see what you have that I could pawn to get enough money to cover what you owe me," Emil said reasonably.

"You can't have anything of ours," Lucas said adamantly.

"Come on, man, you've been a good customer. I need to get to the pawn shops this morning, so I don't have a lot of time."

"Like I said, you're getting nothing of ours."

"Don't make me do this the hard way," Emil said.

"What do you mean by that? Are you gonna pull out your gun again and then just start grabbing our stuff?" Lucas asked.

"Let's look around and see what you got, Lucas. How about jewelry? Surely the pretty little lady has some she can part with."

Just then, Lucas's girlfriend came into the room. She balked at giving Emil any jewelry. "Lucas uses the heroin, not me. You can't have anything of mine."

"Nattie, shut up," Lucas said angrily. Then he turned to Emil. "What she has ain't worth nothing. We ain't rich. You know that."

"Give me what you have. Anything I can't pawn I'll bring back," Emil said, trying to sound like he was being reasonable.

"No way," Lucas responded.

"Then I guess it's the hard way." Emil pulled out his pistol.

"Give him what he wants, Lucas, please. But don't ever tell anybody you got that awful stuff for me. You know I won't use it and hurt our baby," Nattie said.

Lucas finally caved in, and for the next few minutes, they gathered things up and handed them all over to Emil. He finally drove away with some jewelry, a rifle, a shotgun, a small TV, and a box of porcelain dolls. Behind him, he left a raging couple. Lucas was angry with him and had threatened to get even. Nattie was angry with Lucas for getting them in such a bad position that she had to give up things she liked, like her porcelain dolls and her grandmother's wedding ring.

Emil may have just lost another customer, but he had lots more, and most of them paid him in cash when they came to his house for the stuff they wanted.

At the first pawn shop he went to, he was turned away. The owner suspected what he had was stolen and wouldn't take anything from him. The same thing happened at the next place. Discouraged, Emil finally went home, brought everything into the house, and put it in two piles. He put a piece of paper beside each pile—one with the name Bryan and the other with Lucas. Somehow he needed to convince Devonte that he needed another day so he could run to Salt Lake where he was sure he could pawn the items he'd taken. The jewelry wasn't worth much, but the guns were.

Then he had another idea; he could give the stuff to Devonte to pay his bill. That should work just fine. Then it would be Devonte's problem to pawn it.

He still had one more person to talk to who owed him money. Unlike the others, he wasn't sure how to handle Joe Whalen. He'd asked Joe to pay him a couple days ago, but Joe had insisted that he didn't have any money, but he would pay as soon as he could. Joe was different from a lot of Emil's customers in that he actually had a job and came from a slightly more affluent background. And he was not a heavy user.

Joe's cousin was a deputy sheriff with a big bulldog, one who was getting a reputation fast. If Emil pulled his gun on Joe, Joe might get his cousin and his dog after him. That was something Emil couldn't let happen. But he had to get something from Joe. He'd take whatever Joe had of value, like he had done with Lucas and Bryan, but this time, he'd try to do it without having to pull his pistol.

CHAPTER TWO

"I'm telling you, Joe, we gotta find a girl for you," Bo Buckley told his cousin with a grin. "You need a wife."

"So do you," Joe said.

"I'm working on it and making some progress," Bo said with an even wider grin. "You've got to do the same."

"I guess, Bo," Joe agreed reluctantly. "My sister tells me the same thing, but honestly, I'm okay for now."

"Rosina is a smart girl," Bo said. "Listen to her."

Joe frowned. "She's so caught up in her new religion, that Church of Jesus Christ of Latter-day Saints, that she thinks she's better than me."

"Hey, Joe, you're reading Rosina all wrong. She cares about you. It's not her intent to force you to date or to go to church, for that matter, but I'm telling you, my friend, you would be better off if you did both of those things. I went with her and a couple of her friends last Sunday and the Sunday before. Honestly, it made me feel good. I'm going to keep going. You can go with us if it would make it less embarrassing for you."

"I'll think about it," Joe said halfheartedly.

"Well, I guess that's all I can ask." Bo grinned. "There are some cute girls there. They call it a single adults ward. I guess that's enough of that, Joe. Let's go do some ice fishing out on Strawberry Reservoir for our day off. It's not too cold today considering it's the middle of February, and the sun's shining. It'll be a bit of a drive, but I hear the fishing is good there and we can get there by early this afternoon. Are you up for that today?"

"Sure, that I can handle," Joe agreed. "Who were the friends?"

"Do you mean the ones I went to church with?" Bo asked with a grin.

"Yeah, that's who I mean," Joe said.

"One of them is your sister's roommate. You know her: Nyree Morton. She's a nice girl. The other one? Well, let's just say she's someone Rosina and Nyree introduced me to."

Joe chuckled. "So did you feel good because you went to church or because you went to church with a pretty girl?"

"Both, I guess," Bo admitted. "But I liked what I heard in church and the feeling that I got there. And I like what Rosina and her friends have told me about their church. I'm going to look into it."

"Does this girl you went to church with have a name?" Joe asked.

"Of course she does," Bo responded. "Maybe I'll tell you someday."

"Is she cute?" Joe persisted.

Bo chuckled. "You can say that."

"Come on, Bo, tell me her name."

"Well, okay, but don't go making something out of this. She's just a friend, a new friend. Her name is Karmen Ellison. And that's all I'm telling you. Now, let's go fishing."

"How old is she?" Joe asked. He was very curious about this girl Bo didn't seem to want to talk about, and yet just moments ago, he'd said he was working on getting married. This must be a girl he was either serious with or wanted to be.

"Too old for you," was all Bo would tell him.

Joe gave up, and they went fishing.

Emil Eifler approached Joe Whalen's dumpy little house a ways outside of Wellington just as Joe climbed into Bo Buckley's full-size Toyota pickup. He could see the huge head of Bo's English bulldog in the back seat. Lots of people knew about that bulldog. Emil cursed. Joe owed him money and Emil owed his supplier, Devonte, a lot more. He really needed to put the squeeze on Joe today. He needed Joe's money or something he could pawn or give to Devonte.

Even with what Joe owed him and the stuff he'd taken from Bryan Bayle and Lucas, he still might not have enough to pay Devonte off totally, but maybe it would buy him some time to come up with the rest. After all, if Devonte did something to him, Devonte would never get paid. That was in Emil's favor. That thought gave him a little reassurance.

Even though Joe had told Emil a couple of nights ago that he didn't have the money, he had to do whatever it took to get it from him right away. But not while that deputy was with him. He'd come back later, maybe after dark, he decided and drove away. Joe was an okay guy. Emil was sure he'd do what he could to pay his debt. Emil wouldn't have to threaten him as severely as he had the others.

With all the threats he was making, Emil was getting too many people mad at him. It made him uneasy, to say the least. Maybe, he decided, he should raise his price on Joe's weed and some of what he sold to others to help make it so he could buy more from Devonte in the future to keep most of his customers happy.

Joe wouldn't like that, but he also wouldn't like word to get out to his cousin, the deputy with the big bulldog, that he was smoking weed.

Bo didn't let on to Joe that he could smell weed whenever he was around him. It was especially strong in his house. He and Rosina—Joe's sister—had talked about it, and it worried them both. Joe was a good guy, but there were a dozen reasons why smoking marijuana would eventually get him into trouble. Bo knew he could ignore it for only so long. For one thing, he was a cop and had a duty to carry out. Recreational marijuana use was still illegal in Utah, after all. But he'd rather Joe quit before he got arrested.

Bo had seriously considered confronting Joe about it, but Rosina had talked him out of it. He had explained to her that he could turn a blind eye to what Joe was doing for only so long without eventually getting in trouble himself.

Rosina was two years younger than Joe, and she loved him dearly. He had always been a wonderful big brother to her, and as she'd told Bo, she didn't want Joe to get in trouble. Even in high school, he hadn't hung out with the best crowd. She'd mentioned it to Joe, and so had their parents, but it only made him angry.

She'd explained all this to Bo, and Bo could understand how Joe's sister felt. Joe was doing pretty well now. His work at Ron Brady's farm had been good for him. So had getting that collie dog, Herc, a few months back. The best thing Bo could do was try to spend time with Joe whenever he could and set a good example for him—like he was trying to do today.

As they drove the long miles to Strawberry Reservoir, they talked about a lot of things: sports, the weather, girls (a little but not specifically), their jobs, and so forth. "How long do you plan to work on Ron Brady's farm?" Bo asked at one point. "I mean, you know, I was wondering if you'd thought about going to college. You can't work a dead-end job like that forever, you know."

"I'm not interested in college," Joe responded. "For Rosina, it's okay. She likes it. Me, I don't think so."

"What about vocational school?" Bo asked. "There're a lot of good professions you could learn."

"I know, but I like farming," Joe said. "Ron isn't doing very well, and he needs my help a lot."

"Well, if you like it, that's good. Farming is okay, I suppose. It doesn't interest me at all, and I just don't see how working on another man's farm will get you anywhere in life."

"Being a cop doesn't interest me," Joe said with a chuckle. "To each his own, I guess."

"You're right," Bo said. "Tell me about your boss, Ron Brady. I don't know much about him."

"He's a great guy. He treats me really well, but like I told you, he doesn't have good health and can't do much himself. He has a weak heart."

"That's too bad. Does he have a wife? Can she help on the farm?"

"She's dead, and that really has been hard on him."

"Oh, that's too bad. What other family does he have?" Bo asked.

"He had a daughter, but her husband ran off on her, and nobody knows where he is. His daughter, from what Ron said, couldn't handle things after that, and she eventually took her own life," Joe said. "That's been pretty rough on him."

"That's horrible, Joe. Is that all the family he has?" Bo asked as he slowed at the stop sign in Duchesne and waited for traffic to clear so he could turn left onto Highway 40, the highway that would take them to the reservoir.

Joe didn't answer right away. After Bo got onto the highway and headed toward the western edge of Duchesne, he looked over at Joe. "I take it there isn't anyone else."

Finally, Joe said sheepishly, "He has a granddaughter."

"Oh, I see. Where does she live?"

"On the farm with him," Joe said.

When nothing else was forthcoming, Bo pressed him a little. "How old is she?"

"Nineteen," he said. "She's lived with Ron since the end of December."

Bo couldn't suppress a grin. "Three years younger than you. Is she cute?" he asked.

"Yeah, I guess."

"So is she why you like farming?" Bo chuckled.

"No, but it doesn't hurt," Joe answered honestly.

"What does she do?"

"Pretty much what I do. She lived with some distant relatives in Salt Lake after her mother died. She went to college there for a year or so, but then, because she worried about Ron, she came to live with him. Now she says that all she wants to do is help her grandfather. She has a slight frame, but she's strong enough and is a pretty good worker."

"Is she going to run you out of a job?" Bo asked, not entirely joking.

"Oh no, there's plenty of work for both of us with Ron being sickly like he is. And she keeps up his house now, does all the cooking, laundry, and cleaning—that kind of stuff."

"What's her name?" Bo asked.

"I'll tell you sometime," Joe said. He'd had to dig to get Bo to tell him Karmen's name, after all.

"I guess I had that coming," Bo said.

"Yeah, you did. But all right, I'll tell you. Her name is Melia."

"That's a cute name. Does she have a last name?"

"Most people do," Joe answered.

"Are you going to tell me what it is?" Bo asked with a grin.

"She goes by her grandfather's name. So it's Melia Brady. And she likes my dog better than her grandpa's."

"Better not let her meet my bulldog then. He'll be her favorite after that," Bo said with an affectionate glance behind him at the back seat where his dog lay.

Two Face, Bo's bulldog, spent the day with the guys, and he stayed right with them the entire time they fished. He was a nice dog, not what Joe would call beautiful like Herc was, but unique. He was white and brown, but the interesting thing about him was his face. One side was white and the other side brown. That's where his name came from. He was a gentle animal most of the time, but he could be very intimidating and even aggressive if Bo wanted him to be. The deputy hauled him around when he worked, and Two Face was very good at getting the undivided attention of some of the crooks Bo had to deal with as a deputy sheriff. He was a most unusual police dog, but he did the job and did it well. He was very smart and well trained.

The fishing was good that afternoon, and Joe and Bo didn't quit until nearly dark. When they did, they had both caught their limits. "Looks like we two bachelors will have some good frying and good eating for a while," Bo said as they packed up their gear.

"Oh, I won't cook 'em," Joe said. "I'll let Melia do that. I eat with the Bradys most nights since Melia started fixing meals for her grandfather. She's a pretty good cook."

Bo smiled. He had a feeling that this girl might be good for Joe. He wondered if he'd mentioned her to his younger sister, Rosina. Probably not. Well, Bo would do it for him, he decided. He had a feeling she would be okay with it.

Lucas Soto was angry with Emil and wanted to find a way to get back at him for the way he'd treated him and embarrassed his girlfriend. That was not okay. None of this was Nattie's fault; she didn't use drugs and didn't like that Lucas did. All that Emil had done today had only served to draw more attention to his habits, and Lucas didn't appreciate that. So he slipped out shortly after dark that night in black clothing and drove to Emil's house to confront him. He carried a small pistol Emil hadn't known about. If Emil didn't see reason, the pistol would be very convincing. But Emil's old VW was just starting up the street when Lucas rounded the corner.

Instinctively, Lucas followed him. Emil drove out of town and eventually stopped and parked his car off the side of a dirt road way out in the country. Then he walked, keeping to the shadows until he reached an old rundown house in the largely deserted area.

Out of curiosity, Lucas parked up the road and out of sight a short distance from the house Emil had gone to. There were no lights on, so it was likely the resident wasn't at home even though an old truck was there. The house wasn't really in a neighborhood since the nearest inhabited houses were close to a half mile away on either side of the house. And there were abandoned, empty fields and sagebrush flats on all sides of the place, including across the road.

Emil carried a small flashlight, but it appeared that he only used it when he had to. As Emil approached the front door, Lucas, from his vantage point a short distance away, could hear a dog barking in the backyard. He watched as Emil knocked and, after waiting for a minute, tried the door. Apparently, it was locked. Lucas continued to watch, shifting his position in the dark to keep an eye on Emil.

Emil had hoped Joe would be home by now, but when he realized he wasn't, Emil decided he'd get something of value from Joe's house anyway. Joe would never know it was him, and whatever Emil found would help him pay Devonte back in a couple of hours.

He walked around back, a flashlight in one hand and a can of Mace (which he always carried in case he was confronted by a dog) in the other. He didn't like dogs and he'd learned how to deal with them when he had to. He unlatched a gate just as a big dog, looking like nothing more than a shadowy figure, ran to the gate, barking. Emil reached over the fence, shined his light on the dog, and squirted the Mace in his face. The dog ran away, still barking, but this time in pain. Emil grinned, put the little container of Mace back in his pocket, and entered the backyard. The gate, which hung on a strong spring, swung shut as soon as he let go of it.

He was more liberal with using the flashlight now and soon stepped onto a covered porch and approached the back door. He tried the doorknob—also locked. He studied the door for a moment. It was an old-fashioned one with small rectangles of glass that ran up the door from just above the doorknob to within about eight inches of the top.

He pulled his small revolver from a holster fastened to the inside of his belt and struck the glass rectangle closest to the doorknob. It shattered, most of the glass falling inside. He put his pistol away, then reached through the opening he had created and swore as a piece of the glass that still stuck to the edge of the small frame cut his wrist. It drew blood, leaving drops on the door and the floor both inside and outside.

Ignoring the pain, he found the latch to the door and unlocked it. Then he withdrew his arm more carefully and grabbed the doorknob. He thought about the blood his hands left on the doorknob but simply opened the door and stepped in. He would wipe the blood up before he left. His mind was made up now that he was inside. He was going to take what he wanted in order to cover Joe's debt. No one would ever know it was him, and the next time he saw Joe, he would still press him for what he owed but not so hard that he would lose him as a customer.

Lucas had parked off the road on the opposite side of the old house from where Emil had parked. He was intrigued by what Emil was doing. He thought about calling the cops and telling them Emil was committing a burglary. That would serve Emil right, but on the other hand, it would not get Lucas his property back.

Lucas couldn't see well because of the darkness of the night, but he could see well enough to notice a second person approaching the house. All thought of calling the cops left him then as he watched, wondering what the second man was doing. The second intruder also had a small flashlight, and every time he turned it on, even if for just a moment, Lucas was able to track his progress. He approached the back fence not long after Emil had gone in the house. What in the world was that person up to?

The latest intruder did not have to worry about the dog announcing his presence because of something Emil had done to it. He clambered over the fence and silently approached the house. Hatred for and anger against Emil burned deeply in him. When he was sure the person who lived in the house wasn't home, he crept onto the back porch. There he stood and listened to what was going on inside, which wasn't much. He didn't know who the legal occupant of this house was, and he didn't care; he had just followed Emil here. It was for Emil that hatred burned. He frankly hated a lot of people. He was that kind of man. But right now, Emil was on the top of his list of hated people.

Lucas watched the second man enter the house through the back door like Emil had done. Lucas had left his car and watched the scene from behind a tree. He watched for several minutes, eventually backing away from the tree, confused as to what Emil and the second man could be doing inside that house. At last, he decided he should leave and confront Emil another time.

He had only gone a few steps, however, when he thought he heard a shot come from within or near the house. That both unnerved him and made him curious. He crept back to the tree and watched again. He was back to his spot in time to see a figure leaving the yard—the man who had entered after Emil. He was much larger than Emil and moved quickly away and out of sight. Lucas waited for Emil to leave but didn't see him again, even though he stayed for several more minutes.

The house was dark. Surely, he thought, Emil was no longer in the house. He had probably left ahead of the second man in those few moments Lucas had been away from his spot by the tree. Lucas knew that the person who lived there had not returned. He was curious about what the two intruders had been up to, especially considering that he'd heard a shot. So after working up some nerve, he approached the house from the rear, watched for the dog, and when he didn't see it, he climbed the fence and crept forward, his small pistol in his hand.

Lucas didn't plan to spend long in the house. He confirmed it was empty, but something didn't feel right to him. He shuddered, thinking he should leave, but he had come this far, so he forced himself to stay just a little longer. He shined his light about and spotted what he thought was blood. He looked around to see if Emil was lying on the floor, shot and bleeding, but he didn't see him after a cursory check through the house. He looked at some papers on the table in the kitchen: mail. He stirred through it and saw the name Joe Whalen on several envelopes and frowned. Though he didn't know Joe well, he was certainly not a friend. Finally, afraid that Joe could return at any moment, he left out the back door and retreated to his watching spot by the tree. He wanted to see what happened when and if Joe returned.

CHAPTER THREE

It was quite late by the time Bo and Joe got back from Strawberry Reservoir. Bo had to be at the Carbon County Sheriff's Department for work the next morning at six a.m., now only a few hours away.

Joe, on the other hand, was only working about thirty-two hours a week this time of the year for Ron Brady, whose farm was several miles southeast of Price. Joe's hours were somewhat flexible, and it didn't take him long to drive to the farm from his little house near Wellington. So he planned to be at the farm by ten a.m. His employer was fine with that since Joe could work as late as he needed to finish the day's work. Mostly, he filled water troughs and made sure none of them were frozen, fed animals, cleaned stalls in a large horse barn, and performed other mundane farming tasks. He even did some maintenance on the farm equipment during these winter months.

Ron had raised cattle for years as well as registered quarter horses. He kept some of the horses in the barn and some in pens outside. He also boarded horses for a number of other people who had no place to keep their own. So all told, Joe had around thirty horses to care for. The cattle were in a large corral beyond the barn this time of year. They had sheds and enough room to get around in them, even though there were around fifty head.

The cattle only needed feeding and their water troughs maintained. In two or three weeks, they would start calving, and then Joe's and Melia's work would increase substantially. There would also be colts coming along around the first of April.

There was a lot to do, especially inside the barn, where stalls had to be cleaned regularly and the water tended to and the horses fed. As for feed, Ron's fields produced all he needed to keep the animals fed. The hay was kept dry in a hay barn and had to be retrieved daily and distributed to the animals. Oats and barley that Ron harvested in the fall were kept in a separate granary near the barn.

The past few weeks, Joe had been showing Melia what to do when he wasn't there so that Ron Brady wouldn't have to do it. Melia was sweet, pretty, and fun to work with. And even though she was small, she was strong and willing. He looked forward to working with her when summer came and he would be there for well over forty hours a week. Joe and Ron got along great. And he really did enjoy having Melia there now.

At his cheaply rented house, a rundown two-bedroom affair far from any neighbors, there was a backyard of sorts. He'd been able to patch the fence in the back well enough to keep his dog in. He was a pretty yellow-and-white collie called Herc. He always took Herc to work with him to run with his boss's dog—a Border collie-blue heeler mix that went by the name Ace.

Joe had set days to work during the winter months, and his boss used to do the chores on Joe's days off, but that had changed now. Ron was a widower, and between grieving for his dead wife and nursing his health, he could not even come close to keeping the farm up by himself.

What had changed was, of course, Melia, his granddaughter. For this past winter, Ron had asked Joe to come to the farm on Mondays, Tuesdays, Thursdays, and Saturdays. The past two summers, Joe had worked much longer hours almost every day and was promised the same for the next summer. The next day was Thursday, so Joe planned to put in a good day, work late, and be there for dinner. Melia had insisted Joe eat with them just a few days after she had moved in, and since Ron didn't object, Joe did that as often as he could. In the morning, he'd take Melia the fish he'd caught that day out at Strawberry Reservoir. He had a feeling she'd be excited about that.

Joe lived quite cheaply, and if it weren't for his use of marijuana, he'd easily have enough money to cover all his bills, such as rent, utilities, gas for the truck, food for him and his dog, and so on. As it was, he owed Emil, his supplier, around five hundred dollars, which he simply didn't have right now but was determined to save so he could pay him off soon. Joe felt like he could kick the marijuana habit if Emil didn't keep coming around after money. Whenever he did, Emil always managed to sell Joe a little more pot, on credit of course, as that kept Joe hooked. He disliked Emil a great deal but couldn't seem to get him out of his life. He'd thought about reporting him to Bo, but if he did that, he could be arrested himself for possession of the stuff. Bo never asked him about the pot, and yet Bo had to know he used it. He was one of the reasons Joe wanted to quit. He knew it put Bo in a bad spot, him being a cop and all.

That night, Joe entered his house after Bo drove off. Something felt off to him when he got inside. After a moment, he figured it out—it was too cold in there. The house was heated with a propane furnace, and he knew he'd left the thermostat on high enough that it shouldn't feel this cold. He checked it, and it was set at 65, where he kept it most of the time.

Joe walked into his kitchen and to the back door. To his surprise, a rectangle of glass was broken, which accounted for the cold. He could hear Herc whining on the porch. He went to unlock the door, only to discover it was already unlocked. He stood back and studied the door. The break in the glass was large enough for someone to reach a hand in and turn the latch on the lock. He'd been burglarized! A shiver of fear raised goosebumps on his arms. He put his fish in the refrigerator and then quickly checked his house. But he didn't see that anything was missing. He was puzzled. Why did someone break in but not steal anything? Maybe he'd mention this to Bo tomorrow.

He walked out back to spend a few minutes with Herc. "If you weren't so nice, maybe you would have bitten whoever broke in here."

Herc wagged his tail, but he didn't seem quite right.

Joe knelt down and put an arm around him. "Are you not feeling well?" he asked. Herc looked up at him in the illumination of the porch light. Something was wrong with his eyes. Joe felt around them gingerly with his fingers, and when he did, Herc whined.

There was dampness around his eyes, and Herc kept shaking his head like something was wrong. He kept blinking rapidly, and a couple of times, he tried to rub his eyes with one back leg. It suddenly dawned on Joe that something must have been sprayed in his eyes. That worried him, and again he felt a wave of fear. What if Herc went blind? That would be horrible. And what if whoever did this was close by?

Herc growled, not loudly but still in a worrisome way. "Did someone hurt you?" he asked, wishing the collie could tell him exactly what had happened. "I think I'd better get up early enough to take you to the vet in the morning before I go to work." He couldn't afford the extra expense, but Herc was his best friend. He'd find a way to pay the vet bill and still pay Emil off.

Then he had an idea. He hardly ever used his shotgun. If he needed a gun to shoot varmints for Ron, he always used Ron's guns. Joe's guns stayed in his house. He could give that shotgun to Emil, and that should take care of his bill with him. It was a nice gun and hardly used. He'd paid over six hundred dollars for it.

Joe sat and stroked Herc for several minutes while constantly listening for any sounds that might indicate the burglar was still in the area. "I'll get you some dog food and check your water." Joe had a heated water pan on the porch that kept Herc with water all the time, even in freezing weather.

Herc growled again as Joe stepped inside his house, leaving him behind. Something bothered the dog. Joe assumed it was the fact that someone had broken in earlier. It was then that he noticed there was blood on the door handle and some on the floor. He looked closer at the floor as he once again checked through the house and discovered more blood. That really concerned him. He told himself that the blood was from a cut the intruder had gotten when he broke the glass in the door. He tried to dismiss the matter, but he couldn't entirely get rid of the uneasy feeling he had. His mind went to his shotgun again. He decided to load it and keep it by his bed that night in case the intruder came back.

Lucas Soto, dressed in black, watched from a short distance beyond Joe's fence, curious as to what had happened in that house earlier, thinking about the blood he'd seen and the shot he thought he'd heard. The blood made him think someone had been shot, and if so, it had to have been Emil. The other man didn't seem to have been hurt when he'd hurried away. Lucas assumed Joe would figure out that someone had been in his house while he was gone. Lucas continued to watch as lights came on in various rooms in the house, rooms that Lucas was now familiar with, having inspected them just minutes ago.

He watched as Joe came outside. The big collie dog came to him, and Joe knelt beside it for a moment. Lucas shivered slightly and stamped his feet to warm them up. It was quite cold, but he didn't let it bother him. He continued to watch Joe's house, mostly curious to see what Joe would do. He hated the guy because of an altercation they'd had one day in a grocery store where Joe had embarrassed him in front of Nattie. It had been quite an ugly scene.

After reentering his house, Joe began to look around once more when he couldn't rid himself of his uneasy feeling. As before, he still couldn't see anything out of place. And yet for some reason he couldn't explain, the hair stood up on the back of his neck, and a shiver of apprehension raised goosebumps on his arms. It was then that he noticed a kitchen chair was tipped over, and the others seemed to have been moved around. The neat little pile of mail he'd left on the table had been scattered as if someone had looked through it. All of that had to have been done by the burglar. Could that someone still be here? Worry niggled at his brain, and shivers of fear ran up his spine.

He kept three guns in his bedroom: a hunting rifle, a .22 caliber pistol, and the sixteen-gauge shotgun he'd been thinking about giving to Emil to square his debt, the one he now planned to keep loaded that night and near his bed. Why all three guns were still there was a mystery to him. It seemed to him like they were what the burglar would have been most likely to take.

He grabbed the shotgun, loaded it, and then looked around the house for a third time, carrying the gun with him in the crook of his arm. He still didn't see anyone hiding anywhere, but again, it didn't seem like anything had been taken, and he was finally totally convinced no one was hiding anywhere. Whoever had been inside his house must have only stayed for a short while. He couldn't imagine why anyone would break in here. He didn't have much worth stealing. His TV was worth a little, and his guns were worth a fair amount, but that was about it, and all those items were still here. He also didn't have a computer, and his cell phone had been with him.

He wondered briefly if someone had been looking for marijuana or some other kind of drug, but he was out except for a couple of joints of pot in the dresser in his bedroom. He'd looked—they were still there. The presence of blood bothered him, but he decided the burglar had cut himself badly when he broke in and tried not to think too much about the blood.

He finally decided he'd better get to bed. He checked on Herc once more; the dog whined and again rubbed at his eyes with a back foot. Joe stepped back inside, locking the door behind him. He took a few minutes to tape a piece of cardboard over the broken window to keep the cold out.

He was angry but unsure what to do. Finally, he decided to call Bo now instead of waiting until morning. He explained what had happened, and Bo said, "I don't like this, Joe. Should I come out or send a deputy who's on duty?"

They discussed the options for a minute, but Joe really didn't think this was urgent. After all, nothing had actually been stolen, and he had his shotgun loaded and ready if anyone came in again. He mentioned the blood but told his theory concerning it to Bo. "I know you gotta work in the morning," he said. "Why don't you come then if you can? Everything seems to be all right now. I'll be okay."

"All right, I'll do that if you're sure," Bo agreed.

Joe thought about the two joints in his bedroom. He didn't want them here when Bo came in the morning. He lit one and took one puff on it but then put it out. On an impulse, he took both joints outside, climbed over his back fence, and carried them a hundred feet or more beyond it. Then he tossed them. It was time to quit using the stuff. He couldn't help but wonder if tonight's trouble was because of that bad habit.

Herc had followed him as far as the fence, still acting strange and growling. Joe met him there when he came back. Normally, Herc would have been jumping around and demanding Joe's attention. He usually gave him plenty of attention, but this time, he just patted his head and went back inside, already questioning his decision to throw the joints out in the old grass and short brush where he may not be able to find them again if he wanted to. And yet he knew it was the right decision.

Joe thought about the pretty granddaughter of Ron Brady's as he often did lately. He had come to like her a lot. She was fun to be around and treated him better than girls used to treat him when he was in high school. She would frown on his use of marijuana. That mattered to him. That solidified his determination that the next time Emil came around, he would give him the shotgun and not accept so much as another joint of marijuana. He was through with the stuff.

Earlier, Lucas had left his tree and approached Joe's back fence to get a better view. But he silently moved farther away when Joe approached the fence. He couldn't imagine what Joe was doing. Lucas crouched low and watched as Joe first climbed the fence and then passed within fifty feet or so of Lucas's hiding place in the darkness. Joe went a little farther, threw something, then returned, once more passing close to Lucas but not once glancing in his direction. Lucas was pretty sure he wouldn't have seen him even if he had looked his way since Lucas was wearing black clothes in the middle of the night. He figured he'd just appear like another of the dark patches where the snow was mostly melted.

Curious about what Joe had tossed, Lucas waited until Joe was back in his house, and then using his small flashlight, he walked back to where Joe had been. He looked around and then smiled when he saw a joint on top of some snow on the ground. He picked it up with his gloved hands. When he searched farther, he found a second one. He picked it up too but could not find any more despite looking for several minutes. Finally he returned to his position near the back fence and watched. The dog continued to growl, but he kept his distance, so Lucas ignored him.

Lucas decided that another surprise for Joe would be a fun twist to his evening. In fact, it would be a bit comical since he was quite certain Joe's throwing away of the joints was an indication that he was going to quit smoking the stuff. He waited for an hour after the lights had all gone out, figuring Joe would be asleep by then.

Lucas walked all the way around Joe's yard, the dog growling the whole time but keeping its distance. Joe's truck was parked in a short driveway beside his house but on the opposite side of his bedroom. Lucas approached it slowly, making sure no lights came on in the house. He noticed the passenger side window was not rolled all the way up. That was perfect. He flipped both joints through the small opening. They landed on the seat. He smiled to himself and left. Joe just thought he'd gotten rid of the joints.

Snow started falling shortly after Lucas left to return home, and it snowed very lightly off and on during the night.

Joe did not sleep in the next morning. He awoke early to a clear, cold day with a light smattering of new snow on the ground. He worried about his collie, so still in his night clothes, he went outside and checked on him. Herc was acting a lot better, but on close examination of his eyes, Joe could see the edges were red. He determined to take him to the vet after Bo came and before Joe went to the farm to work. It would make him late, but he would work hard to make up for it. He had no desire to cheat Ron or to make him unhappy with him. The last thing he needed was to lose such a great job.

Lucas had left his house earlier. Nattie had been asleep when he'd come in, and she was asleep when he left. He often admitted to himself that she was too good for him. She refused to participate in his bad habits and took his frequent forays away from the house in stride, seldom asking where he was going. If she weren't pregnant, he often wondered if she might leave him.

He shoved thoughts of Nattie from his mind and considered what he was doing. He didn't dare get as close to Joe's house this morning as he had during the night, but since he had nothing else to do, he wanted to watch what happened at Joe's house this morning, if anything. He didn't want to leave fresh tracks in the light covering of fresh snow, nor did he want to be seen, so he stayed back far enough that he was quite sure no one would notice him but where he could see both the front door and the rear one. He watched through a pair of strong binoculars this time. A sheriff's vehicle pulled in and parked behind Joe's truck. The deputy walked past the passenger door and glanced in, did a double take, and looked closer. Lucas knew exactly what he'd just seen. It made him chuckle softly to himself. The joints in his truck were payback for the embarrassment Joe had caused him in front of Nattie.

Bo showed up around seven thirty, just as Joe finished a breakfast of cold cereal and toast. Joe opened the door to his cousin's knock and, after Bo stomped the snow from his feet, said, "This is crazy, Bo. The only things I can tell happened are my mail was messed with, a chair was knocked over and others moved in the kitchen, and the glass was knocked out of one of the panes in my back door. And there's some blood around from where he must have cut himself breaking the glass. I'm also pretty sure something was sprayed in Herc's eyes."

Bo was very fond of dogs. "Let's have a look at Herc first, shall we? Then, if you don't mind, maybe Two Face could go play with him while we look things over inside. They can run around in the snow, even though there's not much, and have a good time."

They walked through the house to the back door, but Bo stopped there. "You taped a piece of cardboard here, but I can see the blood you mentioned on the doorknob, and I can see it on the floor. You were right. He got cut."

"I only taped the cardboard there to stop the cold from coming in," Joe said as Bo continued to look closely at the blood.

"I guess you've touched the doorknob," Bo said, glancing at him.

"Yeah, I didn't think about fingerprints," Joe said sheepishly.

"We'll dust it anyway, that and the chairs in the kitchen, even the mail. Who knows—we might find something helpful," Bo said. "But let me open the door now. I'll wear latex gloves." He put a pair on.

"We'll check the front door too, even though you and I have both touched it, just in case your burglar tried that door first." Bo opened the back door, and they stepped outside onto the porch, where they were greeted by Herc. He'd been some distance from the house, running about in the light, new snow. He seemed to be in a good mood this morning and feeling quite frisky, back to his old self.

Bo examined his eyes and agreed with Joe that something had been sprayed in his face. "I'd have a vet check him just as a precaution," he said. "Although I don't think it's anything to worry about."

"I was going to do that," Joe said.

"Good. Let's go bring Two Face back here and let these two have some fun while we work inside."

They walked past Joe's truck, and Joe noticed Bo glance inside. He did the same and almost fainted. Two joints were sitting right on his front passenger seat. He had no idea how they had gotten there since he never took his marijuana in the truck with him. He was certain Bo had seen them. He suddenly felt sick to his stomach.

Bo didn't say a word about the joints, and as they passed by the truck again with Two Face running ahead of them, Bo did not glance inside the truck. Joe did, and the joints were still there. They were not an illusion, and he was sure they were the ones he'd thrown away; one of them had been lit and then pinched out, just like he'd done to one before deciding to throw them away. He was sunk.

Once Two Face and Herc had gone to play in the backyard, Joe and Bo reentered the house.

"You follow me while I look around, if you don't mind," Bo said with still no word about the marijuana joints in the truck.

"You're the cop," Joe said, trying to keep his voice light.

Bo searched very carefully. Joe would have been glad he'd thrown the joints away so Bo wouldn't have seen them. But his actions last night hardly mattered now because someone had put the joints in his truck and Bo had seen them anyway. He waited for the hammer to fall, for he was sure Bo would mention what he'd seen at some point and then probably have to arrest him.

The last room they checked was the spare bedroom. After looking beneath the old twin bed and in the closet, Bo said, "What's in this old trunk here?" He had stepped over to a very large, rustic trunk that rested against the wall beneath the bedroom window.

"It's empty," Joe said. "I've only opened it once, and that was when I first moved here."

Bo looked closely at it. "You don't dust much, do you, Joe?" he asked with a grin.

"No, do you?" Joe asked, grinning back at his cousin despite the strain he was under.

"Not much, but the reason I mentioned it is that the dust here by the latch and on the front of the trunk has been disturbed. Let's look in it just because I think your burglar did." He glanced around and then added with a frown on his face, "There's blood on the linoleum and on the front of this trunk. See this dark stain right here and right there? I'm sure that's blood."

"Maybe the guy's hand was still bleeding from getting cut on the glass in the window of the door," Joe suggested reasonably. "He must have looked in the trunk for something to steal." Bo made no comment, but his face was grim, and Joe felt a knot forming in his now very queasy stomach. There was really quite a lot of blood, if it was blood, and he was sure Bo knew what he was talking about.

Joe watched as Bo opened the lid, and Joe gasped. A man's body lay in the trunk, curled tightly into fetal position, his face twisted until it was facing up, a neat little hole right in the center of his forehead.

"This is not good," Bo said after both men stared at it for a minute. Without touching the body, Bo leaned down and looked closely. "He's been shot." Bo straightened up and looked at Joe in a way that he'd never looked at him before, his face a mixture of surprise and suspicion. "Joe, have you ever seen this guy before?"

Joe didn't want to answer. He wanted to run, hide, and disappear. How did he tell his police officer cousin that he'd been buying marijuana from the dead man who was crammed in his trunk? How could he tell him that he owed the guy five hundred dollars?

"No," he lied. "I've never seen him before."

"Well, whoever he is, he hasn't been here very long. I mean, he's stiff now, but he can't have been here for more than a few hours in my opinion."

"He must've been killed while we were fishing yesterday," Joe suggested, having a hard time talking. He was shocked beyond anything he had ever experienced. How could Emil Eifler, a man he despised, *but nowhere near the point of wanting him killed*, have ended up dead in a trunk in his own house? It was beyond baffling.

"Okay, let's go back in your living room. I'll need to have some other officers come since your house is now a murder scene," Bo said. Moments later, he made the call, which was short and to the point. "While we're waiting, you and I need to talk, Joe. First, why don't you tell me about the marijuana joints in your truck?"

"Bo, I promise I didn't put them there. I don't know how they got there. Someone must have slipped them in through the window. I didn't have it rolled up all the way. I do that a lot when I have Herc in the truck, even in cold weather like this. And I must have forgotten to roll it back up."

"Yeah, I noticed that. I suppose that's possible," Bo said. Then he studied Joe's face for a moment, making him squirm. "Joe, this is just between me and you. If you will be honest with me, I won't repeat what you say to anyone."

"About what?" Joe asked, feeling increasingly uncomfortable.

"About smoking pot." Joe started to say something, but Bo held up his hand, stopping him. "I'm not an idiot, Joe. So don't treat me like I am. I've smelled pot in your house before and even on your clothes. So again, be honest with me. How long have you been using it?"

The hammer had fallen. Joe took a deep breath, fought back the urge to cry, and said, "About a year. But I don't use much. And I've quit now."

"How long ago did you quit, and don't lie to me."

"Since last night," Joe said with his head down. "I had two joints left, and I threw them out back."

"In your yard?"

"No, I climbed the fence and threw them back there a ways." He pointed to the south.

"It's going to take a little while for other officers to get here, so let's look now."

"Okay, I think I can remember about where I threw them," Joe said.

"Let me take the lead, Joe. This snow, though it's just a small layer, will have covered your tracks a little, but I think I still may be able to see impressions in the old snow or where the ground was bare. Tell me if you think I'm going the wrong way at any point."

They moved slowly, Bo with his head bent, looking closely at the snowy ground beneath them. He was pretty good and didn't once ask Joe when to stop, but he said, "Your tracks end right here. But wait, there are more tracks, some from before this light snow. Someone has tromped all over here."

Joe looked at where Bo was pointing. He could barely make them out, but they were there, just like Bo had said. "Those aren't mine."

"I know that. Joe, someone must have been watching you last night. And it couldn't have been the guy in the trunk." Bo took some pictures of the tracks with his cell phone even though they were faint, and then he said, "You stay right here and let me take a closer look."

Joe watched, sick to his stomach with worry as Bo followed the tracks. He searched the area thoroughly. Finally he walked back to Joe. "Okay, whoever this was must have found your joints. I'm guessing they're the ones in your truck now. Joe, someone doesn't like you. Let's go back."

"Are you going to arrest me?" Joe asked.

"I'm going to collect those joints from your truck, but since I haven't actually caught you with them on you, then no, I won't arrest you. They will be our little secret on two conditions."

With a voice that was not working very well, Joe asked, "What are the conditions?"

"First, that you tell me who the man in the trunk is, and second, that you prove to me that there is no pot in your house—and I promise you that we'll look very thoroughly."

"There's none in there. Nor is there any in my truck but those two joints, and there's none in any of my clothes," Joe said.

"Fine. I hope you're telling me the truth."

"I am, Bo. I won't lie to you anymore."

"Meaning that you do know who's in the trunk," Bo said. It was not a question but a statement of fact.

"I do," Joe admitted with his head hung. "His name is Emil Eifler, and he's the one who I've been buying weed from, and I owe him some money. He's been pushing me to pay him. I planned to give him my shotgun for payment and then not let him give me any more weed."

"I see. One more question, Joe. Was he alive and did you catch him in your house when you got home last night?"

"No! Bo, I would never do something like that," Joe said, alarmed that Bo would even ask such a thing. "I didn't see anyone in here. I had no idea he was in that trunk."

"Okay, so let's go get those joints from the truck now. And you must be prepared to answer whatever questions you're asked by the detective when he and the other officers get here. You will have to tell them that you know the dead man and that you *used* to buy from him but that you haven't for a while. They can't charge you for telling them you used to use it. They could only charge you if they find some."

Lucas had seen the two men search for the joints behind Joe's house. He wished he was close enough to hear what was being said. He shivered with concern when the officer took pictures of the ground—of his tracks, he was sure.

He watched them as they went to Joe's truck and opened the door with Joe's keys. The deputy did something inside the passenger side that Lucas couldn't see, but when the deputy stood up and stepped back, he was holding a small plastic evidence bag. Lucas was certain it held the two joints, an opinion made more sure by how uncomfortable Joe looked. Lucas laughed to himself. Joe was in trouble now, which Lucas was not troubled by in the least. He didn't care for Joe. In fact, he despised Joe.

His mind went back to the day he'd met Joe. Several months ago, when he and Nattie had been shopping in a grocery store, Nattie had accidentally knocked over a display. It was almost empty but had still held several cans of beef stew. The cans had fallen, clattering, and rolled up the aisle. Lucas had laughed and told Nattie that she was a klutz and needed to pick up the cans.

She'd told him she was sorry and asked him to help, but he'd told her that it was her job. She'd started to pick up the cans, tears in her eyes, when this guy, who turned out to be Joe Whalen, had started helping her. Lucas had said, "Hey, that's her job. She's the one who knocked that thing over. She can clean it up."

Joe had looked up and said, "She's a lady. If you aren't gentleman enough to help her, then I will."

Lucas had seethed with anger. When the display was back in place, Nattie had introduced herself. "I'm Nattie. Thanks for helping me. You're a nice guy."

"I'm Joe Whalen," Joe had said. "You're welcome." Then he'd smiled at Nattie and she'd smiled back, a sweet smile, one Lucas thought should only be for him, not for some stranger. The two had looked at each other longer than Lucas liked. It had made him jealous and very angry.

Joe had turned away just then. Lucas had grabbed the back of his shirt and jerked him around. Joe had balled his fists and said, "What do you need?"

"I need for you to get lost. This is my woman," Lucas had said. "No one talks to her or smiles at her like that. Understand, loser?"

"Leave him alone, Lucas," Nattie had said hotly. "He was only being a gentleman, unlike you."

Lucas had let go of Joe's shirt then, but reluctantly. "Get lost."

Joe had held both hands up then and stepped back. "Sorry, didn't mean to offend you." Then he'd smiled at Nattie again. "It's nice to meet you, Nattie. Have a good day."

"You too, Joe," Nattie had said with a brief smile.

Lucas had wanted to punch him for being defiant like that, but Nattie had grabbed his hand. "Don't, Lucas."

Lucas had only seen Joe one time after that. He'd been driving past Emil's old house when Joe was leaving with a package that likely contained some dope. Joe had waved at him with a grin on his face, sending a flash of anger through Lucas, but then Joe and his old truck had gone on by, and Lucas hadn't seen him again until last night. He snapped out of his reverie, hoping Joe would get in trouble. He really didn't like the guy at all.

Joe and the deputy had gone back in the house and were there for several minutes before two more county sheriff vehicles sped up the narrow road and stopped in front of Joe's house. They went inside, and soon, a hearse pulled up, followed by even more officers. That made Lucas squirm. Surely if there was a body in the house, he would have seen it, but he hadn't. Then again, he hadn't looked that closely. But if there was, it had to be the body of Emil Eifler. Lucas didn't particularly care that he was dead, but he would never have killed him. He just wanted to get his property from Emil and even catch him doing something he could turn him in to the cops for to get even with him. Emil *had* done something; he'd broken into Joe's house. But he couldn't use that information now, nor would he get back any of the things Emil had forced him and Nattie to hand over. It was all so unfair.

Getting Emil arrested for burglary would have made Lucas feel better even though that had not been what he was after. All he'd wanted was to get even with Emil for taking his property and scaring Nattie half out of her mind. She hadn't deserved that. But Lucas had never thought about murdering Emil—if that's really what had happened.

He began to tremble. The shot he'd heard had been real, and so had the blood. Whoever the big man was, he must have killed Emil. But Lucas had foolishly gone into the house himself. His fingerprints were in there, and his tracks were outside. He could be accused of murder. But he didn't do it.

He was worried now like he'd never been worried before. And he hated Emil all the more for it.

Joe endured a lot of questioning, and he could feel the suspicion aimed at him by Detective Will Merianos, the lead officer on the case. Joe insisted he was innocent, but no one seemed to believe him. He wasn't even entirely sure Bo believed him. He could only hope he did.

He worried about his collie, and he had to get to work. Ron needed him. Melia needed him.

"We found a small can of Mace in the dead guy's pocket," Bo told him at one point. "That explains why your dog's eyes have been bothering him. You won't need to take him to a vet. Mace has no long-lasting effect. Herc will be fine."

Joe felt better knowing that, but he really felt sick when Bo told him that the detectives were going to take his revolver. "Why do they need that?" he asked.

"Just to make sure it wasn't used to kill the victim. It has been fired recently. Have you shot it in the past day or two?" Bo asked.

"No," Joe responded.

"Then whoever killed Emil probably used your gun. It has an empty shell in one chamber. Also, Joe, we have confirmed that he is who you told me he is. He's a drug dealer who the detectives have been trying to make a case on for the past few months. He's had a few run-ins with the law over the years. He's never been to prison, but he's spent some time in the county jail. There's another drug dealer in the area who we've been watching who apparently has had some run-ins with Emil. His name is Leonardo Augur."

Joe shuddered. "I know who he is. I remember Emil telling me that if the guy contacted me and tried to sell me drugs that I'd better not buy from him. Anyway, back to Emil. I can't imagine why he would be in my house."

Bo cocked an eyebrow. "The detective and the other officers want to search your house very thoroughly. So far, all they've done is take photos of the body and the surrounding area."

"They can search all they want. I'll even sign something saying that."

"No, they are going to get a search warrant. It will take a little while."

"I need to go to work now. And I want to get those fish out to Melia. Is it okay if I'm not here for the search?" he asked.

"Let me check," Bo said. A moment later, he returned to the kitchen where Joe was waiting. "You can go now."

"Thanks," Joe said.

Joe left for Ron Brady's farm with the fish and his collie, feeling like his world was crashing down on him. He was certain the officers suspected he had killed Emil. He hadn't, but they didn't act like they believed him. Admittedly, it did look bad for him. After all, Emil's body had been found in his house, his own pistol had recently been fired, and he owed Emil some money.

Lucas left his watching spot right after Joe got in his truck. He had half expected Joe to be arrested. Better Joe than him. It would have served him right. They should have arrested Joe and hauled him off to jail so they wouldn't look for anyone else who had been in the house. Now, of course, Lucas wished he'd never gone in. He'd heard that a deputy by the name of Bo Buckley was Joe's cousin. Was he the first uniformed deputy who'd shown up? Maybe he had talked the others into letting Joe go. So what would happen now? Would they find Lucas's fingerprints and come after him? What about his shoes? The deputy had taken pictures of his tracks. He needed to ditch the shoes right away.

Lucas hurried to where he'd hidden his car and drove the direction Joe had driven. It might be stupid, but he wondered where Joe was going. He was becoming obsessed with the guy and wanted him to get in trouble. He drove fast and soon had him in sight. Then he slowed down and followed him into a farming area and stopped when he saw him pull into the large farmyard. That must be where he worked. Lucas decided to find a place to hide where he and his car wouldn't be noticed.

He was a little farther away than he would have liked, but his binoculars were high quality. He could see well enough through them to have at least some idea of what was happening on the farm. He leaned against a tree and watched. His car was hidden someplace secure, and he was out of sight of the road or any neighboring farms. Watching Joe beat watching soap operas all day at home.

The cops had to arrest Joe so they wouldn't go looking for anyone else—so they wouldn't come looking for Lucas. He was frustrated. Surely they'd come after Joe in a little while. If they didn't arrest him soon, Lucas didn't know what he'd do. The guy who really needed to be arrested was the guy who had actually murdered Emil, but he had no idea who that was. He simply had to hope that they would arrest Joe.

Another man, the killer, also watched the farm but from a different vantage point. He'd watched Joe's house earlier. He wanted Joe arrested but not because he had any feelings for the guy one way or another. Joe would be as good a person as any to have arrested, and then no one would come looking for *him*. Maybe the cops hadn't figured out yet that Emil had been shot with Joe's twenty-two pistol. Surely that would clinch it. He'd held Emil at gunpoint with his own gun, and when Emil had tried to get away, he'd knocked him on the head, rendering him unconscious. Then he'd looked around the house, and when he found the pistol in the main bedroom, he'd had an idea, a rather good one, he thought.

Emil was just regaining consciousness when he'd dragged him into the spare bedroom and shot him with Joe's twenty-two revolver. He'd first planned to just leave him there on the floor, but then he'd seen the big old trunk. When he discovered it was empty, he'd put Emil's short, skinny body in there. There was a bit of blood around, but the floor was an ancient brown linoleum, and the blood sort of blended in. Not that it mattered. He'd left it at that and gotten out of there. He hadn't wanted to be there when the occupant of the house got home.

The dog hadn't given him any trouble, so he'd hurried back to his truck and left.

From where he was watching now, a short ways from the farmyard, he could see that dog yipping at the heels of an attractive young lady who came running out of the house when Joe arrived. Who was she and what kind of relationship did she have with Joe? Not that it mattered. Joe would go to prison. He would make sure of that because there was no way anyone could be allowed to come looking for *him*. Joe was the perfect scapegoat.

CHAPTER FOUR

Melia was bouncing with energy and had run from the house when Joe pulled into the Brady farmyard. Herc bounded out of the truck and greeted Melia with enthusiasm, his tail wagging and his tongue hanging out. She knelt and petted him for a minute. When she stood up, he ran off to play with Ron's dog, Ace. Melia hurried up to Joe but stopped and stared at him with concern. "Joe, what's wrong?"

"Everything," he said despondently.

"Ah, come on, Joe. It's a pretty day. It can't be that bad. Let's go start our chores." She smiled at him, that pretty, bright smile he'd come to admire. He tried to smile in return, but it didn't go too well. Clearly, she noticed. "Joe, why don't you tell me about whatever is bothering you. We can work while you talk and I listen."

They worked, but he did not talk. Finally, Melia poked a fork in a bale of hay and faced him with a determined look on her face and her hands folded across her chest. "Please, Joe. Tell me what the problem is."

He finally decided that he'd just as well. She would find out eventually anyway. "My cousin Bo and I went ice fishing yesterday," he began, and then he remembered the fish in his truck. "Oh, I almost forgot. We caught a bunch of nice fish. The ones I caught are in the truck. I brought them in case you wanted to fry them for dinner sometime."

"Hey, that would be great. I'll do it for dinner tonight. Let's bring them in the house," she said with enthusiasm.

When they entered the house, Ron was in his recliner reading a book. "Hey, what do you guys have there?"

"Joe caught some fish yesterday. I'm going to fry them for dinner," Melia said.

"That sounds like a mighty fine idea," Ron said. "Just put them in the fridge for now, Melia." He looked at Joe for a moment after Melia went into the kitchen. Joe was trying his best to look like everything was fine, but he just couldn't quite manage. Ron didn't miss it. "Is something wrong?" he asked.

"Oh, no. I'm okay."

"You are not okay," Melia said as she reentered the living room. "I've never seen you like this before. What's going on? Please tell us. We're your friends."

Melia and Ron looked expectantly at him. He cared about both of them. In fact, he cared more about them than anyone in the world besides Bo and Rosina. He felt tears forming in his eyes but rubbed them away. He couldn't cry in front of them. He just couldn't. He had to be strong and face his troubles with some semblance of courage. "Maybe I'll tell you at dinner," he said, hoping to put it off.

"So are you saying that everything really isn't okay?" Ron asked, his face creased with worry.

Joe shook his head. "We'd better get the work done, Melia. Ron's animals won't feed themselves." He forced a grin that he didn't feel.

Ron spoke again, and he did so quite sternly. "That can wait, Joe. Let's all sit down and you can unload your troubles on Melia and me. We're both good listeners, and we care about you a great deal."

"Please, Joe," Melia begged as she gently took hold of his arm and looked into his eyes. "Maybe we can help."

"Nobody can help," Joe said forcefully.

"Please, Joe, just tell us," Ron begged.

"Okay," Joe said finally. "But I'm warning you, it's really bad. So Bo and I got home kind of late from ice fishing at Strawberry Reservoir last night. Bo dropped me off at my place and left. After he was gone, I discovered my house had been broken into."

"Joe, that's horrible!" Melia exclaimed.

"It gets worse," Joe said. "Whoever it was got in by breaking some glass out of my back door and reaching in and unlocking it."

"Your back door," Melia said. "But wasn't your dog back there?"

"He was, and he got Maced by the burglar, but he's okay now. Anyway, I went in and looked around."

"What was stolen?" Ron asked.

"Nothing, as far as I can tell. Anyway, to make a long story short, my cousin, Deputy Bo Buckley, came early this morning to check it out."

"You slept there last night?" Melia asked. "I'd have been scared to death to stay there."

"I didn't really have anyplace else to go, and I kept my shotgun loaded beside my bed."

"You could have come here. I have plenty of room in this big old house," Ron said.

"I didn't think about that. Plus, it was quite late, and I looked all through the house. It didn't feel like there was any danger. So this morning, Bo came after he got on duty and looked through my house. He asked me what was in this large trunk in my spare bedroom. I'd only ever opened it once when I first moved in. There was nothing in it then, but Bo opened it and there . . . there was the . . . the dead body of a man in it," Joe stuttered. "He'd been shot!"

Melia let out a little scream, and then clapped her hands over her cheeks. "Who was it?" she asked with wide, frightened eyes.

Joe thought about the lies he'd told Bo and then fessed up to. He couldn't very well start lying again now, even if it meant Ron would fire him. He supposed that wouldn't matter anyway because he was probably going to end up in prison. His stomach twisted at the thought. For a moment, he looked down, then he met Melia's and Ron's anxious gazes. "It was a guy I knew by the name of Emil Eifler. He was a drug pusher and was in trouble a lot. The cops are still at my place. I think they think I did it."

"You would never do something like that," Melia protested with alarm in her voice, her pretty blue eyes wide with distress.

"I wouldn't and I didn't, but I still think they think I did. I wish Bo had come in with me last night. Then they'd know it happened while he and I were fishing, but as it is, I think they are going to say that I killed him right after Bo dropped me off at home."

"But I don't understand. Why would they think you'd do that?" Melia asked.

"Maybe they think I caught him in my house and shot him," Joe guessed.

"That would be self-defense," Ron said.

"Only if I did it, which I didn't." What he didn't say was that in the eyes of the law, he had motive and it was his pistol that was the murder weapon. He didn't see any way he could avoid being locked up for murder.

They talked a little longer. Joe could see that both Ron and Melia believed him, and they also agreed that the cops might try to blame him. He decided he needed to tell them the rest of the story, as shameful as it was. He bucked up his courage and then said, "There's more, and you'll both hate me for it."

"I don't think so," Melia said, her gaze glued to his face, her eyes full of warmth now. "So what else happened?"

"Well, this is horrible, but the reason I knew the guy who was killed—Emil Eifler—was because I've been buying some marijuana from him," he said.

They both stared at him with blank faces.

"That is disappointing," Ron said finally, "but I'm sure you want to quit using it."

Melia just looked at him with narrowed eyes, the warmth they'd held a moment ago now gone. She looked angry, but then he was certain he saw a tiny bit of moisture in her eyes. She did not rub them; instead, she let a couple tears meander down her cheeks.

"I've already quit—for good—but I still owed Emil some money. He'd been pushing me to pay up. But I didn't kill him, and I wouldn't ever murder someone. Definitely not for something like that. I'm not that stupid for starters. I was thinking that I'd give him my shotgun to cover the debt. It's worth more than I owed him, and that would have been the end of it. But I never got the chance."

"Did the police search your house and truck?" Ron asked.

"They searched my truck before I left to come here, and they're searching the house now, but they won't find any drugs, because I don't have any anymore."

He thought about mentioning the two joints he'd thrown away that had been found and placed purposely in his truck, but he didn't when he remembered that Bo had told him that detail would be just between the two of them.

"You will probably hate me now for being such an idiot," he said with his eyes down.

"We'll never hate you, Joe. We may be disappointed, but I, for one, will never hate you," Ron said.

"I could never hate you, Joe," Melia added.

"Joe, you have my support," Ron said. "So you don't need to worry about that. We all make mistakes, and when we change, we have to hope others will forgive us. I forgive you, so it's done and over with as far as I'm concerned. Now you need to forgive yourself."

"I forgive you too," Melia said as she now rubbed the tears away. "We are still best friends, I promise."

"Thank you both," he said, "but I'm afraid I'll still get arrested for a murder I didn't commit."

After a few minutes, Joe and Melia went outside and began working where they had left off earlier. They worked hard and with very little conversation, and when they did speak, it was only about matters that had to do with their work. A couple hours passed before Melia said to Joe, "I trust you, Joe, and I like you a lot. Grandpa and I will help you in any way we can."

"Thanks, Melia. I like you too, but I don't think there will be anything anyone can do for me. Someone killed Emil, and whoever it was made it look like I did it. I'm afraid they did a pretty good job of it."

Melia cooked the fish early that evening. Joe had helped her a little by setting the table for the three of them, getting things they needed from the refrigerator, and handing her some salt and pepper when she asked for it. Melia, Joe, and Ron had just sat down at the table and said a blessing on the food when the doorbell rang. "I'll get it," Melia said, jumping up and leaving the kitchen. She returned a minute later, giving Joe a look of concern, trailed by two deputies, Detective Merianos and an officer who had been at Joe's house but whose name Joe did not know.

Joe did not get to taste the fish that night. They arrested him, cuffed him, and hauled him away. The last he saw of Melia was her sobbing and Ron drawing an arm around her to console her.

The killer had been watching the officers at Joe's house from a safe distance, and he followed them when they drove to the farm. He had smiled with satisfaction when he saw the officers haul Joe off in handcuffs. The frame-up he'd set had worked after all. It couldn't have been better. Joe was the perfect victim for his frame. Joe would go to prison, and no one would be the wiser about what had really happened at Joe's house. Emil Eifler got what he had coming to him, and Joe would pay for it. He left, feeling quite smug.

Lucas was relieved. He'd watched from a distant vantage point and saw Joe led from the farmhouse in handcuffs. Lucas was off the hook. He'd worried about being accused of the murder of a man he hated, but everything was okay now. Joe, someone else he hated, was being blamed, not him.

And yet . . . Lucas kept thinking about the real killer. That's who should have been arrested, but he had no idea who the guy was. It had been too dark to get a very good look at him. It made him a little nervous to think that the man was getting away with murder. Who might he kill next? Would the guy come after him? Lucas didn't think the guy had seen him, but he couldn't be positive. The guy had no reason to come after him unless he'd seen him, Lucas told himself. But the very possibility made him shudder.

An hour later, Joe had been booked into Carbon County Jail for murder. When he asked to speak with Bo, he was told Bo had been taken off the case by the sheriff at the request of Detective Will Merianos because he was related to Joe but not for any other reason. He had a feeling that he had made Bo angry with Will, but Joe knew Bo could do nothing but accept the decision and keep his mouth shut.

Joe had worried about his collie dog, Herc, when he was first arrested, but Ron had promised to take care of him until he could get things straightened out and get out of jail. He was scared of the other inmates and got very little sleep that night. The next morning, he was taken in front of a judge and formally arraigned on the charge of homicide. An attorney was appointed to represent him, and he was taken back to his jail cell.

The attorney, Dylan Tokery, was a well-dressed man of medium height and weight in his early thirties with short black hair and brown eyes. He went to the jail and met with Joe immediately following the arraignment. The first thing he said to Joe when he sat down across from him was, "Joe, you must be totally honest with me. If you aren't, I'm not sure I can help you. You say you didn't do it, and I will try to prove that."

"I *didn't* kill that guy," Joe affirmed desperately. "That's the truth."

"Tell me about the victim, Emil Eifler," Mr. Tokery said. "Did you know him?"

Joe hung his head in shame. He was in jail and charged with killing Emil. He couldn't see how it could get any worse. So he looked his attorney in the eyes. "Yes, I knew him. I used to buy marijuana from him. I told the officers that."

"I've only had a chance to glance at the report, but I understand you didn't have any of the marijuana or any other illegal drugs in your house, in your truck, or on your person," Dylan said. "Is that right?"

"I had quit using, but I still owed Emil money," Joe said. "I wanted to give him my shotgun. That would have more than paid him off. I despised the man."

"Joe," Dylan said sternly, "everything you tell me is confidential. From now on, you don't speak with any of the officers without me being present. Do you understand that?"

"I do," Joe said.

"Okay. By doing it that way, I can make sure you don't slip up and tell them you despised the guy. They don't need to know that," Mr. Tokery said. "And I'll make sure you don't say anything else that might make you look guilty."

"I understand," Joe said.

"Okay, so let's move on," Dylan said. "I need to know everything you did over the past few days. I need to know who you saw, who you talked to, what you did, and where you went."

Joe spent the next hour explaining his recent life to his attorney. When he had finished, Dylan said, "Okay, Joe, I believe you are innocent. Truly, I do. Now what I've got to do is prove it. I'll warn you that it won't be easy."

"I understand that," Joe said. "Is there any chance I can get out of jail before I have a trial?"

"I'll work on that, Joe. I'll try to get you released on bail. But I can't promise anything," his attorney said. "The prosecutor will try to convince the court that you're a dangerous man and that you must be kept in jail in order to protect others. I'll show the court that you have never been in trouble before and will stick around for your trial if it comes to that."

"What do you mean by *if it comes to that*?" Joe asked.

"I mean that someone killed Mr. Eifler, and since it wasn't you, that means it was someone else. If I can, I'll find out who the real killer is, and if I succeed at that, you will never have to go to trial," Tokery said.

"I don't see how you can do that. He made it look pretty bad for me," Joe said.

"Yes, he did, and it will be hard, but I'll work on it. For now, you have to understand that it could be several days at the very least before we'll know if the judge will set bail and, if so, how much. So plan to be patient, and whatever you do, stay out of trouble with other inmates."

"I might spend the rest of my life in jail," Joe said despondently.

"Not if I can help it," Mr. Tokery said. He sounded both sincere and determined, but for some reason Joe couldn't quite define, he wasn't at all sure. For one thing, he didn't see how Mr. Tokery could possibly find the real killer. He honestly didn't think anyone could.

The killer had gone back to the farm and had begun to watch through his binoculars. He'd driven by Joe's house earlier and noticed it was surrounded by yellow police tape, but Joe's truck was gone, so even if he got out of jail, he wouldn't be able to go in his house. But perhaps he would go to the farm. He might have already been released from jail and done so. Joe's boss might be willing to pick him up at the jail and take him to the farm.

He did not want to watch the jail to see if Joe got out, for there were too many cops coming and going. So he settled in with his binoculars trained on the farmyard. He didn't have to wait long before a young lady, the one he'd seen the day before, came out of the house and started feeding animals. Joe was not with her. So far so good.

Melia was exhausted as she went about doing the chores for her grandfather that morning. She had cried most of the night. Her grandfather had tried to comfort her, but it hadn't worked—he was as sad as she was. They both liked Joe a lot, and they needed him on the farm. Melia was a hard worker, but there was no way she could do it all, and Ron tired very quickly. Joe's dog needed him too. Herc stayed right with Melia while she worked as if she was the closest thing to a friend he had in Joe's absence. He ignored Ace, Ron's dog.

A white car pulled into the yard just as Melia was walking out of the barn with Herc at her side. She stood there and watched with a heavy heart as two young women in winter coats, both probably around her age or maybe a little older, got out and looked around. Then they spotted her and started walking in her direction. Herc ran toward them, jumping in excitement. One of them patted Herc's head, and he writhed with joy. He clearly knew them. Melia stood where she was until they reached her.

"You must be Melia," one of them said, an attractive girl with long chestnut hair and eyes that reminded her of Joe. She was a little shorter than Melia. "I'm Rosina Whalen, Joe's sister," she continued. "And this is my friend Karmen Ellison."

The second girl was several inches taller than Melia and Rosina. She was also quite attractive. She had long brown hair and was slender and graceful. Melia took an instant liking to both of them. "Hey, it's nice to meet you guys. I'm Melia Brady, Joe's friend."

"And his boss's granddaughter, right?" Rosina asked with a smile.

"Yes, I am. And I don't know what to say. Grandpa's brokenhearted over what's happened to your brother." Melia choked up a little. "I am too. He's a great guy."

"Yes, he is," Rosina agreed. "And I am very sad about what happened to him. So is our cousin, Bo. Can we talk to you for a little while? We'd like to talk to your grandfather too if it's okay."

"He's in the house. He's not in good health. I don't know what he's going to do—what either of us is going to do—if Joe doesn't get out of jail real soon. We need him here," Melia said, and to her dismay, tears started to trickle down her cheeks. "I'm sorry. I thought I got cried out last night."

"Me too," Rosina said. "I'm shocked, but not for one second do I believe Joe killed that awful man. I am so angry at the cops; not Bo, but the others. They think he did this." She balled her fists as she spoke, and her eyes flashed.

"Why don't you guys come in the house where it's warm? Grandpa doesn't like to come out in the cold very much. It really bothers him," Melia said.

Herc was still sticking with them, but it was clear to Melia that he knew and liked Rosina.

"Herc," Rosina said, dropping to her knees and putting her arms around the big collie's neck. For a moment, all her attention was on the dog. Melia petted Ron's dog when he joined them. Then Rosina stood up. "I have no place to keep a dog."

"Don't worry, Rosina. Herc has a home with us as long as he needs one. He'll be just fine. We'll take good care of him."

Ron stood up from his recliner when the three girls entered the house. "You must be Rosina, Joe's sister," he said to Rosina. "He talks about you a lot."

"I hope it's mostly good," Rosina said.

Ron smiled. "Nothing but good. He's very fond of you, and I am very fond of him. He's become like a son to me. My late wife and I only had one child, Melia's mother. Here, won't you girls sit down? Could we get you a glass of water?"

"I'm fine," Rosina said. "This is my friend Karmen Ellison."

"It's nice to meet you," Karmen said. "I don't need water either."

After they were all seated, Ron said, "So what can I do for you girls?"

"We'd actually like to know what we can do for you?" Rosina said with a sad smile. "Until Joe gets out of jail, you must need help."

"I'll do the best I can," Melia said.

"Melia can't do all that needs to be done by herself," Ron said with a long face. "I have a lot of animals, and they require a lot of work. And I can't do much anymore. I honestly don't know what we're going to do. I may have to hire someone else, and I don't want to do that. Joe would be very hard to replace. I don't like to even think that I may have to do that."

"We are both in college right now and have part-time jobs, but we also have some free time since we are not actually carrying a full load at school. We were wondering if we could come out a few days a week and help out for a couple hours."

"Oh, Rosina, you guys don't have to do that," Ron said.

"I know, but I'd like to. Joe is a wonderful brother, and well, I hope he won't be in jail for very long. Karmen and I would like to help so you won't have to hire someone else."

"I appreciate that, Rosina. Maybe it would be okay for a while if you are sure you have time. Melia can show you what needs to be done." Then he looked at Karmen. "Why would you want to help? Not that I don't appreciate it."

She smiled. "I'm dating Bo Buckley."

"Oh, I see," Ron said with a smile. "Joe thinks the world of him. He must be pretty shook up over what's happened."

"He's devastated, and he's angry," Karmen said. "He knows that Joe is innocent, but he can't convince the detective who's in charge of the case to look at other possible suspects. Detective Merianos is very arrogant, and he's also, in my opinion and Bo's, power hungry, and he thrives on publicity. Anyway, the sheriff told Bo that he can't have anything more to do with the case since Joe and Bo are cousins. That wouldn't have happened if it hadn't been for the detective. He didn't want Bo involved at all. Bo knows Joe's innocent. We know it too. So the question is what can anyone do to prove his innocence?"

For the next half hour, the three girls and Ron talked. There wasn't much that Rosina and Karmen could tell them about what had happened at Joe's house that Joe himself hadn't already explained. Ron explained to the girls that Joe had opened up to them and admitted everything he'd done regarding the use of marijuana but adamantly denied killing Emil.

"Melia and I suspected before that he used marijuana, but he never told us about it. He says he's through with it, and we believe him. He has our full trust and support."

"Grandpa and I thought we could smell it on him sometimes," Melia said. "I knew some kids in high school who smoked marijuana. I know the smell. But I know that Joe is telling the truth when he says he's quit."

"Bo and I suspected it too, and we'd been trying to figure out a way to tell him we knew and get him to admit it so we could help him, but that's all moot now. So I guess that's that," Rosina said, rubbing at her eyes. "I'm going to visit him at the jail, and when I do, I'm sure he'll admit this to me like he did to you guys. Then I can assure him that I will help him in any way I can. I also hope I can get him to tell me who might hate him bad enough to frame him for murder. He's had to have had a run-in with someone, as unlikely as that seems. I need to get him to tell me since the detective on the case won't even consider anyone else as a suspect."

They talked a little longer, but then at last, Melia said, "You guys can stay and talk with Grandpa, but I need to get back to work."

"We'll help you," Rosina said. "You just show us what to do."

The man who had killed Emil right there in Joe's house with a revolver he'd found in Joe's bedroom had seen the two young women drive into the farmyard. He'd watched them enter the house with the other young woman. Then after around an hour, the three came out together and went to working around the corrals and in the barn.

He had no idea who they were, but when they left, so did he. He was able to follow them back into Price. One girl dropped the other one off at an apartment complex and then drove to a different one nearby, where she went inside. He memorized where each of them lived. He might not need to know that, but then again, it might be helpful at some point. He did not want them or anyone else to mess up his plans to see Joe pay for the murder of Emil Eifler so that he could get on with his own life without having to worry about the cops coming after him. Joe had made a perfect scapegoat.

CHAPTER FIVE

Joe was told on Sunday afternoon that he had visitors. He assumed it must be his sister and possibly Bo, although he had convinced himself that Bo believed him to be guilty of killing Emil. He was taken to the visiting area, but to his surprise, it was Ron and Melia who had come to see him.

"You guys didn't need to come," Joe said, even though he was glad they had. "I'm just sorry I can't be there to help you. What are you going to do, Melia? You can't handle it alone and still keep up the house and meals."

"I'll do what I have to," she said. But Joe knew how hard the work was and how much there was to do. He knew there was no way she could handle it by herself.

"Have you seen your sister yet?" Ron asked.

"No, I expected it was her when they told me I had visitors. Maybe she'll still come," Joe said. "Or maybe she won't."

"I'm sure she will," Ron said. "At any rate, she and her friend Karmen insist that they're going to come out and help Melia for two or three hours a few times a week."

"But they both have part-time jobs and college classes," Joe protested. "They don't have time."

"They insist that they do, that they don't have a full load at school, so I showed them what we do on Friday when they came out, and then they came again yesterday. They both worked for several hours."

"That's great," Joe said, not sure what else he could say.

"Have you got an attorney yet, or would you like me to find one for you?" Ron asked.

"The judge appointed one," Joe said. "He seems like he'll be okay. He says he believes me and that he will do what he can to prove I didn't do it."

"How is he going to do that?" Melia asked skeptically.

"I don't know. He says he needs to figure out who actually did it. But I don't know how he will go about that or if he was just saying it to make me think he could actually help me."

"Honestly, Joe, my guess is that he was just saying that to make you feel better," Ron said. "Something has to be done. I'm going to give it some thought and then get back with you. It might be best to hire a more experienced attorney, one with some background on this kind of case."

After leaving the jail, Ron and Melia stopped at the store for a few groceries and then drove back to the farm. Melia put the groceries away, and then she headed for the barn to do some work. To her surprise, there was a piece of paper taped to the outside of the small barn door she usually used to enter the barn since the big door was latched from the inside. The note had been typed and left unsigned. She tore it down and gasped when she read it.

> *Miss Brady, you and your grandpa leave the matter of Joe's murder charge alone. He is guilty, and if you do anything to try to prove otherwise, he could be hurt very badly.*

She pulled the note from the wall with shaking hands and ran to the house, her heart pounding.

The killer was at his former spot with binoculars around his neck. He smiled wickedly to himself. He'd watched Melia (for he had done some quiet snooping around and learned that was her name) read the note and then rush for the house. He guessed officers would be coming, but there was nothing they could do. No one could ever catch him. He had worn latex gloves when he'd handled the note. It couldn't be traced to him by fingerprints, so he wasn't worried. He just hoped that Ron and Melia took the note seriously. If they didn't, he knew someone in Carbon County Jail who could and would carry out the threat.

He didn't wait to see officers come. He had someplace else to be and something else to do.

Joe was told he had more visitors. This time it was his sister and a friend of hers whom he hadn't met before.

"Are you doing okay?" Rosina asked. "I can't believe this is happening. Oh, and this is my friend and Bo's, Karmen Ellison."

"It's nice to meet you," Joe said. "I'm just sorry you have to meet me in here. I hate it here. There are some guys that scare me."

"We've got to figure out a way to get you out of jail," Rosina said. "We all know you didn't do it."

"Detective Merianos thinks I did," Joe said dejectedly. "Because of him, the sheriff won't let Bo have anything to do with the investigation. I think I'm going to be stuck in here."

"Hey, big brother, you hang in there and don't think that way. You've got to be positive. You're innocent, and somehow, someone will find a way to prove it."

Joe doubted that, but after a little while, he said, "That's nice of you guys to help Melia on the farm. But you don't have to do that. Ron could hire someone else to take my place. He's probably going to have to do that anyway."

"Think positive," Rosina reminded him, pointing an index finger at him and cocking an eyebrow.

"Joe, Bo wants to come see you, not as an officer but as a visitor. He couldn't come when we did, but he'll be here tomorrow for sure. He's really worried about you," Karmen said.

"I hope he can."

"Joe," Rosina began with a very serious look on her face, "there's something I need to know: who hates you enough to frame you for murder? I assume you've been thinking about it."

"I have," he said. There was an idea in the back of his head, but he didn't want to tell his sister, for he was afraid it would put her in danger, and there was no way he would do that. "I don't know, but I'll keep thinking about it."

"You do that," she responded. "I don't know what I could do with a name once you think of one. Maybe I could tell your attorney."

"Maybe, but I don't have a lot of confidence in him," Joe responded. "He's a nice guy, but I don't think he's had much experience. I sure wish I could get out of jail. I'm scared in here. I know that sounds pathetic, but I really am." He could feel his chin trembling as he spoke and was ashamed.

"Of course you are," Rosina said. "Anybody would be. But I'm sure the officers will keep you safe."

Their visiting time ran out, and Rosina and Karmen left. Joe was taken back to his cell. He hadn't been kidding when he'd told the girls that he was scared, and in all honesty, he didn't trust the jail officers to keep him safe. There were some mean-looking dudes in here, and they were often together. He almost wished he could stay locked in his cell. He would prefer isolation to being around some of the men in the jail.

Rosina dropped Karmen off and then drove on to her apartment. She parked her car and headed for the door. She stopped when she reached it. There was a note taped there. Why? Her roommate, Nyree, was at home studying hard for an upcoming test; her car was parked in the spot next to Rosina's.

Rosina reached for the note, and then she hesitated. Maybe she should read it first. She leaned close. It was typed.

> *Rosina, you and your friends leave the matter of Joe's murder charge alone. He is guilty, but if you do anything to try to prove otherwise, he could be hurt very badly.*

She felt sick to her stomach as the blood drained from her face and her knees began to shake. This was terrible.

Now she suspected Joe's fear of the jail had a stronger foundation than she'd thought. Maybe he wasn't safe there. Somebody was out to see that he never went free again. That somebody was probably the person who killed that Emil guy. That somebody had left a note on her door. With shaking hands, Rosina unlocked the apartment door and called out, "Nyree, are you home?"

"Yeah," Nyree said, coming from her room. "Didn't you see my car?"

"I did, but, Nyree, someone taped a note to the door. Did you see or hear anyone?"

"No, nobody rang the bell or knocked. What kind of note? My word, you look like you've seen a ghost. You are shaking like a leaf."

"Seeing a ghost wouldn't be as bad as this note. Come read it. It's frightening. I'm going to call Bo," Rosina said.

She pulled out her phone as Nyree read the note. Her face went white, and she said in a weak voice, as Rosina listened to her phone, hoping that Bo would answer, "Rosina, this is terrifying. What can we do?"

"I wish I knew," Rosina said as the phone continued to ring in her shaking hands and finally went to voice mail. She left Bo a message telling him to call her as soon as he could and that she had something extremely urgent she needed to show him. When she hung up, she collapsed on the sofa and put her head in her hands.

The watcher chuckled as he drove off. He was certain he had both Joe's sister and her roommate scared out of their wits. He had plans that would soon make Joe's situation worse unless people kept their noses out of the investigation as he had warned them to do. Emil got what he had coming, and Joe was going to have to pay for it. He patted himself on the back for being so much smarter than the cops.

Bo was the officer who responded to Melia's 911 call. He had no idea what was wrong as all she'd told the dispatcher was that she needed to see him right away. It worried him, and he'd gone lights and siren all the way out to Ron's farm. When he got there, she and Ron had both been waiting in the house, worried looks on their faces. Melia had been crying. Her eyes were red, and her hands shook as she gave him the note. He read it, and anger flared to life within him. The real killer was out there, and he was playing games with Joe's life. Unfortunately, that idiot Will Merianos would never believe it. He was out to make a name for himself, and he wouldn't even think about looking for someone else in the murder investigation.

His phone rang while he was talking to Ron and his granddaughter, but he let it go to voice mail. It was not until he was almost back to the sheriff's office with the note that he remembered the call. He pulled off to the side of the road and checked his phone. Rosina had left him a message. He listened to it with growing concern. Then he called her back.

"Bo, somebody put a note on my door while I was visiting Joe at the jail," she said the moment he answered.

"This is unbelievable. Someone wants to make sure Joe is convicted!" he said. "I'm just coming from Ron Brady's farm. Melia found a note on the barn door. Read me the one you have."

"Just a minute. It's still on the door. I didn't want to touch it," she said. "I'll take a picture of it and text it to you."

Bo had a feeling he knew what it contained. He quickly turned his car around and headed Rosina's way. "You do that," he said, "but read it to me anyway." When she read it to him a moment later, the anger he'd felt over Melia's note doubled. The killer was brazen, and Bo feared he would stop at nothing to make sure Joe was convicted of the murder that this scumbag, whoever he was, had most likely committed.

Whoever the guy was, he was apparently pretty sure of himself because he was clearly keeping track of Joe's family and friends and harassing them. But what worried Bo the most was the fact that there was a chance Joe could be in real danger in the jail. He picked up the second note from Rosina and then drove to the sheriff's office to find Detective Merianos. He reported what he'd found to him and gave him the notes.

"This does look fishy in a way, but then again," Merianos said, "as much as I hate to say this, your cousin is almost certainly guilty. But don't worry, I'll look into this."

Bo had tried to follow the sheriff's orders and stay out of the case, but he couldn't stop himself from arguing with the detective. And he doubted that Merianos would truly follow up on the notes. In the detective's mind, he had a slam-dunk case and probably would not want to jeopardize it. "Why would Joe put the body in a trunk in his own house, leave blood around, and call me to come in if he knew the man he'd killed was hidden in his house? Detective, it just doesn't make sense," Bo argued. "And these notes should tell you something."

"Bo, you should know by now that criminals are not the brightest people in the world," Detective Merianos said flippantly. "Maybe the notes are someone's idea of a morbid joke. They probably mean nothing."

"This is my cousin we're talking about, Will. I know him well, and he's not stupid. I don't for one minute believe he's a killer, but if he was, he wouldn't do something this idiotic," Bo said.

"Bo, you need to back away from this case like the sheriff told you to. You are too close to Joe to be objective," the detective reminded him.

"Okay, I will. But I did get the call on these notes here," he said, pointing at the papers, which he had enclosed in evidence bags where Detective Merianos had dropped them on his desk. "I had to deal with them, and now, I've given them to you, but I think you should make sure that Joe is safe in the jail."

"These are nothing to worry about," the detective said dismissively. "Maybe whoever typed these notes was a friend of the victim and simply wants to make sure justice is carried out."

"You may want to check them for fingerprints," Bo suggested.

"Deputy, I know my job. But crooks aren't always stupid. I'm sure whoever put these on the doors they were found on wore gloves," Detective Merianos said.

Bo couldn't help himself. "You just said criminals are stupid. Now you say they aren't."

Merianos glared at him. "Hey, Bo, leave it. I didn't say the person who wrote the notes was a criminal. Just the friend of one: namely Emil Eifler."

Bo knew he'd better shut up, so he simply turned and left Merianos's office. He didn't have any idea what Merianos would do with the notes, but as a precaution, Bo had photographed them both with his cell phone and then emailed them to his personal email account.

Back in his patrol car, he worried that he'd probably gone too far with Merianos, but then he was convinced the detective was being stubborn and extremely shortsighted by not wanting to consider that he didn't have an open-and-shut case. But he didn't want to make matters worse for Joe. He made up his mind right then that even though he was off the case officially, he could and would do some sleuthing on his own time, very quiet sleuthing.

In the meantime, despite knowing it would possibly jeopardize his career, he headed for the jail. He was turned away after being told that the jail staff had received instructions Bo was not to be admitted at the jail to visit Joe while on duty. When off duty, he could come only during regular visiting hours. Detective Merianos had left those instructions. Frustrated, Bo returned to his regular duties.

Monday morning, Joe was brought before the judge. His attorney, Mr. Tokery, requested that bail be set for his client. The prosecutor strenuously objected, and a hearing was set for the next morning during which both sides could argue the matter before the judge.

With discouragement written all over their faces, Ron, Melia, Rosina, and Karmen left the courtroom. Bo Buckley was on duty and was unable to attend.

The killer was a short distance from the courthouse, heavily disguised, watching who came and went. He shook his head. Clearly the notes he had delivered were being disregarded. Well, he told himself, they had been warned. What happened after this would be their fault.

The killer waited until visiting hours that afternoon and then went to the jail. Heavily disguised again and using a false ID, he visited an inmate by the name of Gus Hammond, a big, strong man with a very violent criminal history. They talked very softly as the killer applied pressure to the inmate without revealing why he was making the request or, rather, giving the order. The killer made it clear to Hammond that he had better do as he was told or there would be consequences. The inmate, a man who relished violence, readily agreed. Not that he had much choice. Gus was being blackmailed, but that didn't mean he wouldn't enjoy what he'd been told to do.

Joe was in an exercise area with some other inmates who were awaiting trial on their cases. One of them, an inmate the others called Gus, began to taunt him. At first Joe ignored the taunts, but it became more difficult when the other inmates joined in with Gus. Gus was a natural bully. And he was a large man at well over six feet tall and at least two-hundred fifty pounds. The other inmates sided with Gus. Probably for their own safety.

They all crowded around Joe so that the cameras, if there were any pointing at them, wouldn't catch any violence that might occur. Joe felt a shiver of fear. He couldn't imagine why Gus would want to pick on him. But it didn't matter. Joe could tell that Gus was trying to goad him into throwing the first punch. He resisted, but suddenly Gus shouted, "Hey, you guys see that? Joe hit me."

Before Joe could proclaim his innocence, Gus hit him hard in the face. It felt like he'd been kicked by a horse, and he reeled back into the men crowded around.

He straightened up and tried to fight back, but that punch left him woozy, and it was all he could do to stay on his feet. Gus had no intention of allowing that, and he threw a flurry of punches that laid Joe out on the floor. He curled into a ball as Gus, joined by others, began to kick and stomp on him. Suddenly, someone shouted that the corrections officers were coming. Gus leaned low and hissed, "You tell them I did this, and next time, you'll die." Then Gus and the other inmates stepped back to the far side of the room, leaving Joe writhing in pain on the floor.

As he was being carried from the room, he could hear one of the officers asking the other inmates what had happened. They all spoke at once, blaming Joe for punching Gus. Joe knew that even if he told them what had happened, no one would believe him. He, on the other hand, believed Gus's threat. He didn't want to die, so he said nothing.

A nurse checked him out and reported that nothing was broken and that he would be okay. He was placed in an isolation cell after she gave him some pain pills. He lay on his bunk, curled up and in pain. He felt like crying, but he did not. He just couldn't understand why he was in so much trouble.

Bo went to the jail that evening after his shift and asked to see Joe. He was told that Joe was in an isolation cell for starting a fight and would not be allowed to have any visitors. When Bo asked who he started a fight with, he was told that Joe had punched Gus Hammond. Bo knew who Gus was and so also knew this couldn't be true. If Joe was stupid enough to start a fight, it wouldn't be with a violent and tough man like Gus.

After leaving the jail, Bo called Dylan Tokery, Joe's defense attorney. He explained what had happened. "I know Joe very well," Bo said. "There's no way he would start a fight. They won't let me talk to him, but they can't stop you."

"I'll go right now," Dylan said. "I hope he'll tell me what really happened."

"I can't imagine why he wouldn't," Bo said. "Please, will you call me as soon as you finish meeting with Joe? I'm worried about him."

"I think I'm going to be able to get him out on bail tomorrow," Dylan said. "His boss, Ron Brady, has agreed to do whatever he has to in order to raise what's needed to pay a bondsman."

"If the judge will agree to bail, you mean."

"Yeah, there is that," Dylan agreed. "But I think I can get him to. I'm sure going to give it my best shot. I'll call you later."

Bo answered his phone as soon as he saw it was Dylan calling him back. It had been over an hour, and he was tense with worry. "Deputy Buckley," Dylan began, "I'm afraid this is more serious than I thought. Joe has been badly beaten. According to the nurse, he didn't have any broken bones, but he is badly bruised and has a black eye, a bruised kidney, a bloody lip, and a hurt mouth."

"Did he say why he started the fight?" Bo asked.

"He refused to talk about it, but I'm sure he didn't start it," the defense attorney said.

"He has a bail hearing tomorrow. Is he going to be able to be there?" Bo asked.

"He says he is, and he hopes he can get out. He may have been accused of starting the fight, but Joe is terrified. Frankly, Deputy, I believe his life is in danger in the jail. This will give me more ammunition to argue for bail."

"What else are you going to argue?" Bo asked.

"Well, the killing took place in Joe's own home. The victim had clearly broken in. If Joe killed him, and I'm sure he didn't, it would certainly make an argument for self-defense possible," Dylan said. "I will also point out that he has no previous record of any kind of crimes. His past is clean as a whistle."

"I'll be on duty, but I'm going to try to be there," Bo said.

As soon as his call with Dylan Tokery ended, he called Rosina and told her what had happened. She was understandably incensed and extremely worried.

"I'm going to go help Mr. Brady and Melia this afternoon," she said. "I'll tell them what happened."

"Then I won't call them," Bo said. "I'll leave it to you."

CHAPTER SIX

MELIA LET OUT A SMALL cry of horror when Joe was ushered into the courtroom Tuesday morning—not because of the handcuffs or leg irons but because of the condition of his face and the painful manner in which he moved. "He's hurt badly," she whispered angrily to her grandfather. "The judge has got to let him out today before they kill him."

Ron nodded his agreement. Joe was clearly in a lot of pain, and when he was asked a question, all he could give was a slurred response. Judge Leitner, who presided at the bail hearing, looked at him very sympathetically. But the prosecutor, Nate Vesey, a stocky man around forty years old, insisted that the defendant had been the one to cause the fight that resulted in his obvious injuries and that there should be no sympathy shown to him.

"Mr. Whalen had taunted and then punched another inmate, which resulted in a fight that, in turn, resulted in Joe's injuries."

"Your Honor," Dylan Tokery spoke up, "does the state expect us to believe that Mr. Whalen, who until this latest charge has never had an offense of any kind, would be so stupid as to attack Gus Hammond, a man much larger and with a long history of violence?"

"Mr. Vesey, is Hammond the other party in the assault?" the judge asked.

"Yes, Your Honor, and he was pushed to the extreme by Mr. Whalen."

The judge shook his head. Then he said to Dylan Tokery, "Counselor, do you feel that your client is in danger in the jail?"

"I certainly do," Tokery said.

"He's a troublemaker," Vesey countered.

"Also, Your Honor, I would ask the court to note that the alleged homicide took place in the defendant's home after it had been broken into. I think bail should be set in this matter for that reason, if none other."

"The state strongly opposes that," Vesey said. "The defendant shot and then hid the victim's body in a large trunk. That is not something someone would do in self-defense. At trial, we intend to prove that it was cold-blooded, premeditated murder. We believe the defendant lured the victim to his home on some pretext or other and then shot him in the head in cold blood."

"How did the sheriff's office come to learn of the trouble at Mr. Whalen's house?" Judge Leitner asked.

"Joe Whalen himself reported that his house had been broken into, and it was a deputy sheriff who responded and found the body in the trunk. There was blood all around, and no attempt had been made to clean it up," the defense attorney said.

The arguments went back and forth for several more minutes, but finally, Judge Leitner raised a hand and said, "Enough, gentlemen. Bail in this matter is set at $50,000. We are in recess."

Melia heaved a sigh of relief, a sound that was echoed by others around her. An hour later, Ron Brady and a bail agent had posted the bond, and Joe hobbled from the jail. Melia threw her arms around him, and then Rosina did the same.

"Thank you," Joe said to Ron. "You will not regret it."

Bo congratulated Joe but said, "Joe, you'd better watch your back. You were in danger in the jail, but you're still in danger now that you're out. I would suggest you stay with me for a while."

"I'll be fine," Joe said stubbornly. "I've done nothing wrong."

"I agree with Bo," Ron said. "You are very much in danger. I have a big house. You're welcome to stay with Melia and me."

Once again, Joe declined. "I appreciate it, both of you," he said, having a very hard time speaking. "But my dog will be with me. I think I'll let him sleep in the house after this even if my landlord doesn't like it."

Rosina spoke up then. "We sure won't tell him. I am taking you to see a doctor. You don't look very good."

"I'm fine," he said.

"Joe, you are not fine. But let me ask you this: why did that Hammond guy beat you up?"

Joe said nothing except, "I just want to go home. And Ron, I'll be at work tomorrow." He refused to say anything about the beating he'd taken.

After Joe went with Rosina to her car, Melia asked Bo, "I know he didn't attack that Hammond guy, so why doesn't he say so?"

Bo shook his head. "He's probably been threatened if he says anything different from what the other inmates stated. It works that way quite often.

Gus Hammond is a vicious man, and other inmates wouldn't dare oppose him any more than Joe does."

"That's horrible!" Melia said angrily, shaking her fists.

"We need to find out who killed Emil Eifler," Bo said evenly. "That's the only way to end this trouble for Joe."

"How can we do that? You aren't allowed to help investigate, and that detective is convinced Joe is guilty," Melia said. "All he wants is to see his name in the paper and on TV for arresting a murderer. He doesn't care about the truth, only his own image."

"You're right about Merianos. As for who killed Emil, I'll just have to think of something I can do. I have an idea of who is behind all this trouble," Bo said. "Gus had a visitor at the jail right before the assault on Joe."

"Who was it?" Melia asked.

"I don't believe the guy signed his real name on the visitor roster."

"Didn't he have to have some ID?" Melia asked.

"Of course, but he could have produced false ID. I read the name on the roster and did some digging. A person by that name doesn't exist."

"But he does," Melia protested. "He must be the guy who left the notes."

"I'm sure he is, and whoever he really is, he wants Joe convicted so that no one will look for him in the case. He must know who killed Emil, or he might be the actual killer, and I have to find out who he is, even if I have to do it on my own time. If Joe goes to prison, the real killer will get away with murder."

"Don't they have a description of him from when he visited the jail?" Melia asked.

"Yes, of course. He can be seen on a camera at the jail, but who's to say he wasn't disguised? Mr. Tokery, the defense attorney, was allowed to view the video, and he also believes the guy was heavily disguised. So, you see, we can't know for sure who he is."

"Is Joe going to be able to work?" Melia asked. "He looks like he's in a lot of pain."

"If he says he can, you can bet he will. Joe is a determined guy," Bo said. "I just wish he wouldn't insist on staying alone at his house. That's just plain foolish, suicidal even."

Rosina took Joe out to the Brady farm to pick up his dog and his truck. Ron had kept the old truck for him in his equipment barn. He helped a little with some chores, but Joe realized he was not in good shape. He hurt all over so bad it made him nauseated. But he figured that he'd feel a lot better by the next morning. Rosina helped Melia as well, and both girls tried to talk Joe out of staying at his own house, but he stubbornly insisted that he would be okay.

Rosina took him home and walked to the front door with him after he'd put Herc in the backyard. "You will let him stay in the house, won't you?" she asked as Joe unlocked his front door.

"I guess I should, but he's not really housebroken, and you know what my landlord thinks," he said.

"Better to have an accident or two to clean up than to be alone in the house," Rosina said sternly.

"I'll see. I think I will let him be inside, at least when I go to bed," he said and pushed the door open.

"Joe, what in the world has happened to your house?" Rosina asked as the two of them stared dumfounded at the mess inside. The place had been ransacked. There were broken dishes and plates on the floor. A kitchen chair was busted into several pieces; the rest of them were also too broken to use again. The sofa cushions had been cut open and the stuffing spread around the living room. His TV screen was smashed.

They went into Joe's bedroom. Similar destruction had occurred there. His drawers had all been opened and the contents scattered around the room. In the bathroom, the mirror had been shattered. The clothes in his closet were scattered all over the room, and some of his shirts had been ripped.

"Joe, what about your guns?" Rosina asked.

"Detective Merianos took my pistol. He says it was the one Emil was shot with, *the one I shot Emil with*," he said bitterly. "I had Bo take my other ones. Let's look in the other room."

The only room that wasn't trashed was the room with the trunk that Emil's body had been stuffed in. But on the lid of the trunk was a typed note.

> *You killed Emil and you know it. You either confess and plead guilty or you will pay with your life. This is just a sample of what you have coming if you don't admit that you killed Emil.*

Of course, there was no signature.

"We mustn't touch the note, Joe," Rosina said. "I'm going to call Bo. And what in the world is that awful smell? I noticed it when we first came in, but it's strongest in this room."

"I don't know," Joe said, sitting on the twin bed with his head in his hands.

Bo wasn't the only one who showed up. Detective Merianos also came with another deputy, twenty-five-year-old Jim Grizzel. The arrogant detective showed no sympathy for Joe. Bo and the other deputy, on the other hand, were both appalled. Rosina got on her phone and called Karmen, who promised to come out and help clean up the mess.

"It smells bad," Detective Merianos said as he wrinkled his nose. "Is there another dead body in here, killer?"

"That's uncalled for," Bo said hotly as he inspected the back door. The cardboard Joe had taped in the empty pane had been taken out and dropped on the porch. "Here's how they got in."

Detective Merianos gave Bo a dirty look, but he did at least examine the door and agreed that someone could have come in that way. "I want to know what the smell is," Merianos said. "Are you going to tell me or not?"

"Will, as you know, Joe has been in jail. How would he know what it is?" Bo demanded.

The detective snorted but gave no response.

"It's strongest in the spare bedroom," Rosina said.

The officers entered that room and looked around for a moment. Joe and Rosina stood at the doorway. "Maybe we should look in the trunk," Bo said with a shake of his head.

Will opened it and stepped back, his fingers pinching his nose. "Poaching, too, are you, Joe?" Detective Merianos said. "When did you put this little deer in here?"

"Detective, like I just reminded you, Joe has been in jail. So you know very well that he had nothing to do with this deer," Bo said. "You need to lighten up here."

The other deputy agreed with Bo, but Merianos just smirked. "One of you guys call Wildlife Resources," he said. "This is their problem now, and don't let Joe touch this deer. I don't think there's anything more for me to see here." He paused and scowled at Joe. "You already know this, Joe, but now *I* know that two inmates heard you tell Gus Hammond you killed Emil because you owed him money for pot that you refused to pay for." Then he spun and left the house at a fast walk.

No one was sad that the detective left. In fact, Bo and Rosina were steaming with anger.

"How can there be a fair investigation into the murder of this Emil guy with that jerk in charge of the case?" Rosina said. "We all know that Joe didn't say that. Did you, Joe?"

Joe did not respond.

"Perhaps I should try to find out who the other inmates are," Bo said, "and who's visited them recently."

The other patrol deputy, Jim Grizzel, spoke up then. "Bo, let me do that. You don't need the sheriff angry at you."

"He's going to know what his star detective said and did here today," Bo said angrily. "It can't be ignored."

"Let me handle that too," Grizzel said.

Bo actually smiled then and pulled out his cell phone. "Merianos doesn't know it, but I recorded everything he said in here. I had a feeling he would act this way, so I took precautions. I am going to lodge a complaint with the sheriff. Jim, thanks for the offer, but I'll do it myself. I would appreciate it though if you would figure things out for me at the jail if it can even be done."

"I can do that later, but, Bo, I'm coming with you to see the sheriff. And don't argue," Jim said.

"All right, maybe that's best," Bo agreed. "Then we can both try to figure things out at the jail."

Karmen arrived at that point, and the first thing she said after giving Bo a rather tender hug was, "What is that awful smell?"

Rosina explained. "Let's open some windows. Then you and I can start to clean up this mess."

"Not until we take some pictures," Bo said. "Jim, would you take the bedrooms and the bathroom? I'll get the rest. We can just use our cell phones."

By the time a couple of officers from Wildlife Resources arrived, the pictures had been taken and the girls had started to clean the mess in the kitchen. Joe, despite hurting badly, pitched in and worked as best he could.

The killer finally put his binoculars away. He'd seen enough. Joe was going to cave in and confess, or there would be a lot more trouble coming his way. Maybe even to his family and friends.

The killer was a master at disguise. He could make himself look any way he wanted to, and no one would ever recognize him. Joe would take the fall for what he'd done, for what he, the killer, had had to do. *Emil had needed to die.* And Joe was a nobody who had angered him one day, a day he hadn't forgotten. It made him chuckle again at his good luck at having killed Emil in Joe's house. It wouldn't hurt Joe to spend his life in prison.

If he lived long enough.

The house cleaning was going well and the wildlife officers had taken the deer and left. They didn't even attempt to accuse Joe the way the detective had.

Bo and Jim had also left since they were on duty and had other matters to attend to. They hadn't been gone long, however, when there was a knock on the front door. Rosina answered it. She'd straightened up Joe's bed as much as she could with the slashed mattress, and it was in good enough shape that he'd finally agreed to lie down. He was hurting, sick to his stomach, and extremely tired. He'd admitted to Rosina that sleeping in the jail had been almost impossible.

"Hi, Melia. Come in," she said as Melia held out a hot casserole and some rolls.

"Thank you. Grandpa's waiting in the truck, so I can't stay. I just wanted Joe to have something to eat. How's he doing?"

"Not great. He's resting," Rosina said. "We insisted, and he wasn't much help in cleaning up the house the way he was hurting."

"What happened?" Melia asked with wide eyes as she suddenly became aware of the damage in the house that had yet to be straightened up. "This is horrible!"

"Oh, it's much better now than it was. Why don't you have your grandpa come in, and we'll explain the best we can," Rosina said as she took the meal from Melia's hands.

When Ron Brady came in, he was visibly upset. "How come someone can't leave the poor guy alone?" he fumed. "Enough is enough. What happened here?"

Ron sat on what was left of the sofa. Melia stood beside Rosina and Karmen while they explained what they had found, including the dead deer. "So that's why the windows are open," Ron observed. "I thought it was awfully cold for that."

"We need to go to the store and get some things. We'll get an air freshener when we do," Rosina said.

Melia was close to tears. "I can't believe this is happening. Joe is such a nice guy."

"Yes, he is," Rosina agreed.

Melia turned to her grandfather. "Grandpa, if these guys will give me a ride home later, you won't need to stay. There's more casserole in the fridge at home. All you'll need to do is heat it up. I want to help these guys."

"I guess I'd better," Ron agreed. "It's a bit of a shock to me, and my weak heart can't stand a lot of this kind of thing."

"Should we eat the casserole while it's still warm? I made a lot," Melia said.

"We'll have to go to the store first. All of Joe's plates, bowls, and glasses are broken," Rosina revealed. "We've cleaned them up already, but we plan to get some paper ones to tide him over. He'll also need a few other things."

Just then Joe staggered into the kitchen.

"Joe!" Melia cried and rushed to him, throwing her arms around him. In a broken voice, she said, "I'm so sorry."

"Yeah, this is almost as bad as the jail," he said. Then he gave a very small, painful smile and added, "Almost, but not quite."

"Melia brought some casserole and rolls," Rosina said. "But you need something to eat on. We washed your silverware, but all the plates, bowls, cups and glasses are destroyed. Karmen and I will go get some paper ones and a few other things. It won't take us long. Melia, you can come too if you'd like."

"No, I think I'll stay with Joe," she said. "He can rest some more while I keep cleaning things up."

The other girls left, and Melia began to straighten things up in the living room as best she could. Joe hobbled around and helped her. He refused to lie down again. In a way, Melia didn't mind. She was glad to have him near. She liked him a lot and hoped and prayed that he would be able to overcome the terrible thing he'd been accused of.

Later, after they had all eaten, Melia said, "Joe, please come stay at Grandpa's house tonight. I'll be so worried about you being here alone."

"Well, this place is kind of a mess. Are you sure it wouldn't be too hard on Ron?" he asked.

"He'll be fine. So you will come?" she asked with pleading, hopeful eyes.

"I guess so," he said. "It is going to be kind of hard to stay here until . . . well, until it looks better in here and smells better. It's mostly the smell that bothers me."

So a few hours later, Karmen went home, and Rosina delivered Joe, Herc, and Melia to Ron Brady's farm.

CHAPTER SEVEN

"YOU'D BETTER STAY IN AND rest today," Ron told Joe on Wednesday morning.

"No, I want to go out and work. There's a lot to do. As soon as we feed, I'll start cleaning stalls."

"But you're in really bad pain," Melia said urgently. "And you still can't open that one eye very far."

Joe forced a smile. "I may hurt a little, but I will hurt whether I'm inside resting or outside working. I can see okay. Don't worry about me."

"It's quite cold today," Ron warned.

"Hey, will you guys quit trying to get me to be lazy? I lay around in the jail enough to last me a long time. You let me stay here last night, and you didn't even charge me rent." Joe forced a painful grin. "So the least I can do is go out and take care of the chores." With that, he put on a heavy coat, a hat, and some insulated leather gloves.

"If you're going out now, so am I," Melia said stubbornly. She also began putting on warm work clothes.

Yes, it was cold, and yes, he was hurting, but Joe relished the work. He was so glad to be out of jail, at least for a while, that the last thing he wanted to do was lie around indoors. He and Melia worked pretty much side by side for the next three hours. To Joe's amazement, he hardly considered the pain when he was busy. He did notice the pretty girl he was working with. If only . . . But he forced useless thoughts from his mind and concentrated on enjoying the work and the sweet companionship.

Deputy Bo Buckley had stewed over the events in Joe's house all night long. Detective Merianos was being a real jerk over the whole thing, refusing to look at the possibility that someone else may have been the killer, not Joe. All he wanted was publicity. It was causing a lot of trouble for Joe for no honest reason.

Bo met Deputy Grizzel at eleven o'clock in the parking lot of the sheriff's office. "You really don't have to stick your neck out, Jim," Bo said. "I can do this alone. After all, it's my cousin who's being hurt by Merianos's bad attitude, arrogance, and sloppy police work."

"I want to do this, Bo," Jim said. "I love my job, and I love this department. Sheriff Hermock needs to know that a very serious case is being intentionally mishandled. I just can't figure out why Merianos is being so lazy about this case."

"He has a suspect, and he has some evidence that points to Joe. He made the papers, the radio, and TV. That's what he cares about. He isn't inclined to consider any other suspects. And you are right about him being lazy. It would require a lot of effort on his part to look for the real killer. So anyway, if you're sure, we'll go in together. The sheriff's truck is here, so I suppose he's in his office now. Let's do this. I may be out of a job in a little while, but I can't stand by and see such a blatant miscarriage of justice taking place and not do anything about it."

Sheriff Pete Hermock was a tall, dark-complexioned man in his midfifties. He'd been an officer for over thirty years, sheriff for ten. He welcomed Bo and Jim into his office, closed the door, and said, "Okay, men, what seems to be bothering the two of you?"

"I know you told me that I was not to be involved in my cousin's case, but I was dispatched to his house shortly after he was released on bail from the jail yesterday," Bo began.

"I take it there was a problem," the sheriff said as he leaned forward and placed his hands on the desk.

"You can say that again," Bo said. "And it's a big one."

Before he could go on, Sheriff Hermock said, "Deputy Grizzel, were you sent there too?"

"Yes, and so was Detective Merianos, and that's what we need to talk to you about," Jim responded.

The sheriff looked both of them in the eyes. "Okay, gentlemen, tell me about it. I'm all ears."

Bo did exactly that. Jim added a little from time to time. The sheriff did not look pleased. A frown creased his face, and he narrowed his eyes. Bo was afraid he would be in trouble, but he had made up his mind to report what he perceived as serious misconduct. He would not back down now. "Sheriff," he said, "I recorded what we just told you about. I would like you to hear it so you'll know we aren't lying. What you do about it after that is up to you."

"Okay, let's hear it," the sheriff said. Bo pulled out his cell phone and began to play the recording. The sheriff's face looked grim as he listened. His dark-brown eyes burned with anger, and he kept running a hand through his thick black hair. The recording ended. Bo put the phone back in his pocket without another word.

For a full minute, silence filled the sheriff's office. Finally, the sheriff spoke, his voice slow and deliberate. "I won't stand for it," he said. He picked up his phone and buzzed his secretary. "Locate Detective Merianos and tell him to come to my office right now."

"Well, I guess Jim and I should be going," Bo said. "I'm sorry about all this."

"Stay put, men," Sheriff Hermock said. "I want you to be here to hear what Will has to say about his actions. The contents of that recording are extremely serious, and I'm not going to allow that kind of thing to occur in any investigation conducted by officers of my department. Will had better have a very good explanation for why he acted like he did."

Joe and Melia went in the house for lunch, which she fixed while he sat on the sofa and took it easy. He had offered to help her, but she'd said, "Nope, you are going to rest for a while. And I mean it, Joe. I can finish the rest of the work outside this afternoon. You look awful. You shouldn't do any more work today."

Joe not only looked awful, he felt awful now that he was no longer working and moving around. Ron sided with his granddaughter, and that was that. Ron was the boss. So Joe rested and visited with Ron while Melia worked in the kitchen. He had to smile as he heard her singing softly while she worked.

She was something else, and he was a stupid jerk. Why he had ever starting smoking pot seemed a mystery to him now. All it had done was cause him a lot of trouble. He wished he'd never met Emil Eifler. *But he hadn't wished him dead.* Nor could he imagine who had killed him, unless someone else owed him even more money than Joe did, and Emil had threatened him if he didn't pay. Of course, that was only a guess.

"Joe, we're going to help you get through this," Ron said. "You're a good man, and I don't want to lose your help. If I need to, I'll go talk to the sheriff about Detective Merianos. He needs to know that Merianos has shut his eyes to the truth."

"You don't have to do that," Joe said. "It could cause trouble for my cousin, and he's a good guy. It's my fault that I'm in trouble. I should never have let

Emil talk me into using pot. I knew better. But I did it anyway, and now I've got to pay the price."

"Not with a murder conviction you don't," Ron said grimly.

"Hey, you guys, lunch is ready," Melia called from the kitchen, interrupting further discussion. They both went in and joined her. "Let's make a deal," she continued. "No talking about trouble while we have lunch." She tried to show that she meant it, but she could not suppress a smile. Joe couldn't believe how cute she was when she tried to sound firm.

"You needed to see me?" Detective Merianos asked as he stepped into Sheriff Hermock's office. Then he looked at Bo and Jim. "What are these guys doing here? Don't they have to work?"

A third chair had been placed in front of the sheriff's desk, right next to where Bo was seated. The sheriff pointed to it. "Sit down, Will. You have some explaining to do."

Will's face grew dark, and anger shot from his eyes, but he sat down. "If these two guys have been making up lies about what happened yesterday at the killer's home, then I'll explain what really happened."

"I think I know what happened," the sheriff said. "But I'd like to hear your version."

He heard it, and it did not even resemble the recording Bo had taken. "And that is exactly what happened," Will concluded. "Bo's cousin is trouble. That's not my fault. And anyway, you told Bo to stay out of my investigation. He's lying for Joe. It's that simple."

"Really?" the sheriff said. "Bo, get out your cell phone and play what you recorded."

Bo retrieved it from his pocket, and then at the sheriff's direction, he started the recording.

"What's this crap?" Detective Merianos asked angrily.

"Be quiet and listen," the sheriff ordered.

Will listened, but it wasn't quietly. He kept interrupting, and the sheriff kept telling him to be quiet. Finally, the recording ended.

"Now, tell me what really happened, Detective," the sheriff said.

"These guys are troublemakers," Will said with a red face. "Can't you see that? They're protecting Bo's cousin."

"I'm afraid that your own words, the ones Deputy Buckley recorded, tell the true story. Will, you are off this case as of this moment, and you are no longer a detective. You will go on patrol in the patrol division in Bo's place. Bo, I am promoting you to detective. Joe may be your cousin, but I am going to trust you to make sure this case is handled properly from this point on. It's up to you now. Deputy Grizzel, since you had the guts to come in here and support Bo, you will be temporarily assigned to assist him. I'll have the patrol commander make what adjustments he needs to. When the case is over, you can go back to your regular patrol duties."

Merianos cursed. "This is stupid, Sheriff. You can't do this. I'm an experienced investigator."

"It sure doesn't appear that way to me. I am the sheriff, and I *can* do this. And if you don't like it, you can submit your resignation. Which will it be? You can either go back into the patrol division or quit."

Will stood up, shook a finger at the sheriff, and said, "I won't quit, and you will find out you made a bad mistake believing these jerks."

"My mistake was in trusting you, Will. Give me everything you have on the Emil Eifler murder, and then take the rest of the day off. You will take orders from the patrol commander in the morning. Be here at eight sharp in uniform and ready to go on patrol."

Bo released his breath after Will had stormed out, slamming the door behind him. He didn't even realize he'd been holding it. Tension seeped from his shoulders.

"You two go to work," Sheriff Hermock said. "This is not the first time I've received a negative report about Will, but it is the worst. I appreciate both of you for coming forward with what he was doing. And Bo, keep me updated on your investigation."

Emil's killer, in yet another disguise, had observed Deputy Buckley talking to the young deputy who had been at Joe's house the night before. Then he'd watched them go inside the sheriff's department building. He waited patiently and after a while, Detective Merianos showed up as well. He was inside for a long while. Buckley and the young deputy left before Merianos did. And when Merianos finally left, the killer could see through his binoculars that the detective was extremely angry. What had happened? Whatever it was, he had a feeling it was not good for him. Merianos had been doing the investigation the way he'd hoped he would. He needed to take further action. Joe could not be allowed to get off. There had to be a way to make the murder charge stick.

Joe had helped Melia finish the essential chores on the farm, insisting that he felt better when he was working than when he was sitting around. Finally, he said he was ready to go back to his house and see if there was anything else he could do there.

"Melia, you go with him," Ron said. "The house cleaning here can wait. I want you to keep an eye on Joe. I don't want him to overdo it. Although I believe he probably already has, haven't you, Joe?"

"I'm fine," Joe said, although he knew that was not quite true.

"I'll bet Rosina and Karmen have his house in pretty good shape," Melia said. "I doubt there's much to do. You have a good sister, Joe."

"Yes, I do, and it's time I start listening to her. She may be younger than me, but since she joined The Church of Jesus Christ of Latter-day Saints, she has become an amazing person," Joe admitted. "I've seen a really big change in her. She's been trying to get me to go to church with her, but I've been stubborn. Now I regret it."

"I guess you know that I'm a member of the Church too," Melia said. "You can go with Grandpa and me on Sunday."

"I'd like to, but right now, I'm not a very popular person. I would be an embarrassment to you."

"Never!" Melia said firmly. "Come on, Herc. Let's go."

Herc jumped in the back of Joe's old truck. Joe took a moment to pet him with Melia giving a few friendly strokes. Then Joe opened the door to Ron's truck for Melia to get in. She smiled at him. "You are a real gentleman, Joe. Thank you. I'll follow you to your house and help for a while if there is anything to do."

Joe was surprised to see Bo's police vehicle pull up to his house just as he and Melia were approaching it. He had that other deputy with him, the one who had been at the house the night before and had sided with Bo when Bo got angry with Detective Merianos.

He pulled up and stopped in his driveway and helped Melia out of the truck. Bo and the other deputy waited for him at the front door. "Hi, Joe. How are you, Melia?" Bo said. "Do you mind if we join you two inside?"

"Let me put Herc in the backyard first," Joe said. He called Herc, and the pretty collie jumped out of the back of his truck.

"Is it okay if I put Two Face back there with him?" Bo asked. "We may be a few minutes."

"That would be great," Joe said. He patted his dog's head for a moment, and when Two Face joined them, he opened the gate to the backyard to let both dogs enter.

"How are you feeling this afternoon, Joe?" Bo asked.

"He says he's fine, but he really isn't," Melia answered feistily before Joe could. "He worked part of the morning and again for a little while after lunch."

"I'm okay," Joe responded, giving Melia a fond smile. "So what are you guys up to?"

"You remember Deputy Jim Grizzel from last night?" Bo said.

"I didn't remember his name."

Jim grinned. "Just think grizzly bear. Then you'll remember my name."

"Let's get in so we're out of the cold, and then I'll tell you what we're doing," Bo said.

Joe unlocked the door, and they trooped in. To Joe and Melia's amazement, the old ruined sofa was gone. A different sofa, clearly not new but in good shape, was sitting where the old one had been. "How did this happen?" Joe asked, looking at Bo with wide eyes and spread-out hands.

"Your sister has a key, remember?" Bo said with a grin. "She and Karmen borrowed my personal pickup truck this morning and went to the thrift shop. Rosina's roommate helped too. They took your old sofa, your ruined mattress, your TV, and the broken kitchen chairs to the landfill and got this sofa for you, and some other stuff."

Melia walked into the kitchen. A moment later, she came back into the living room with a smile as wide as a river. "Joe, you have dishes and some nice kitchen chairs. Like I thought, things are pretty well cleaned up."

Joe shook his head. "They shouldn't have done that. I don't deserve it."

"Joe, Rosina loves you. So do I, for that matter," Bo said. "You do deserve to be treated right. Let's look in the bedroom and bathroom too. I suspect they have things looking better in there as well."

"I still don't know why you and Deputy Grizzel are here," Joe said without moving from where he stood in the kitchen.

"Call me Jim," the young deputy said.

"Let's see what else the girls have been up to, and then Jim and I have some good news for you. Not great news but good news, I think," Bo said.

Things were pretty much put right throughout the house, and even though it was used stuff, such as a used mattress and a small TV, Rosina and Karmen had replaced most of what needed replacing. There were even a few groceries in the refrigerator and cupboards. "I don't know what to say," Joe said, fighting back tears. "I've got to find a way to pay Rosina back."

"When you see Rosina, you can say thank you," Bo said. "As for paying her back, you can work that out with her. Now, let's go sit down, and we'll tell you what Jim and I are up to."

CHAPTER EIGHT

"Jim and I met with the sheriff a couple of hours ago and explained what happened here last night and how Merianos was mishandling things in general," Bo began.

"Bo, you shouldn't have done that. It could get you fired," Joe said, feeling his stomach take a concerned tumble.

"I suppose it could have, but it didn't," Bo responded with a characteristic grin. "It did, however, get Merianos taken off the case."

"More than that," Jim chimed in. "He's no longer a detective."

"I can't say I feel bad about that," Joe said as he digested the information with a now more settled stomach.

"Yeah, he was treating Joe really badly," Melia added. "Detectives shouldn't act like that."

"Yes, he was doing things that he shouldn't have. That's for sure," Bo said. "And we don't know for sure why he did what he did, although publicity was part of it. Apparently the sheriff had received complaints about him before. He said he was not going to allow it to continue."

"So who's going to take over for him?" Joe asked hesitantly. "I hope it's somebody who will look at other suspects besides just me."

Jim spoke up. "It is, Joe. I'll be assisting *Detective* Bo Buckley."

Joe was shocked, and his face showed it. "But the sheriff wanted you off the case because we're related, Bo."

Bo shook his head. "No, Merianos was who really wanted that. The sheriff said that he trusts Jim and me to be totally objective. So that's why we're here. We want to go over everything with you. I'm hoping we can convince the prosecutor to drop the murder charges against you. Don't think that it will happen automatically, because it won't. Jim and I need to dig deep and find who actually murdered Emil and why. A lot of evidence in your house has been destroyed now that could have been helpful, such as fingerprints. But we do have the tracks of whoever was out back when . . . well, you know . . . when we were worried about Herc being sprayed with Mace. We don't have much helpful evidence from your house, but Jim and I will do all we can. You have my word on that."

"And mine," Jim added, punctuating his words with a firm nod of his head.

Joe felt huge relief, and he felt bad for thinking Bo may have thought he was guilty. Joe knew now that wasn't true and never had been. Bo was an honest man and would follow the evidence. Right now, that evidence was very much against Joe. But he was sure Bo would keep digging until he found the truth. "So what are you guys going to do now, Bo?"

"First, I want to ask you some questions," Bo said. He turned to Melia. "I noticed that you drove your grandpa's truck here. We're going to be a while. You might not want to stay."

"Yeah, I'd better get home," she agreed. "Joe, I'll see you when you come to the farm in the morning. You are coming, aren't you? Or better yet, why don't you stay with us again tonight?"

"I'll be there in the morning, Melia," he said firmly. "I'll be fine staying here tonight. Thanks for following me over. I'm glad you didn't have to help me clean up more. You've worked too hard today."

She smiled at Joe, making his toes tingle, and a moment later, she left.

Bo then had Joe sit down as he and Deputy Grizzel did the same. "Tell us where and when you first met Emil," Bo started.

Joe scrunched his eyes and thought for a minute. "It was the day after I turned twenty-one. Like an idiot, I went to a bar."

"We had a party for you on your birthday. Isn't that right?" Bo asked.

"Yes, you and Rosina and her roommate," Joe said.

"But you went to a bar the very next day? Why?" Bo asked.

Joe hung his head. "Cause I could, I guess. Cause I was old enough. I know it was stupid."

"Not necessarily. Lots of people go to bars. I've gone a few times myself, but of course, I don't go anymore. Is that where you met Emil?"

Joe nodded. "He was sitting at a table with another guy. I felt lost and out of place in there, so I kind of wandered around for a minute," Joe said. "I decided to leave, but when I started toward the door, a guy came up behind me, touched my shoulder, and asked, 'Are you new here?'"

"Was that guy Emil?" Bo asked.

"Yes. He introduced himself and led me over to his table. He sort of introduced me to a guy who was sitting there," Joe said. "He didn't actually tell me his name. Then he asked me to join them."

"Do you have any idea who the other man was?" Bo asked.

"I thought he was a friend of Emil's, but as it turned out, he was not a friend, more like an enemy. But I didn't learn that until after the guy got up. He said something about Emil leaving his customers alone or he would regret it. Then he walked out of the bar. The dark, angry look on the guy's face told me he was a long way from being a friend. The guy had left his drink untouched, so Emil pushed it toward me and told me to drink it. I picked up the glass, looked at it for a minute, and took a sip. It burned, and I coughed, splattering some on the table. Emil laughed and said something about it being my first time. I told him it was, and he told me to try it again. He said it would grow on me."

"Did you try it again?"

Joe grinned sheepishly. "Yes, but it wasn't any better that time than the first. I did manage to swallow a little, but I told Emil that I didn't care for it and that I thought I'd go home."

"I take it you didn't," Bo guessed.

"Actually, yes, I did leave the bar, but so did Emil. He followed me to my truck and said that if that stuff wasn't to my liking, he had something better. I asked him what it was. He told me it was pot, and he said he knew I'd like it."

"Did he sell you some right then?" Bo asked, his eyebrows creased.

"No, but he told me to follow him to his house, and he'd let me try some for free. So like the idiot I am, I followed him."

"And he gave you a joint?" Bo asked.

"I smoked it in his house," Joe admitted. "I guess I sort of liked the feeling it gave me, so he gave me some more but said I'd have to pay for it. I asked him how much, and he said a hundred dollars, so I bought it."

"Did you leave then?" Bo asked.

"Not for a while. Me and Emil talked a little, and then he mentioned the guy that he'd been with in the bar. He told me I would do well to stay away from him."

"Why did he want you to stay away from him?" Bo asked.

"He said the guy was dangerous, sold pot that was poor quality, and threatened people if they tried to find a new source. Emil claimed the guy came into the bar that night looking for him. I guess Emil must have sold some pot to a customer of this other guy, and he didn't like that," Joe explained.

"Did the other drug pusher threaten Emil?" Bo asked.

"Yeah, he did, at least according to Emil. He said the guy told him just before I came into the bar that if he ever sold to one of his customers again he'd kill him. Well, let's see," Joe said as he squinted thoughtfully. "No, he didn't say that exactly. I think Emil said that the guy told him he'd need a burial plot in the graveyard if he did."

"Sounds about the same to me," Deputy Grizzel said.

"Yeah, that's what I thought," Joe agreed. "Anyway, I told him I wouldn't buy from the guy. Emil told me I'd better not."

"Did Emil threaten you then?" Bo asked.

"No, but I got the message," Joe said. "I was his customer now and had to stay that way. I left right after that."

"Who was the other pusher? Did Emil ever tell you his name?"

Joe thought for a minute, rubbing a hand over the stubble on his chin. "I didn't ever hear a last name, but I'm pretty sure the first name was Leonardo. I only remember that because that was the name of a character in a book I was reading at the time. Anyway, the guy approached me in the grocery store a few days later and told me he needed to talk to me. That made me nervous, but I agreed to meet him outside after I got my groceries."

"So did you?"

"I didn't want to, but he was waiting by my truck when I came out with my groceries. I asked him what he wanted, and he said something about how I should buy my pot from him because Emil was overpriced and had low-quality product."

"Joe, had you bought more from Emil by that time?" Bo asked.

Joe lowered his eyes. "Yeah, I had."

"Where did you meet Emil to buy more pot?" Bo asked.

"At his house in Price."

"Could this Leonardo guy have seen you go to Emil's house?"

"I suppose, but I don't know."

"Did you ever buy any from Leonardo?"

"Yeah, I did that day because the guy was pushy and scary. But it was only a couple of joints. I told him I didn't want to buy more from him, and he told me I should think seriously about that."

"He threatened you?" Bo asked.

"I guess, sort of. It felt like a threat. It wasn't so much his words as his eyes and the way his voice sounded."

"Did you ever buy more from him?" Bo asked.

"No."

"Did you ever see or talk to him again?" Jim Grizzel said.

Joe looked at him and frowned. "Yes. He forced me to stop one day right after I left Emil's house. That time he really did threaten me. He said I would wish I hadn't gone to Emil's place and that if he ever saw me there again, I'd wish I hadn't. I guess he'd been watching Emil's house or else how could he have known I'd been there?"

"That's a good question. Joe, can you describe Leonardo to us?" Bo asked.

"Oh yeah, that's easy," Joe said. "He's taller than me but probably not quite six feet. He's pretty heavy."

"As in fat or obese?" Bo asked.

"No, just big. He has big muscles and lots of tattoos on his arms and his neck. And I remember a scar on his cheek. His left cheek, I think."

"Let me guess," Bo said. "He has black hair, which he usually wears in a ponytail. His eyes are very dark, almost black. He has a flat nose."

"Yeah, Emil says the nose is flat from being in fights," Joe revealed. "Do you know him?"

"I'm afraid so. He's a nasty actor. We've had him in jail a few times. He spent a couple years in prison a few years back."

"I know he's bad. When I went to Emil's one time to buy some marijuana, Emil didn't look so good."

"Are you telling me you went back to Emil's again after Leonardo threatened you?" Bo asked.

"I told Emil on the phone what had happened, and he said to ignore the guy, that he was all bluff. He didn't look like bluff to me, but anyway, that one night, Emil had a black eye and bruises on his face. I asked him what happened, and he said that he'd had a run-in with Leonardo. I asked him what it was about, and he said that Leonardo accused him again of selling to some of his customers," Joe explained.

"And did he admit that he had?" Bo asked.

"Yes, he did, but he said that one of them was me and another one was a guy he called Lucas, but he said that me and Lucas were both his customers, not Leonardo's. He told me that he wasn't afraid of Leonardo and that the next time he came around, the guy would be looking at his gun barrel."

"He didn't kill Emil; he just beat him up," Jim said thoughtfully. "Sounds like he had it in for Emil. That doesn't sound like someone who bluffs."

"You sure picked some dangerous guys to buy pot from," Bo said.

"I know. I wish I'd never gone in the bar that night. Trouble is, I thought I liked the stuff."

"Where did Emil meet Leonardo's so-called customer, the one he called Lucas, when he sold him some marijuana?" Bo asked.

"It wasn't marijuana. He sold meth to Lucas," Joe revealed.

"Whoa. So Emil dealt with the hard stuff too?" Jim asked.

"Yes, he and Leonardo both did. He tried to get me to try some heroin or meth, but I didn't. In fact, I was thinking then that I needed to quit smoking pot and try to avoid those guys. I owed Emil some money, and I didn't want to get in any deeper. Anyway, I was thinking that I didn't need to use that stuff to be happy. I had my job at the farm, and I liked being around the animals. Plus, I had Herc and you and Rosina," Joe said honestly.

"Joe, when did this happen, this fight between Emil and Leonardo Augur?" Bo asked.

"About two months ago, I think. Maybe it wasn't quite that long ago."

Bo looked at Jim. "I think we need to take a closer look at this Augur guy."

"Do you think he killed Emil?" Joe asked in alarm.

"I'd say it's possible, wouldn't you?"

"But he doesn't know where I live," Joe said.

"Did Emil?" Bo asked.

"Yeah," Joe said. "I was scared to go to his house to get more of the stuff after that day. He followed me home so he'd know where I live and started to bring pot to me there in the evenings. He was getting pushy, and that's when I started to dislike the guy. But he kept giving me more pot than I could afford. He'd say he needed more money and then push more stuff on me."

"I see," Bo said.

"Yeah, and a few days before he was killed, he told me that I needed to pay up right away."

"Did he threaten you then?" Bo asked.

"He just said that it would be best for me if I did. That's all, but it was the way he looked at me. I can't explain it, but I knew then that I needed to pay my debt to him and then refuse to let him give me more on *credit.*"

"Okay. So Leonardo Augur could have followed Emil there while you and I were fishing, killed Emil, and set you up."

Joe felt a faint tremor and licked his lips nervously. "He must have watched Emil's place other times too."

"I was just thinking that same thing," Bo said. "We'll have a visit with him. He could be the one who left the notes too."

"This makes me nervous," Joe admitted.

"As well it should," Bo said seriously. "You had better be careful. I don't think you should stay here tonight."

"I'll see," Joe said, but he intended to, even though he knew it wasn't smart.

"We'll see if we can figure out who Lucas is," Bo said. "Can you think of any other people that Emil might have been selling to?"

"Well, yeah. I happened to go to Emil's one night when there was another guy there. I could tell that they'd just made a deal," Joe said.

"Tell us about him," Bo said.

"Emil called him Bryan. He didn't say a last name. Bryan seemed upset. I remember him saying something about Emil charging him too much. I think Emil told the guy that he was a businessman and had to make a profit."

"Describe Bryan for us."

"He is probably in his thirties. He's a big guy, even bigger than Leonardo, but with less muscle," Joe said. "He's about the same height, probably around six feet. Let's see . . . he wore a short scruffy beard the same color as his hair, which was brown, long, greasy, and messy. He was really dirty and smelled bad. I remember that. I'm pretty sure he had brown eyes. And he had kind of a round face."

"That's a pretty good description, Joe. Can you think of anything else about him that might help Jim and me find him?" Bo asked.

"Yeah, the way he talked. He had a lisp. He was a little hard to understand."

Jim and Bo looked at each other. "That's got to be Bryan Bayle," Jim said decisively.

"You guys know him too?" Joe asked in surprise.

"Carbon County is not that big, Joe. We get to know most of the less upright citizens at some point," Bo explained. "Can you think of anyone else who we might need to locate and speak with?"

"I've never seen the guy and I don't know his name, but whoever Emil buys from had been putting pressure on him to pay up. Emil let that slip when he told me I had to pay him real soon."

"But you have no idea who it is?" Bo asked.

"I'm pretty sure he isn't from around here," Joe said as his phone began to ring.

He excused himself and answered the second he saw the call was from Melia.

"Joe, I need help."

CHAPTER NINE

Melia stood beside her truck, which was off the road and in a snowbank. When Bo and Jim got there, she was wringing her cold, purple hands. Both officers got out of their vehicle as quickly as they could after they stopped.

"Melia, are you all right?" Bo asked with concern.

"Yeah, just scared," she said.

"Joe's on his way," Bo said. "What happened? This is a straight stretch of road, and you aren't far from your home."

"A guy ran me off the road," she said with a shaky voice.

"Intentionally?" Bo asked.

"Yes, he came up behind me real fast, and then he slowed down and drove right up behind me. Then his car bumped the back of Grandpa's truck. I started to slide, and he backed off but then came up alongside me and swerved at me. He was laughing. I jerked to avoid having him hit me, and I ran off the road. He honked and sped off," she said as tears filled her eyes and she shivered. "He scared me bad. He waved something at me. I'm pretty sure it was a gun."

"What did he look like?" Bo asked as Joe parked behind his sheriff vehicle and hurried to join them.

"Are you okay?" Joe asked. "What happened?"

"Someone intentionally ran her off the road," Bo said. "She was just about to tell us what he looked like."

"Did you know him?" Joe asked.

"No. He was quite large, I think. He had large, dark glasses on. I guess that was sort of crazy because it's overcast and not at all bright out here this morning. He was also wearing a black hoodie. So I couldn't tell much, and anyway, I didn't really have time to look at him other than a few glances," she said, "mostly through my mirror."

"What was he driving?" Bo asked.

"A big gray or silver SUV. I can't tell you more than that," she said.

"I don't suppose you saw his license number," Bo said.

"No," she responded. "I was too scared and didn't have time."

"Okay. We'll see if we can pull you out. I have a tow rope in the Explorer," Bo said. "But first we need to call dispatch."

Jim got on the radio and called in the description of the driver and the vehicle, but neither he nor Bo was very hopeful about the guy or his SUV being found.

Joe looked at Melia, and the fear in her eyes made him angry. He noticed how cold her hands were. "Do you have gloves in your truck?" he asked. When she nodded, he waded into the snowbank and reached in the open door of the truck as Bo hooked a tow rope to the back bumper. The gloves had fallen on the floor on the passenger side. He climbed into the cab and retrieved them, and then he climbed back out and onto the road. He handed them to Melia. "Here you go."

Melia put her gloves on. "Thank you, Joe. I'm so scared I didn't even think about my gloves."

A few minutes later, Melia's grandfather's truck was back on the road. A close inspection showed a small scrape and dent on the rear bumper. It was not very obvious, but once they found it, there was no question about what had caused it.

Bo offered to follow her home after she'd begged Joe to come stay with her and her grandfather again that night. "I don't feel safe now, and Grandpa isn't well, as you know. I would feel so much safer if you were there."

Her forlorn request melted his heart. For her, he would stay at Ron's house. "Okay, but my dog is at home. I'll need to go get him first."

She thanked him, and then she turned to Bo. "Okay, I'm ready."

"Hey, don't leave your house until we get there," Bo called out to Joe. "We'll just see that Melia gets home okay and then come. We need to finish what we were talking about when Melia called."

"Okay, see you in a bit," he said.

The officers pulled out behind Melia, and Joe turned and went the opposite direction.

Joe hurriedly packed a bag for another night or two at Ron's place. He wanted to get back there as soon as he could for Melia's sake. He was angry someone was dragging her into his mess. And who was it?

He carried his bag out to his truck and then walked around to his backyard to retrieve his dog. He was going to put Herc in the truck so that he could head to Ron's as soon as he finished speaking with Bo and Jim.

There was no sign of Herc in the yard. He called his name, expecting to see him emerge from his doghouse. But he did not. Joe looked in it, and it was empty. He felt a stab of panic.

Joe's heart beat fast as he hurriedly searched the yard, looking behind every bush and tree trunk while continuing to call for his collie. He even looked over the fence, although he knew it was too tall for Herc to jump over.

By the time Bo and Jim arrived, Joe had admitted to himself that Herc was gone. The latch on the gate was fastened, and he couldn't find anywhere Herc may have made a hole and crawled through or under the fence. That could only mean one thing: someone had let him out of the yard.

"What's the matter, Joe?" Bo asked as he came out the back door.

"Someone's either turned my dog loose or taken him," Joe said angrily.

Bo's eyes narrowed, and Jim shook his head. They looked at each other in what Joe thought was suspicion. "Probably someone in a gray or silver SUV," Deputy Grizzel suggested with a scowl.

"He was here when I let Two Face out of your yard to go with us to help Melia," Bo said. "Where do you keep Herc's leash?"

"On a hook on the back porch," Joe said and led the way to the back. "It's gone! Why would anyone take Herc?" Joe was so upset he felt like screaming and pounding on something with his fists, but he didn't. He just stood with his fists clenched and his face red.

Before Bo or Jim could offer a guess, Bo got a call on his cell phone from the dispatcher. After the call was finished, he said to the others, "An SUV, a silver Chevy Suburban, has been abandoned on a county road about ten miles from where Melia was run off the road. This may not surprise either one of you, but it was stolen from the Walmart parking lot between an hour and two hours before it had been used to force Melia off the road."

Joe listened while Bo gave orders to have the stolen car towed. He arranged over the phone for other officers to process the vehicle while they—Bo, Jim, and Joe—attempted to locate Joe's missing dog.

"I have a feeling that the dognapping could be tied in with the murder, Joe, but I don't think we'll learn much from the car that hit Melia. I've ordered it dusted for fingerprints on the off chance that the guy had not been wearing gloves. I think, and Jim probably agrees, that the driver of the car is somehow tied to the problems that have been plaguing you."

Jim did agree.

"The officers who located the car have no idea where the driver went after abandoning it."

Joe was getting more upset by the minute. "Hey guys, I need to find Herc," he said. Then in the next breath he said, "I sure hope Melia's okay." In a third breath, he asked, "What did I do to deserve so much trouble? Is it all because I was an idiot and smoked pot?"

"That may have been the start, but apparently whoever killed Emil thinks you know something that could lead us to him," Bo explained.

"But I don't," Joe insisted. "I wish I did. Then I'd tell you."

"Not that you know of anyway, and even if you don't, the fact that *he* may think you do is dangerous to you and, frankly, to Melia and Ron as well. My guess is that the killer wants to make sure you go to prison for killing Emil instead of him. But that is not going to happen. Joe, extra precautions need to be taken. Be really careful and watch behind and around you at all times. Ron and Melia need to do that too."

Joe shook his head. His most urgent concern at the moment was for his best friend, his dog. "Where do I start looking for Herc?" he asked the two officers helplessly.

Bo rubbed his chin for a moment. "I have an idea. Let's see if Two Face can track him."

Joe was all for that.

Bo got his big bulldog out of his vehicle and took him around to the backyard. Two Face sniffed around the fence, the doghouse, and the back porch. He was whining. "He misses Herc," Bo said. "I'm going to put Two Face's leash on him now and take him out through the gate to see what he can tell us."

As he got near the gate, Two Face began to tug hard on the leash. Joe opened the gate, and the bulldog went through. He followed the fence clear to the east corner and then circled around to the back. He was tugging on Bo the entire time. At the corner where the fence turned and went along the back of the yard, he headed straight out into the empty, abandoned field behind it.

"I can see some tracks here in the snow," Bo said. "And Two Face can smell his scent. We're going the right way."

The three men followed Bo's dog, jogging to keep up. They ended up nearly a half mile away near another road, a seldom-used one. They crossed a long-ago tramped-down fence. There were some scruffy trees on the other side. Two Face sniffed around the trees for a minute, and then he simply stopped at the edge of the road. From there, he would not go any farther.

"What's Two Face doing?" Joe asked anxiously.

"The scent ends here," Bo said. "Herc must have been loaded in a vehicle and driven away." He turned to Jim. "Let's take a look at the impounded car and let Two Face check it out."

"What good will that do?" Joe asked.

"Two Face may be able to tell us if your dog was ever in that car," Bo said.

"Let's go then."

"Jim and I will handle it from here, Joe. Why don't you go back out to the farm and work for the rest of the day if you feel well enough to this afternoon. Melia could use the help, I'm sure. She's upset, and you may be able to calm her some."

Joe reluctantly agreed. "Will you let me know what Two Face does?"

Bo grinned. "He'll tell me if Herc has been in that SUV, and of course I'll let you know."

When they got back to Joe's house, he locked the doors, for all the good that would do, then climbed in his truck and left. Bo and Jim left at the same time.

At the sheriff's impound yard, the fingerprinting was still ongoing. Bo had the other officers step back, and then he told Two Face, "Find Herc."

Two Face didn't find Herc, but he left no doubt in Bo's mind that Herc had been in that vehicle. Bo gave instructions to have it carefully vacuumed so he could later check for hair that matched Herc's. "Jim, I wonder if Detective Merianos searched Emil's house and car."

"You mean *Deputy* Merianos. Let's go to the office and look at his reports. That should tell us."

It told them all right. Merianos had neglected to search the dead man's car and his house. "Let's get a search warrant to be on the safe side, although I don't think we need one," Bo said.

"Bo, I wonder if it might be best to contact the county animal control officer and let him know about Herc," Jim suggested as they worked on the search warrant.

"That's a good idea. Will you make the call while I finish up here?" Bo asked.

When Jim ended his call a couple minutes later, he related his findings to Bo. "He hasn't seen anything about a dog that fits Herc's description, but he'll let us know if he does."

A short while later, they arrived at the impound yard where Emil's rusty Volkswagen was impounded. They found some suspected drugs, including marijuana, heroin, cocaine, and meth tucked under the seats, both front and rear. "I can't believe Merianos didn't search his car. Emil must have been planning on making some sales somewhere other than at his home the night he went to Joe's and ended up dead," Bo told Jim.

They bagged the drugs and continued to search. Jim found one other thing of interest in the glove box on top of an owner's manual, the registration, and an insurance card. It was a small black address book. It didn't contain any names besides Emil's, but it did have quite a number of initials and a few phone numbers in it. Each phone number corresponded to a set of initials.

"I think this could be important," Jim said when he showed Bo the little book.

"Ah yes, those initials could refer to customers, and customers could be potential persons of interest in Emil's murder," Bo said.

They found nothing more of value in the car, so they proceeded to Emil's house. Inside they found some items that interested them greatly. There were two stacks of items on Emil's floor amidst a bunch of trash that had been pushed back to make room.

With gloved hands, the two deputies began to inventory the objects in each pile. Bo worked on one pile and Jim the other.

"Hey, Bo," Jim said suddenly. "Look at this shotgun. It has *Lucas Soto* etched on it."

"Interesting. This pistol has some etching too. It has the initials *BB*. Jim, these items probably belong to the Sotos and the Bayles, if my guess is correct. It will be interesting to see what the Bayles tell us when we interview them."

They continued the inventory until every item had been noted. "Is the jewelry in your pile valuable, Jim? Can you tell?" Bo asked after putting the last item down.

"I'd say it's mostly cheap stuff, but this ring looks like it might have a real diamond in it, and it's not a small one," Jim said, holding up the ring, which Bo took and examined. "I can't imagine anyone just handing something like that over to Emil Eifler."

"It will also be interesting to see what Lucas has to say about not knowing Emil," Bo said with a chuckle.

Bo took pictures of all the items with a small camera and then prepared to take the items back to the office to be secured in the evidence room. When all those things were safely stored in their vehicle, Bo and Jim continued to search the house. They found a lot of drug paraphernalia, as well as a small number of illegal drugs.

"Too bad Emil is dead," Jim joked. "We could have arrested him for intent to distribute all this stuff."

"Or at least for possession," Bo said. "Well, I think we are finished here. Let's pay a visit to Bryan and Belle Bayle. They may be able to help us, especially when we ask them about the things that are probably theirs." He paused thoughtfully for a moment. "Actually, let's not tell them about the things we found until we see if they also deny knowing Emil. Then when we tell them what we have and where we found it, we might be able to get them to tell us more. Once they know we've made a connection between them and Emil, they might be more cooperative."

Bo parked in front of the home where the Bayles lived, and the two of them, accompanied by Two Face, approached the front door. Before they could reach the door, it opened and Bryan Bayle came out, followed closely by his wife.

"What do you guys want?" the big man asked with a nasty snarl.

"We need to talk to you and your wife for a minute," Bo said.

"We got nothing to talk to you cops about," Bryan said. "We ain't done anything illegal, so we don't have to talk to you."

Bo gave his dog a command, and Two Face circled around the Bayles. Bo stepped up to Bryan, who backpedaled, but the dog stayed right with him until he stopped.

"My dog just told me that he can smell drugs," Bo said. Then he had the dog check Belle Bayle with a similar result. "It looks like we will need to search you two and your house."

"I'm going back in," Bryan said belligerently. "And you guys ain't."

"Neither of you is going back in. You are going to wait right here while I go to the computer in my car and prepare a search warrant."

"You can't do that," Belle screeched. "We have rights. You pigs are on our property."

Jim walked behind them so they had to go past him to enter the house.

"Deputy Grizzel and my police dog will keep an eye on you two while I prepare the warrant," Bo said.

"It's cold out here," Belle whined.

"Yes, it is. I'll tell you what; you may go inside if you allow Deputy Grizzel and Two Face to accompany you," Bo offered.

"What did you come here for?" Bryan asked, some of his belligerence slipping.

"We came to talk to you about Emil Eifler," Bo said.

"We don't know anything about him. Don't even know who he is," Bryan said with shifting eyes. Bo noticed that Bryan did have a lisp, as Joe had told him.

"Don't lie to us. That won't help you any. We already know that's not true. He sold you drugs, and if we find any on you or in the house, you will both be going to jail. If that happens, then we'll talk to you there later."

Belle and Bryan looked at each other. They both suddenly appeared to be very nervous, fidgeting and moving their eyes around rapidly.

"Look, I know you guys have drugs," Bo said. "My dog doesn't lie about these things. Do you want to go in and sit down, or do you want to stand out here in the cold? It may take a while to get the warrant. We're not leaving until we have it and you, your house, and your car have been searched." Bo stared hard at Bryan. He thought that if he didn't threaten too much that maybe the couple would be more likely to open up about Emil. So he said, "Or you can make this easy by simply getting the drugs for us and then answering our questions. We're not nearly as concerned about you and your drugs today as we are about finding out who killed Emil Eifler, your drug supplier. If you cooperate, we won't need to take you to jail." He hoped that would help loosen their lips.

"I tell you we don't know him," Belle said, but her rapidly shifting eyes told a different story.

Bryan finally gave in. "Okay. We'll get you the stuff if you promise not to haul us to jail."

"That works. I already told you I wouldn't," Bo said decisively. "Should we all go inside? We'll watch you get your stuff and give it to us. Then we'll talk."

"Okay, but like I said, we don't know anyone by the name of Emil," Bryan said with averted eyes.

CHAPTER NINE

Herc was walking very slowly, limping along. He had long hair, so he didn't notice the chill in the air, but he did notice the pain in his shoulder. Small drops of blood dripped occasionally onto the snow-covered ground. The snow was less than a quarter-inch deep, although there were deeper drifts from earlier snowfalls that he had to go around.

He had a good memory—by sight, by sound, and by smell. If he ever got near the man who had forcibly taken him and then turned him loose before shooting at him, he would remember. Although several shots had been fired, only one hit him. He'd been running and dodging, instinct telling him that he was in extreme danger.

That was past. He'd escaped with his life. Right now, what the big collie wanted was to find his master. Herc's instincts told him he was much closer to the farm than to his home, and he was painfully working his way in the direction of the farm now.

He could not get over several obstacles since his ability to jump was badly impaired from his shoulder injury. So he'd had to steer around those obstacles, making the trek longer than it would normally have been. But not once did he fail to correct his direction of travel when he'd passed the obstacles, most of which were fences. Instinct directed him to the Brady farm.

He'd crossed a couple of roads. Once a car had stopped and someone had tried to approach him, but he'd bared his fangs and growled a clear warning. He was not about to let another stranger touch him after what the last one had done. The fellow had persisted for several minutes but had finally given up and driven off. Herc had resumed his arduous journey as soon as he felt safe again.

Herc became increasingly weaker as he limped along, but he finally was within sight of the farm, and he could hear two familiar voices; one was his master, and the other was the girl. He barked as loudly as he could, and then he started forward again, but after only a few more yards, his strength gave out, and he collapsed in a heap behind a large bush.

"Did you hear that, Melia?" Joe asked.

"Hear what?" she asked as she shoveled some manure into a wheelbarrow sitting just outside the barn door.

"A dog barked," he said. "Look at your dog. He heard it. Ace, take us to the dog you heard. Come on, Melia. It might be Herc."

"Then why isn't he running to us?" she asked sensibly.

Ace was already moving in the direction the sound had come from. Melia and Joe propped their shovels against the wheelbarrow and followed Ace.

"I don't know. Maybe he's hurt . . . but I sure hope that's not the case." They had to run to keep up with Ace. He soon left them behind, but they were able to keep him in sight.

He had led them out of the farmyard, across the road, and into a large abandoned field on the other side. They had to go through an opening where years ago there must have been a gate. They dodged around clumps of brush and dead weeds, snowdrifts, and clumps of tall grass that stuck above shallow snow, still keeping Ace in sight. Then suddenly Ace stopped, looked back toward them, and began to bark.

Joe and Melia hurried as fast as they could, both of them gasping for air from their run. Joe, who was ahead of Melia despite the pain he was in, first spotted the yellow-and-white form on the ground, partially concealed by a large clump of brush. "It's Herc," he shouted over his shoulder and sprinted for all he was worth. Ace stood next to Herc and moaned as if in mourning. Herc was deathly silent and motionless.

Joe's heart nearly stopped at the sight of his dog. He spotted the bloody shoulder, which frightened him, and he sank next to Herc in the snow, fearing that he had died since barking earlier. But when Joe touched his head, his beautiful dog shuddered and his eyes opened briefly before closing again.

"I'm here, old boy," he sobbed just as Melia sank down next to him.

"Is he dead?" she asked between gasps for air.

"No, but he's been shot."

"Oh, Joe, I see the blood. This is horrible."

"Do you have your grandpa's vet's number in your phone?" he asked. "I remember you called him about one of the horses a few weeks ago."

"Yes, I'm pretty sure I saved it to my contacts," she said as she stood up and reached for her phone.

"I'm going to pick him up and head back to the road," Joe said.

Herc weighed about seventy pounds, and even though Joe was exhausted from running and weak because of the beating he'd taken in the jail, he got his arms around Herc and staggered to his feet. He had to catch his breath for a minute and then stood sucking in deep lungsful of cold air. He was aware of Melia talking on the phone as he finally started lugging his beloved canine friend toward the road. It was all he could do to carry him. His injuries were far from healed and hurt worse with each step he took. But he was not about to stop, no matter how bad the pain became. He had to save his dog.

Melia finished her call. "Joe, we're supposed to take Herc to the vet as soon as we can. I'm going to call Grandpa and see if he can drive his truck so you can hold Herc. Or if he wants me to, I'll drive it."

"Thanks," Joe said. "Or you can drive my truck. Oh, Melia, I hope he lives."

"Me too. I'm praying for him, Joe. I know prayer helps," she said.

"Thanks," he said again. He wasn't so sure about that prayer thing, but he decided that it couldn't hurt. He'd never prayed in his life, but he did believe in God. So if God cared, maybe He would help Herc.

Bo and his partner had collected the contraband that Bryan and Belle had gathered up. There wasn't much—just some much-used drug paraphernalia. After that was done, they'd once again begun to talk to the couple about Emil Eifler. They both denied knowing the man even though Bo had told them he knew this wasn't the truth. They'd gone round and round for several minutes.

Finally Bo pulled out his phone. "Let me show you some pictures. Maybe this will help you remember. Tell me about the objects I show you."

The first picture was of the pistol with the initials BB etched on it. Bryan looked at it and admitted in a whisper, "That's my gun." He hesitated, looking around the room like that might help him. Finally, he said, "It was stolen. Where did you find it?"

"You tell me," Bo said.

"How would I know?" Another hesitation. His eyes met Bo's. "Someone broke in here and took a bunch of our stuff a few days ago."

"Were you able to give a complete list of what you were missing to the officer who came when you reported the theft?" Bo asked, watching as well as listening for Bryan's reaction while glancing briefly at Belle's face. They both had that deer-in-the-headlights look.

"Ah, we . . . we . . . didn't report it," Bryan stammered as he looked at Belle in what appeared to Bo to be a warning of some kind. It made Bo wonder if she was afraid of her husband.

"Yeah, we didn't figure the cops could help us get it all back," Belle chipped in with downcast eyes, finally getting herself together enough to back up her husband in his lies.

"What else was stolen?" Deputy Grizzel asked.

"Oh, just some jewelry and stuff," Bryan said.

"Like this?" Bo said, showing them another picture.

"Yeah, that jewelry is mine," Belle said. "Where did you find it?"

"It must have been pawned," Bryan said. "I've heard that's what thieves do with stuff like this when they steal it."

"That's often true," Bo said. "But in this case, that hadn't been done yet. Your drug supplier, Emil Eifler, still had it. We found it in a neat little pile in his house."

Both Belle and Bryan gasped, and their eyes opened wide.

"We don't know that guy, but . . . ah . . . apparently he must be a . . . a burglar," Bryan said.

"Bryan, the game's over," Bo said sternly, staring hard at Bryan's shifting eyes. "It's time you stopped lying. We need help finding out who killed Emil. You both knew him well." Then Bo decided to bluff a little. "Why would he have your names and address in his little black book, one he carried in the glove compartment of his car?"

This time, both of them went rather pale. Bryan cast another dark look at his wife, and then neither of them attempted an answer.

After letting them think about their situation for a full minute or more, Bo finally said, "Emil wanted to be paid, didn't he? And you didn't have the money to pay him, so he forced you to give him your gun, jewelry, and those other items we found in his house. That's true, isn't it?"

Bryan hung his head. "Okay, so yeah, we knew him. But he pulled a gun on us and threatened to kill us if we didn't give him our stuff. He scared us. I can tell you that. He stole our property."

Just then, Bo's phone rang. He looked and saw that it was Joe's number. "I need to take this," he said. "Deputy Grizzel will stay with you while I step outside." As soon as he had closed the door behind him, he answered the call. "Joe, what's going on?"

"Herc has been shot," Joe said in an emotional voice.

Bo gasped in alarm. "Is he alive?"

"Barely. We're taking him to the vet right now. Ron's driving us in his truck, and Melia and I are holding Herc."

"Where did you find him?" Bo asked.

Joe explained. "If he dies, I don't know what I'll do."

"He won't die," Bo said, hoping he was right. "If he made it back to the ranch from wherever he was shot, it means he's a fighter, that he wants to live. He won't die. Have faith and let me know what happens. In fact, as soon as Jim and I finish what we're doing, we'll meet you. Do you have the address of the vet clinic?"

"Let me give the phone to Melia. She can tell you," Joe said.

After speaking with Melia, Bo ended the call and went back in the house. "Deputy Grizzel and I need to go in a couple minutes. But before we do, we need to have you tell us where you both were on the night Emil was murdered." He then recited the date.

"Why do you need to know that?" Bryan asked. "You've already got his killer in jail."

"That was the wrong person. He's free now," Bo said. "So tell us where you were."

"You don't think we killed him, do you? We would never do something like that," Bryan protested.

"Somebody did, and you guys sure had a reason to if he actually pulled a gun on you and robbed you like you say he did."

"Okay, okay," Bryan said. "We were right here at home watching TV until after midnight, and then we went to bed."

"What would you say if we told you that we found your fingerprints at the house he was killed in?" Bo bluffed.

"No way, man," Bryan said. "We didn't kill him."

"Tell me what you were doing and where this morning," Bo said.

"I was home all morning," Belle said. "Bryan was only gone for a little while. He went to see a friend."

"What's the name of the friend?" Bo pressed.

Belle got another dark look from her husband. "I don't think this friend would want me telling you who he is. He likes his privacy."

Bo and Jim glanced at each other.

"We will need the name of that friend whether he likes his privacy or not," Bo said. "We will be getting back with you two. Don't leave town. If you do, that will make us believe you really did kill Emil. And if you're smart, you'll tell us where you were this morning, Bryan."

"What does it matter?" he asked.

"Take my word for it; it does matter," Bo said ominously.

Bo and Jim left with Bryan continuing to proclaim his innocence and Belle looking like she was afraid, her skin moist and her eyes avoiding her husband's.

"Bryan could be our killer," Jim said when they were back in the county vehicle. "And his wife is scared to death of him."

"Yeah, could be, and I could tell Belle was frightened," Bo agreed. "Right now, we've got to get to a vet clinic. Joe's dog was shot and is being taken there."

"Where were you that night, Bryan?" Belle asked Bryan with a shaky voice as soon as the officers were in their car. "You told the officers we were here watching TV, but I was the only one here. You never did tell me where you went that night. For all I know, you killed Emil."

Bryan's face hardened. "You'd better watch what you're saying, woman," he said with burning eyes. "How many times have I told you that?"

"Or what, Bryan? You'll beat me up again? I'm sick of it. I want to leave. I can't stand what you do to me anymore," she said foolishly, even as fear of her husband caused her stomach to clench. "I don't care if you did kill Emil, but at least you can tell me the truth."

"I didn't kill Emil," he said, barely holding his anger in check. He advanced toward her, and she backed away. She was very frightened now, but she was angry too and not backing down.

"Where were you this morning?" she asked. "And every other time you've never explained to me? You've been gone a lot, and you don't even have a job, so where were you?"

"Belle, it's best you don't know. Just trust me. I'm not a killer," he said with clenched fists.

"You know who Joe is, don't you?" she asked, even as she began to feel the fear inside of her building.

"Yeah, so what?" he asked. "I've seen him a couple of times."

For a moment, she said nothing more, but finally, she asked, "Do you know where he lives?"

"I don't," Bryan said as his face took on a rigid, angry look, one she'd seen before. She'd seen it just before the time she suspected he'd done something terrible to his own brother. That memory came flooding back. Bryan had told her to leave and not come back for an hour. She'd done that, and when she did come home, Bryan was gone. When he finally got home, she'd asked him where his brother had gone. He hadn't answered, but she never saw the brother again. Nor did she ever again ask Bryan about him. She was afraid to. Bryan had told her never to mention his brother's name again. She wished she'd left her husband then, but she didn't have the courage.

That was two years ago. Belle had tried to tell herself that his brother had recovered from whatever Bryan had done to him and then left the area. Now, as she looked in dread at Bryan's angry face, she had a feeling his brother was dead and no one but Bryan had any idea where his body was. She couldn't deny it anymore. She should never have denied it, but fear of her husband controlled her life. Now, she was almost as sure that Bryan had killed Emil too.

Belle was suddenly deathly afraid of her husband, and she began to tremble. Sweat poured from her forehead into her eyes. She knew she had gone too far, and tried to back down as she lifted her hands in surrender. "Okay, okay, I'm sorry. I'm sure you didn't kill Emil, but I sure wish you would tell me where you've been all these times you've been gone. That way I could help keep the cops away from you."

"It's not your business!" he shouted. Moving with amazing speed for a man as large as he was, he leaped forward and slammed a fist into her narrow face. Belle flew backward, hit the wall, then crumpled to the floor. "You need to learn to keep your mouth shut, woman, or you'll be where my brother is."

Bryan looked at his wife there on the floor. He wished she would just learn to keep her mouth shut. "Hey, Belle, get up!" he ordered angrily.

Belle did not respond. Bryan leaned over her. Blood was seeping from her mouth and soaking into the ancient carpet. As soon as Bryan could see her skinny chest slowly rise and fall, he stood back up. He felt the impulse to kick her as he had done before, but he fought it off. He didn't have time to stick around. He'd deal with Belle later. She would learn to do as he told her or else! Right now, he had things to do. He hurried out the door, got in his car, and drove off.

CHAPTER TEN

Joe stood up from where he and Melia had been sitting with red and swollen eyes and arms around each other. Ron was sitting on the other side of his granddaughter. He also had an arm around her.

"Thanks for coming, Bo," Joe said.

"Is Herc still alive?" Bo asked.

"The vet is operating on him. He said he's lost a lot of blood, and he can't believe Herc almost made it back to the farm."

"Of course, we have no idea how far he walked to get there," Bo reasoned.

Joe shook his head. "No, I guess not, but the vet also said he must be a strong dog to have walked any distance at all in his condition."

"Any idea how long he'll be in surgery?" Bo asked.

"No, but I guess it might be a while."

"Joe, tell me exactly where you found him."

Joe explained and then said, "You can see our tracks in what snow is left on the ground."

"Jim and I will be back. I'm going to see if Two Face can backtrack and take us to where Herc was shot. It might not help us, but then again, maybe it could."

Joe looked at Ron, and then his eyes lingered on Melia's tearstained face. Neither she nor Ron had stood up.

"I'll call you as soon as we learn anything," Bo said.

"I'm not feeling too well," Ron said as he slowly and laboriously got to his feet. "Since you men are going back to where Herc was found, perhaps you could give me a lift home so Joe and Melia will still have a truck to drive when they're finished here."

"Do you need me to go too, Grandpa?" Melia asked, concern etched into her already sad face.

"No, Melia, I'll be fine. I just need to rest. You stay here and keep Joe company," he said. "Oh, and let me know how Herc does."

Melia promised to do so, and the two lawmen and the farmer left the clinic.

Belle Bayle tried to move, but her thin body was not cooperating very well. The pain in her face was excruciating. Bryan had hit her lots of times before but never as hard as he had this time. She finally managed to reach her face with one hand. She touched her jaw, and it moved and grated in an unnatural, painful way, so painful that she screamed. It was badly broken. Fear stoked her to greater movement. She had to get away before her husband returned, but she was not sure how she could manage it. The old car she'd driven for years had finally died, and Bryan had towed it into the backyard where he'd left it to rot away along with a lot of other junk that had accumulated back there over the years.

Belle wanted out now. She'd pushed Bryan too far today, and now, fear of what Bryan might do to her when he came back caused her to attempt again to get to her feet.

Bryan probably had their other car, which was not in great shape either but seemed to get him around just fine. She listened for him now. She couldn't hear him, so she was pretty sure he'd left.

She finally managed to get to her feet and leaned unsteadily against the wall. Blood still seeped from her mouth. She wiped it with the back of her right arm.

She couldn't repress another scream of pain as the motion caused her broken jaw to move, grating and crackling.

Belle felt very dizzy, but she had to do something. She was desperate for help. Finally, by keeping her bloody hands on the wall to steady herself, she walked slowly and unsteadily into the kitchen where she'd left her cell phone on the counter. She punched in 911.

"Help . . . me . . ." she tried to get out when the call was answered. "My . . . husband . . ." She knew she wasn't sounding right and couldn't get any more out. She simply could not talk properly with her jaw broken and her mouth full of blood. She coughed, causing her to double over, and a tooth that had been under her tongue flew out and dropped onto the kitchen counter. The dispatcher asked her who and where she was. She tried to talk, but she could only groan. She was attempting to give her address, and finally managed to say a couple of words, but she only had it partly out, and even that was garbled when she began to choke on the blood in her mouth and throat.

She'd kept a pen and notepad on the counter, and she managed to get a hold of them both with her bloody hands. Slowly and painfully, she wrote, *Bryan killed Emil and me.* It took all the energy she had. When she'd finished, the pen slipped from her trembling, bloody fingers and fell on the floor. The pain and dizziness overcame her, and she fumbled for her phone again. She could faintly hear the voice of the dispatcher still coming from the phone, but she could not respond. Belle fell face forward onto the floor, smacking her face violently on the faded linoleum. Her cell phone slid underneath the kitchen table.

She couldn't cough, she couldn't even scream. She felt blood going into her lungs, drowning her. After a minute Belle Bayle's heart stopped beating.

Bo was pleased with Two Face's progress. He could see Herc's tracks at times in the snow, and he saw spots of blood along the way, staining small amounts of snow crimson. But he didn't pay a lot of attention to that as Two Face was tugging relentlessly on the leash. He had Herc's scent, and he was not to be delayed.

Jim was in the county SUV and patrolling the area as he awaited Bo's call to tell him where to meet him. They didn't want to waste valuable time walking all the way back to the Brady farm when Bo finally led them to wherever it was that Herc had been shot.

Bo had his portable radio on his hip, and he could hear the constant calls being made to various officers of different jurisdictions. He had mentally tuned it all out, knowing that Jim would call him on his cell phone if he needed to talk to him. Before long, that is exactly what happened.

"Bo," Jim said, "a Price City officer has been dispatched to a call at an address that sounds like it could be the Bayles' place. The dispatcher could only say that a female voice requested help, but the voice was indistinct, and it sounded like the caller was choking and groaning. She didn't get an address or a name before the person calling failed to continue to respond. They've discovered the address now and are on the way. Should I go there too?"

"Maybe you should," Bo agreed. "I don't have any idea how far I still have to go, but we're right on Herc's tracks. We've crossed some roads and long empty spaces. We've also had to make detours, as the collie did, around fences and other obstructions. Call me if you learn anything. I'll let you know when Two Face finds where Herc was shot."

Two Face continued to pull hard on the leash, and at times, Bo jogged so the dog could make better time. The snow was very light, and in some places, it had melted away, leaving only mud behind. He checked his watch. They'd been tracking for almost an hour. He hoped they would soon reach where Herc had been shot.

Five more minutes passed and then ten. They came to a dirt road, and as soon as they were on it, Two Face slowed down and began to shift his head back and forth. Bo peered closely at the ground and could see traces of blood. Suddenly, Two Face stopped, whined, and looked up at Bo. Bo studied the small pool of blood for a moment and then told his dog to continue on. Obediently, Two Face did as he was told, but a short distance up the road, he stopped again. Then he whined once more, barked, and attempted to pull Bo back the way they had just come.

"Good boy, Two Face," Bo said. "This must be where he got out of the car. The guy who took Herc probably shot him as he was running."

Two Face watched Bo's face, waiting to see what he wanted him to do next. Just then, Bo's cell phone rang. "What do you have, Jim?" he answered.

"You're not going to believe this," Jim said. "It looks like somebody did a number on Belle Bayle."

"What do you mean?" Bo asked.

"Her face is a mess. She's bloody, and she has a shattered jaw."

"Is an ambulance there yet?" Bo asked.

"They don't need one. She's dead," Jim said. "Her husband and their car are gone."

"Did Bryan do it to her?" Bo asked as he and Two Face slowly walked back to where Herc had been shot.

"The dispatcher said she was having a hard time understanding Belle, but she is sure she tried to say she needed help, and she thinks she heard the word *husband*. The city officers will listen to the tape, but we all think it must have been Bryan. Should I come get you now?"

"Yes, and then I want to go to the Bayle place and have a look around," Bo said. He then told Jim about where he believed he was and ended the call.

As he was waiting for Jim to arrive, Bo took several photos of the spot the blood first appeared and then some of the trail heading off the road. Jim roared up in the SUV just as Bo was putting his cell phone back in his pocket. He had Two Face get in the back seat and then climbed in the front with Jim. "Let's get back to the Bayles' as quickly as we can."

As Jim drove, he told Bo as much as he knew about the crime scene, which wasn't a lot since he'd mostly stayed out of the way and let the Price City officers conduct their investigation during the short time he was there. When Bo and Jim arrived, they exited the county SUV, passed the crime scene tape that had now been placed around the house, and entered through the broken front door.

Bo briefly talked with the city detective, Gary Costello, who was now overseeing the investigation. "Do you mind if I look around?" Bo asked. "I'll be careful not to disturb anything."

"Sure, Deputy Buckley," Costello said. "We've really not done much yet." He waved a hand around. "As you can see, there's a lot of blood on the floor and on the walls. At some point, I need to talk with you and your partner about this woman. I understand you were here not too long ago."

"That's right," Bo said. "We're working a case that involves them. We will help in any way we can."

Bo was careful not to step too close to where the body lay on the floor of the small kitchen, but he did look closely around the room. Jim, standing beside him, asked, "What are you looking for?"

"I don't know, just whatever I might see that is of interest," Bo said as he noted a bloody pen on the floor against the kitchen counter. "She touched that pen," he said, pointing toward it. Then he looked up at the surface of the counter. He quickly spotted a notepad smeared with blood partially hidden by a dirty casserole dish.

"Detective Costello," he said. The detective looked up from where he was kneeling close to Belle's body.

"See something?" Costello asked. "I heard you say 'pen' to your partner."

"Yes, there's a pen right there at the base of the kitchen counter. It's bloody, so I think your victim may have touched it. Also, there's a small pad of paper on the counter with blood on it. You might want to look at that pad and see if she happened to write anything."

"I'll do that," Detective Costello said as he rose to his feet, stepped carefully around the body, and with his gloved right hand, picked the pad up. He read it to himself, and then he turned to Bo. "Isn't Emil the name of the murder victim you guys found out in the country?"

"Yes, and I'm the investigating officer on that case now," Bo said. "What have you got there?"

"I think your murder case is solved," Gary said with a grim face as he walked toward Bo and Jim. "Take a look at this."

Bo pulled on a pair of latex gloves and then accepted the proffered notepad. "This is a huge break," Bo said with excitement. "She says her husband killed Emil."

"I thought Will Merianos was the investigating officer," Costello said. "How did you come to get assigned the case?"

"Sheriff Hermock promoted me to detective first thing this morning and told me to take over the case," Bo said as he thought about all that had occurred since then. It had been a busy day to say the least.

"Merianos has been assigned to the patrol division," Jim added.

Despite the question in Gary Costello's eyes, Bo made no effort to clarify. He read the note again. "I think Mrs. Bayle was trying to solve your case for you as well." He held the note out to Gary, who took it and read it once more.

"It appears that you're right, although we suspected her husband from the very beginning."

"We need to find him fast," Bo said.

At that exact moment, Bryan Bayle watched from almost a block away as the sun sunk low in the sky. He cursed Belle for calling the cops on him. All he'd done was hit her one time to teach her a much-needed lesson. This was not good. Now the cops would be after him. The car he'd driven here, which was not his, was well hidden, and he could use this one or steal a different one if he needed to.

It seemed to Bryan that having so many police cars at the house was unusual for a simple little thing like a domestic disagreement—for that is what he considered it to be. He and Belle had had them before, but she'd never called the cops. He kept thinking about the fact that the two officers who'd been harassing him earlier were there, and that made him nervous. He thought about it for a little while, and suddenly, he figured out what was probably happening. Belle was probably spilling all the beans, and that would be very bad. She knew way too much.

He needed to slip home in the middle of the night, take Belle with him, and order her to stay someplace where she couldn't be found. He would have to come back, however, for he had other interests to take care of. He continued to watch, but suddenly, he jerked in surprise as a hearse pulled up in front of his house.

Surely . . . she was not . . . no . . . she couldn't be dead! He didn't hit her that hard. There must be some mistake.

But when several men came out a few minutes later with someone on a covered litter, he knew he had a serious problem. He'd always managed to get away with the things he did, even the really bad things, but this? The cops would be hot on his trail, and he'd have a hard time blaming it on anyone else. He couldn't let them catch him. They'd say he murdered Belle, but all he did was give her a little smack to remind her to behave herself. Well, maybe a *big* smack, but not one hard enough to kill her.

It was time to get away from here. He had several things to do. At least he had a safe place to stay, and that was where he headed. When he arrived, he was invited in with a hug and a kiss. Life wasn't so bad, he guessed. He had to be careful. The cops were looking for him, but they would not find him. In fact, if they did see him, they wouldn't know him. His girlfriend could help him alter his appearance so radically that no one would know him.

CHAPTER ELEVEN

The veterinarian, Dr. Eugene Scanlon, walked into the lobby of the clinic and smiled at Joe and Melia. "Your dog is going to be okay," he said with a thumbs-up gesture. "The surgery went very well. No bones were broken, nothing too critical was damaged, and I was able to put him back together just fine. The worst problem is that he lost a lot of blood. You got him here just in time. What's his name?"

"I call him Herc, short for Hercules," Joe said with an embarrassed grin. He was feeling a whole lot better now that he knew Herc would live. He loved that dog. "So can we take him home in a little while?"

Dr. Scanlon shook his head. "Since he lost so much blood, I'll need to keep him here for a couple days until he gets stronger. He sure is a beautiful creature. I can't imagine why anyone would want to shoot such a wonderful animal."

"Yeah, he's a great dog."

"I assume the police know about him," Dr. Scanlon said.

"Yes, and they're trying to find out who did this to him," Melia said. "Thanks for saving his life."

The vet smiled. "You two saved his life by getting him to me so quickly. I just finished the job."

"It might take me a while to pay you," Joe said. "But I have a good job, and I'll pay as soon as I can."

Dr. Scanlon nodded. "I'll give you a discount for being such a good dog owner and because you work for Ron Brady. I've treated his animals for a long time. He's a great man. And payments will be fine, Joe. My secretary will get a bill to you. You can give her an address before you leave."

"Thanks," Joe said. "Can we see Herc before we leave?"

"Sure. He's groggy, but come on back," the doctor invited.

Herc lifted his head when Joe softly spoke his name. Joe stepped next to him and gently stroked his head. "I'm gonna keep you close after this, big fella."

After a few minutes, Joe and Melia left in Ron's truck with Melia driving.

"We are sure lucky, aren't we?" Melia said.

"We are," Joe agreed.

"I was praying for him," she said softly, glancing at Joe.

"Thank you," he said. "I sort of did, but I don't really know much about God or praying and stuff like that."

"I'll help you learn," she said. "Would that be okay?"

Joe looked at her profile as she watched the road ahead. A lump rose in his throat. He felt lucky to have such good friends as Melia and her grandpa.

She glanced at him and smiled. "Well?"

"Yeah, I'd like that," he told her.

"Will you go to church with me and Grandpa on Sunday?" she asked.

"I don't have any church clothes," he said.

She pushed on the brakes, pulled off at an intersection, and did a U-turn. "What are you doing?" he asked, lifting an eyebrow as he glanced at her.

"Deseret Industries, the thrift store. We'll find you something to wear on Sunday. And it will be my gift to you. The clothes won't be new, but they'll look good. I'll make sure of that. And don't argue, Joe. I'm very serious," she said.

Joe watched her for a moment, and finally, he just smiled at her. "Okay." He needed to make some changes in his life. His bad habits had gotten him into this mess, and it had now affected Melia. He would do his best to be a better person, not just for her and Ron but also for himself.

After leaving the Bayles' home, Jim asked, "Where to now, Detective?"

"We're going to visit Lucas Soto and his girlfriend," Bo responded.

"Why? We know who killed Emil now," Jim protested mildly.

"Maybe we do, or maybe we don't," Bo said.

"What do you mean? We have that note Belle wrote. She told us Bryan did it."

"I've been giving that some thought. I'm afraid that isn't good enough, Jim. What if she just *thinks* he did it? She's dead, so we can't question her about why she accused him."

"Okay, but still, isn't that pretty likely? I mean, surely she'd know if he did it."

"I suppose, but we're going to be thorough, something Merianos was not. We'll start by talking to Lucas Soto," Bo said. "We need to find out why Emil had items that belong to him and his girlfriend."

"Okay, I see now," Jim agreed as Bo's phone began to ring.

It was Joe.

"How's the dog?" Bo said when he picked up.

"He's going to make it," Joe said. "Thank goodness."

"Oh, I'm so glad. Are you headed home with him now?" Bo asked.

"No, Dr. Scanlon says he needs to keep him for a couple days since he lost so much blood. We're heading to Deseret Industries," Joe said.

"What are you after?" Bo asked. "I thought Rosina and Karmen got you pretty well set up."

"They didn't get me something to wear to church," he said. "I'm going with Melia and Ron on Sunday. I'll talk to you later." With that, the call ended.

The call had been synced to the vehicle, so Jim heard it all. He began to chuckle. "I bet you didn't expect that, did you?"

"No, but I'm glad," Bo said. "I invited him to go with Rosina and Karmen and me, but I think Melia has more pull than we do." He grinned. "And that's okay with me. She seems like a nice girl."

Bo and Jim rode the rest of the way to the Soto apartment in silence. When they got there, Lucas was not at home, but his girlfriend, Nattie Shrader, was. She was a small young lady, attractive with long dark hair and dark eyes. She was pregnant and, in Bo's estimation, fairly close to having her baby.

Bo introduced themselves to Nattie as deputy sheriffs. "Where is Lucas? We need to speak with him."

"I don't know where he is," Nattie said with a sad face. "He's been gone a lot. He says he's looking for a job, but nobody looks for a job at night."

"What time did he leave this morning?" Bo asked even as he considered what she'd just said about him being gone at night.

"He hasn't been home for a couple of days. He's mad at me. I don't know what I'm going to do," she said as her eyes filled with tears.

"May we come in for a moment?" Bo asked.

"Oh, yes. I'm sorry. I'm just so upset. I'm almost out of food, and I only have a few dollars," she said as she stood back and let them enter.

Her house was more orderly than Bo would have expected. Even though Nattie was upset and worried, she looked very nice. Her hair was brushed to an ebony sheen, and her face was clean. Her teeth were white, and Bo suspected that if she smiled, it would be a pretty smile. But right now, she was not smiling.

She invited them to sit down, which they did, and then Bo asked her, "Has Lucas done this before—left for days at a time?"

She shook her head. "No, he has never done this to me. I worry that something has happened to him."

"Nattie, tell us about what happened before Lucas left. You said he was mad at you. Had you had an argument of some kind?" Bo asked.

She hung her head for a moment, and then she rubbed at her eyes and looked back up. "Yes. There was a man who came here. I had never seen him before. He came twice. Lucas sent me to the bedroom, but I could hear what he and the guy were saying because I kept my door partly open and listened to them talk. The guy was angry, and he threatened Lucas."

"What was the man's name?"

"Lucas called him Emil," Nattie revealed. Bo and Jim exchanged glances, but before Bo could go on, she spoke again. "Lucas lied to him. He told him he needed drugs for us, but I don't use the stuff that he brings home. You know, drugs. Lucas uses a lot. That's what we were fighting about. I told him he shouldn't tell anyone that I use drugs, because I don't."

"Have you ever?" Jim asked.

Her eyes were downcast when she responded. "Yes, a couple times, but that was before I got pregnant. I don't want to hurt my baby. Lucas laughs at me and says it will make our baby stronger. But that's a lie. I told him that a lot of times."

"You said this man Emil came twice. Was your argument after the first visit or the second?" Bo asked.

"The second. I saw him that time. The guy had a gun, and he threatened us if we didn't give him something to make up for what he says Lucas owed him for drugs," she explained.

"What did he take?" Bo asked.

"My jewelry, including my grandmother's wedding ring. It was a valuable one. I hated that Lucas made me give it to that little man," she said.

"I don't blame you for being angry," Bo said. "What else did he take?"

She thought for a minute and then proceeded to list every single item they had found in the pile that had the shotgun with Lucas's name etched on it. Bo pulled out his phone and showed her the pictures he'd taken, and she identified each item.

"You got them back?" she asked in surprise.

"They were at Emil's house," Bo revealed. "We've got everything, but we can't return it to you for a while since we may need it as evidence. But eventually we'll return it all to you."

"Emil will be really angry. He might do something to Lucas." Suddenly her dark eyes shot wide open. "Oh," she moaned. "Maybe Emil already did something to Lucas. Maybe that's why he hasn't come home." She dropped her head into her hands and cried. "What am I going to do? My baby is due in a few weeks, and I won't be able to take care of it. Why did Lucas have to go and get himself in trouble?"

Bo and Jim looked at one another as she sobbed. Bo could tell that Jim was feeling bad for Nattie, just like he was. Finally, Nattie wiped her eyes and looked up at Bo and Jim. "I'm sorry. I thought I loved Lucas, and I thought he loved me, but now I'm not sure. I'm so confused."

"I'm sure he did," Bo assured her, even though he had no idea if that was true or not. "Nattie, Emil can't hurt Lucas or anyone else now. He's dead."

Her mouth dropped open. "Dead?" she asked. "How did he die?"

"He was shot, murdered," Bo said.

"Oh," she said with a groan. "That's why Lucas hasn't come home. He never will now. I'm so ashamed, and I'm going to have to ask my parents for help. I think they will, but they're angry with me for moving in with Lucas. They told me Lucas would bring me nothing but sorrow. I should have listened to them."

"Nattie, what do you mean when you said that's why Lucas didn't come home?" Bo asked.

She shook her head, smoothed a lock of her dark hair from her face, and said, "I think he killed Emil. He was angry. I've never seen him as mad as he was when he left. He was angry at me, but he was also mad at Emil. He shouted to Emil that he would kill him when Emil drove away with our things. Lucas is gone now, and he'll never come back."

Once again, Jim and Bo looked at each other.

"I guess it's good we came here," Jim said.

"It is," Bo agreed and turned to Nattie. "What kind of vehicle does Lucas drive?"

"A Nissan pickup, one of the small ones. It's black and in pretty good shape."

"Does he have a cell phone?" Bo asked.

"Yes. He took it with him. We only have one, so I can't even try to call him. I can't even call my parents unless I go somewhere and borrow a phone," she said. "I don't know what I'll ever do."

"Do you know the number of his phone?" Bo asked.

"Yes." She recited it to him. Jim wrote the number down.

"Nattie, describe Lucas to us," Bo said.

"He's Hispanic, but I guess you probably knew that," she said. "He's probably about four or five inches taller than me—so about five six. Of course, he has black hair and dark eyes, like mine."

"How long is his hair?" Bo asked.

"It's to his shoulders," she said.

"What was he wearing when he left?" Bo asked.

"A western shirt, denim jacket, blue jeans, and his brown cowboy boots. That's what he usually wears. No, wait. He may have been wearing sneakers. I don't remember the color of the shirt. He has several. The rest are in the closet."

"Do you have any pictures of him?" Jim asked.

"In my purse, I do," she said. "I'll get it." She left the room and came back a minute later with her purse. She pulled a wallet from it, and from the wallet, she extracted a small photo, which she handed to Jim. He looked at it for a moment, then handed it to Bo. "You can keep that. I don't want anything to do with him ever again. I'm sure he's a killer now. He deceived me, and I let him."

"Thanks. We'll keep it," Bo said. Then he asked her for Lucas's birthdate, which she told him. "Thanks for your help, Nattie. Really, you've been a big help."

"I can't stay here," Nattie said, suddenly becoming emotional again. "I'm afraid of Lucas now, and I'm afraid of that other guy too."

"What other guy?" Bo asked with a creased brow.

"Oh, I guess I didn't mention him. I don't know his name, but he came to the door between when Emil was here the first time and when he came back and stole my jewelry," she said after she had controlled another round of sobs.

"Can you describe him to us?" Bo asked.

"I'll try," she said and then she closed her eyes. When she opened them, she said, "I think he's probably nearly six feet tall and quite heavy. His hair is almost as black as mine, and he had it in a ponytail. His eyes were dark like mine too. Let me think for a minute." Once again she closed her eyes. "I remember seeing a scar on his left cheek, and he had sort of a flat nose. He looked like he'd been hit a lot of times in the face. I remember thinking that at the time. Oh, and he had tattoos on his arms and neck. He was wearing a T-shirt without a jacket even though it was cold outside. That's how I saw the tattoos."

"Anything else?" Bo asked as he glanced meaningfully at his partner.

She slowly shook her head, causing her long dark hair to sway gently.

"Did you happen to see what the guy was driving?" Bo asked.

"Yeah, I did. When I answered the door, there was a pickup at the curb—a small Nissan like Lucas's, but it was tan and a lot newer than Lucas's."

"Did you hear anything the two of them said?" Bo asked.

For the first time since they had come, Nattie smiled. It was a very thin smile but quite pretty. "Lucas sent me to the bedroom like he did that first time Emil came. But I didn't close the door, and I listened to them. The other guy—I think his name started with an *L*, like Leon, or something like that—told Lucas that he could sell him some good stuff for cheaper than Emil. Lucas wanted some, but when he told the guy . . . wait. I just remembered his name. I'm good with names. It's Leonardo. I don't think he ever said a last name."

"Good, Nattie. So did Lucas buy something from Leonardo?" Bo asked.

"No, he didn't have any money, so he couldn't, and the guy wouldn't let him take it on credit," Nattie responded.

"What else was said?" Bo asked.

"Well, I do remember that the guy, Leonardo, told Lucas that he could meet him somewhere when he had some money, and he'd sell him some heroin. I remember they exchanged phone numbers and . . ." Nattie paused. "Wait! I remember something else. He told Lucas that he would sell to him from then on, that his prices were cheaper than Emil's and his stuff was better, a higher grade. But Leonardo said that didn't really matter because Emil probably wouldn't be selling drugs anymore."

"Nattie, you have been most helpful," Bo said after she told the officers that she couldn't remember anything else. "Now if you'd like to call your parents, you could do so right now on my phone."

She hesitated for a moment, but then she reached out and accepted the phone. All she had to do was punch in the numbers. She looked at the phone and back at Bo.

"Feel free to go in your bedroom where you will have some privacy."

"Thank you, Detective," she said. "I don't deserve how good you've been to me." She hurried down the hallway, entered another room, and shut the door.

"I guess you were right," Jim said wryly. "We now have two suspects."

"Three," Bo corrected, and Jim looked at him with a question in his eyes. "We need to find this Leonardo guy. He threatened to kill Emil, according to what Nattie just told us."

"In that case, I'd say four," Jim said.

"Four?"

"Yeah. What about the guy who was pressing Emil to pay him, the bigger supplier who was the reason Emil was using threats to get what he needed?" Jim asked.

"Right. Okay, so it looks like we have our work cut out for us. I'd like to think that one of the two women who have been wronged will turn out to be right, but we can't ignore the other suspects."

For the next few minutes, the officers discussed what to do next. Finally, Nattie, her eyes red from more tears, rejoined them and handed Bo his phone.

"Thank you," she said. "My dad is at work, but I talked to my mom. Even though she's mad at me and says Dad will be too, she says they love me. They'll bring Dad's truck and come get me and my belongings as soon as he gets off work."

"Do they live in Price or somewhere close by?" Bo asked.

"No, they live in Sandy, so it's going to be a while before they can get here. And I'm scared. What if Lucas comes back before they get here?"

"You can't stay here, Nattie. Let me see if I can find a place where you can stay until your folks get to Price," Bo offered. "And you'll need to let them know where you are so they can find you when they reach town."

"You guys are so nice. I didn't know cops could be so nice," she said as Bo began to punch in a number on his phone.

CHAPTER TWELVE

Bo's first call was to Rosina, his cousin. She answered and he told her what he needed.

"I'd love to help," she said, "but my roommate and I are in Provo, and my apartment is locked. I'm sorry."

"That's okay. I'll call Karmen," he said.

"She's with us," Rosina said. "Are you saying this girl needs a safe place to stay until her parents can come get her?"

"That's right. Maybe as a last resort I can let her stay at my place, but she would be alone," Bo said.

"Why don't you call Ron Brady? I'll bet she could stay there until her parents get to Price," Rosina suggested.

"Hey, that's a good idea. I think I'll do that. Thanks, Rosina. And tell Karmen hi for me."

"I'll do you one better," she said, and a moment later, Karmen was talking on Rosina's phone. Bo explained briefly what he was doing, and then the call was ended.

Bo punched in Ron Brady's number, and after a moment, Ron came on the line. "I hate to ask favors of you, Ron, but I need one right now."

"If I can do it, I will. Melia and Joe are back. Melia took Joe to DI to outfit him with some clothes to wear to church on Sunday. I'm pleased that he's agreed to go. Melia thinks a lot of him, and I want to make sure he's worthy of her in case something comes of their friendship down the road," the farmer said. Bo explained what he needed, and Ron did not hesitate. "Of course she can come here. Does she know how to get here?"

"She has no car. My partner and I will bring her out right now. Thanks so much for your help." He ended the call and turned to Nattie. "Okay. We're taking you to someplace safe. When we get there, I'll let you borrow my phone again, and you can call your mother and give her the address. It's quite a ways out of town, but she should be able to find it."

Lucas watched Nattie and the two cops exit the house together from a short distance away. He was not pleased. Nattie should have kept her mouth shut. He was afraid the cops might suspect him now of Emil's murder. He didn't do it, but there was little he could do about what they might think. It might be best if he were to find some other place to stay for a while, at least until he could see that either Joe or the real killer, a man whose identity he did not know, had been arrested for the crime. Oh well, he thought, he'd just go on in and get some of his things while the cops were taking Nattie to wherever they were taking her.

He drove his old truck to the back of the apartment and then went to work. It was almost dark, so he didn't expect any of the neighbors to notice him. He took a bunch of his clothes and some of what little food they had. He didn't touch Nattie's stuff. He didn't need it.

Joe and Melia were just leaving the farmhouse when Bo drove into the yard. Melia skipped happily to his SUV as he got out. "You've got to take a minute and see what we found for Joe to wear to church on Sunday," Melia said proudly to Bo. "I can't wait. He'll look so good."

Joe, for his part, was beaming. "I thought we'd find worn-out stuff that I would be embarrassed to wear," he said. "Come in and see what Melia picked out."

"Okay, but we don't have a lot of time," Bo said. "We have a lot going on right now. And by the way, let me introduce Nattie Shrader. She's in some danger, and Ron said she could stay here until her parents come to pick her up sometime later tonight."

"Hi, Joe. I know you. It's good to see you again. You were nice that day in the store when you stood up to Lucas for me. Thank you," Nattie said.

"You're welcome," Joe said. At that moment, Ron, who had just left the house, joined them. "This is my boss, Ron Brady, and his granddaughter, Melia."

Bo was looking back and forth between Joe and Nattie. "So you guys know each other?"

"Sort of," Joe said, acting quite uncomfortable. Nattie just nodded.

Ron broke in and said, "Come on in and get a bite to eat, you guys. We always have something in the fridge since Melia loves to cook and does a great job. You're hungry, aren't you, Nattie?" Ron asked. "We'll be having dinner in a few minutes."

"I hadn't thought about it, but yes, now that you mention it, I am hungry. I'd love some dinner, but I don't want to be a bother," Nattie said with an attempt at a smile that didn't quite come off.

They all trailed into the house, and Melia and Joe showed off the Sunday clothes they'd found at DI. "Hey, those are pretty nice," Bo said. "That was really great of you, Melia."

"Hey, Joe deserves it," she said as she looked at Joe and brought a blush to his face.

"Bo, you and Jim probably need to eat. It will only take me a minute to get dinner on the table, and then you can go back to work with your stomachs full." She grinned.

Bo glanced at Jim, who said, "I won't argue with that, as long as it doesn't take too long. We still have some things we need to do tonight."

"Yeah, they have to find my boyfriend, Lucas. I mean my *former* boyfriend. He killed that guy Emil," Nattie said with bitterness in her voice. "And now I'm afraid he will kill me if he finds me."

Melia's face drained of color. "That's horrible. I'm sorry."

"I'll get through it. My parents warned me about Lucas," Nattie said. "I didn't listen, but they're going to help me out even though I don't deserve it. Can I help you in the kitchen?"

"Sure, that would be great," Melia said and led the way.

As soon as the two young ladies were out of the room, Bo said, "It sounds like you know Lucas but not in a good way."

"Yeah, he's a jerk," Joe said, then he changed the subject. "So you know who killed Emil?"

"Not for sure," Bo said. "Nattie believes Lucas did it. She claims he had threatened Emil. But there are three others we can't rule out."

"Who else?" Joe asked.

"Can you keep this to yourselves for now?" Bo asked.

"Of course," Ron said.

"I won't say a word," Joe promised.

"Okay, I guess you deserve to know what's going on after all you've been through, Joe. Let's sit down."

After the men were all seated, Bo began. "While I was looking for the location where Herc was shot, Jim responded to an emergency call from a home we had been to earlier. After we left, it seems that the two owners, a man and his wife, had a nasty fight. The husband apparently hit his wife really hard in the face, and well, to make a long story short, he left, and she died a short while later."

"She died from just one punch?" Joe asked with creased brows. "It's a good thing one punch didn't kill me in the jail."

"This woman was a small, very thin person, and her husband is very large. It's more than that though," Bo said and explained how they assumed she later fell hard on her face. "We think she may have drowned in her own blood, but the medical examiner will tell us for sure."

"Why is this guy a suspect?" Ron asked.

Bo told them about the bloody note. "Oh, so it was him, not Lucas?" Joe asked. "I wouldn't put it beyond Lucas though."

"We don't know. Since the woman died, we obviously can't question her. It's going to be hard to figure it out, but both of those guys had threatened to kill Emil, and both could have carried out their threats."

"You said there are others who might have done it. Who are they?" Ron asked.

Bo and Jim didn't get a chance to say anything more before Nattie entered the room. The change in her was rather nice. She looked almost relaxed. "Melia says to tell you guys to come and eat."

"A couple of drug pushers," Bo said quietly in answer to the earlier question after Nattie had retreated. "That's all we'd better say for now."

Dinner was a friendly but subdued affair, which was only natural, considering what Nattie was going through. She and Melia seemed to have found some common ground during the meal preparation, for they chattered about nothing important. Bo watched and listened to the way Nattie was talking.

"Nattie," he said finally, "you seem different."

"I guess I feel safer," she said with a weak smile. "It will be hard living at home with my parents, especially with the baby coming in a few weeks. But I think I made a mistake by going with Lucas. I just have to get through it if I can."

"You can do it," Bo said with feeling. "What about your baby? Is it Lucas's, and will you be able to take care of it?"

"It is, as much as I hate to admit it," Nattie said. "Lucas only let me see a doctor one time, but I learned then that my baby is a girl. He didn't like that. He said it should have been a boy. He ranted about it, and several times when he was high on heroin, he would say that there was no way we would keep a baby girl. I didn't want to fight with him, so I didn't argue, but I would have never let him hurt her."

"That's awful, Nattie," Melia said. "I know this is none of my business, but do you mind if I ask how old you are?"

"I'm eighteen. I was seventeen when I ran off with Lucas, much to my parents' displeasure. But I thought he was a great guy. He was a real smooth talker, and at times, he was really sweet to me. He treated me okay most of the time. I guess I was a fool," Nattie said. "How old are you, Melia?"

"Nineteen," Melia said.

"You're smarter than me, Melia. What I did has really messed up my life," Nattie said. Her eyes darted back and forth between Joe and Melia for a minute while everyone at the table was silent. "You two like each other, don't you?"

Both of them blushed. Joe wished he could just disappear. He felt really stupid right now. He didn't know how to respond. "We're . . . just . . . good friends," Melia managed to stutter.

"Joe," Nattie said with sudden seriousness, "don't ever hurt her, and don't treat her the way you saw Lucas treat me that day in the store. And both of you, stay away from drugs. Lucas always tried to get me to use with him. I had no idea he used drugs until I'd moved in with him. I'm ashamed to admit this, but I did try his drugs a couple times at first, but I didn't like the way they made me feel. It scared me, to be honest. So I refused to touch them after that. I should have left him when I first learned about his drug use, but I had nowhere to go. My parents were really angry with me. And then I found out that I was pregnant with my little girl, and I simply didn't think I could have the baby on my own. Now I'll have to, but at least I think my parents will help me."

Joe squirmed uncomfortably because of his own foolish use of pot and eventually turned his full attention to his dinner. After they were all finished, Joe stood up. "I better get some work done outside. Melia and I didn't quite get finished today, so even though it's dark out, I need to get it done."

"We need to get it done," Melia corrected him.

"I'm sorry about your dog, Joe. Melia told me about him. I hope he'll be okay," Nattie said before turning to Melia. "I'll help clean up the kitchen, and then, would you and Joe care if I go outside and work with you? I need to stay busy so I won't think so much about what a mess I'm in tonight. Being around you guys makes me feel good, the best I've felt since before I met Lucas."

"Sure, that would be fine if you can in your, ah, condition."

"I can work," Nattie said firmly.

"In that case, you'll need a warmer coat, but we have more in our coat closet. We also have extra gloves. You can borrow whatever you need," Melia said.

The men went outside, and Joe walked to Bo's SUV with them. "Can you tell me the names of the other people you suspect? I probably don't know them, but if I do, maybe I could help a little."

"What do you think, Jim?" Bo asked.

"Maybe it wouldn't hurt," Jim said.

They debated it for a moment. "It seems that we are in agreement, Jim," Bo said finally. "Okay, so the man who killed his wife this morning and who she says killed Emil is a guy by the name of Bryan Bayle. You told us before that you know who he is."

"Big guy," Joe said, nodding his head.

"Yeah, more fat than muscle but strong enough to do what he did to his wife," Bo said.

"Like I told you, I've seen him before. I saw Lucas too, but I tried to keep him from seeing me. I know you realize that I had met him in rather a bad circumstance. We had a run-in at the grocery store one day. He was being rotten to Nattie, and I stood up for her, even though I didn't know her, and told him off. It made him mad. Anyway, who are the other two?"

"We only know the name of one other: Leonardo Augur," Bo said.

Joe nodded. "Oh yeah. The guy I told you about wanting to sell to me."

"According to Nattie, she heard Leonardo tell her boyfriend that he'd never be able to buy from Emil again because he wouldn't be selling anything after that."

"Like maybe he planned to kill him?" Joe asked perceptively.

"Yeah, like that," Bo said. "We know nothing about the other guy except that he was who Emil was getting his stuff from. And according to Lucas and Bayle, he'd been threatening Emil if he didn't pay up."

"Emil told me about that too. Emil was scared. But he didn't pull a gun or anything on me when I saw him just a couple of days before he was killed," Joe said. "He did give me a hard time though. That's why I was going to give him my shotgun."

"I think he was getting desperate because he'd been threatened more by this mystery drug supplier," Bo said. "I'll bet that's why he was at your house the evening he was killed. My guess is that you were about to get threatened as well."

"I feel like such an idiot," Joe said, hanging his head and looking at his boots. "I wish I'd never gone in that bar to celebrate turning twenty-one."

"Hey, Joe, there is no use worrying yourself about it now. What's done is done. You're a good man, Joe, and don't forget it," Bo said.

Jo looked up. "Thanks, Bo. I'd better get to work. My dog getting shot really messed up my day, and Melia and I are way behind on our work."

"I'll be in touch," Bo promised. "You just be careful. Whoever shot Herc has it in for you, I'm afraid."

"I'll be fine," Joe said.

Bo hoped that was true but doubted it.

Joe headed for the barn as soon as Bo and Jim got in the SUV and flipped on the lights. The horse barn really needed to be cleaned. He and Melia had started when he heard Herc bark, but they hadn't gotten much done. For the next half hour, he worked hard, wanting to get as much completed as he could before Melia and Nattie joined him. He'd made great progress when Melia, accompanied by Nattie in a warm but overly large coat and a knit cap and insulated gloves, joined him.

"Wow, Joe, you've gotten a lot done," Melia said.

"How can I help?" Nattie asked. "I want to. I mean, like I said, I want to get busy. But I owe you anyway for what you did for me that day. By the way, I told Melia about it. She said that was the kind of thing you would do."

Joe felt uncomfortable. "I don't want you to cause a problem for your baby," he said hesitantly. "This is hard work."

"It will be fine," Nattie said. "I can work if I'm careful. In fact, it would be good for me."

"All right, then here's what we're doing." Joe took a few minutes to explain in some detail. "You stick by Melia, and the two of you will keep me hurrying." He grinned.

The three of them had worked for close to an hour when Joe's cell phone rang. He looked at the screen, saw it was Bo, and answered, wondering if he and Jim had made some progress on the case that he wanted to tell him about.

"Have you caught one of the suspects already tonight?" Joe asked Bo.

"No, but I just got a call from Nattie's parents. She doesn't have a phone, so I let her call them on mine earlier to ask for their help. They need to speak to her again," Bo reported. "Would you mind letting her call them on your phone? She has their number, of course."

"Sure," Joe said.

He walked back in the barn where Melia and Nattie were cleaning out the last stall and filling a wheelbarrow. They'd been doing that, and Joe had been wheeling the manure outside to an ever-growing pile that he was going to have to get onto the fields in a few weeks. Since they were using two wheelbarrows, the girls were keeping him hopping. He'd barely get one dumped and wheeled back to the barn when they'd have another one ready. It was hard working outside this late, and he was grateful that a full moon came up and made it easier for him to see.

"We've almost got it, Joe," Melia said. "Nattie is amazing. She works so hard." When she noticed the phone in Joe's hand, she frowned. "What's going on?"

"Bo just called me. I guess Nattie's folks need to talk to her for a minute. And the only number they had was Bo's," Joe explained. "Here, Nattie, you can call them on mine."

"Thanks," Nattie said as a shadow crossed her face. "I wonder if they're going to be late. Or maybe they want to come in the morning."

"Maybe," Joe said. "Melia and I will step outside so you can have some privacy."

"It's okay," Nattie said. "I don't care if you hear what I have to say." She accepted the phone and punched in her mother's cell phone number.

CHAPTER THIRTEEN

Nattie listened with the phone to her ear, but Joe could hear it ringing. It rang a number of times before he finally heard someone answer. He couldn't tell what was said or even if it was a man or a woman.

"Hi, Mom. This is Nattie. I'm using a friend's phone to call you this time." She then listened for a moment before saying, "So Dad's not home yet? It's getting late." Nattie listened again. Her face clouded over, and she slowly sank to the barn floor. When she spoke, her voice was all choked up. "Mom, please, you can't do that to me. I'm sorry I left with Lucas. You and dad were right about him. I did a terrible thing. But I need you guys. Please," she begged and began to cry.

Joe could tell something bad was going on, so he motioned for Nattie to activate the speaker. She nodded in understanding and did so. At that point, he and Melia could both hear what was being said by Nattie's mother. What he heard made him seethe. Mrs. Shrader could be clearly heard to say, "Your father is not happy with you, Nattie. He said you made your bed and that you can lie in it."

"But, Mom, you said you would come get me," Nattie said, sobbing. "I don't know what to do. I'm afraid of Lucas. I can't go back to his apartment."

"I'm sorry, Nattie. You should have thought about something like this happening when you went against our wishes and left home to be with Lucas. We told you he was rotten and you shouldn't go with him, but you defied us and did it anyway," Mrs. Shrader said coldly.

"Mom, please, I'm going to have a baby, your granddaughter. Don't you care about that?" Nattie begged.

"Oh, your father just came in. Here, I'm going to let you talk to him. It's Nattie, Sean," they all heard Mrs. Shrader say. "You talk to her. It's your decision to let her work out her own problems."

"My decision? I thought we agreed on this, Eugena. Here, give me that phone." A moment later, Sean Shrader was on the phone, and he was shouting in anger. "Nattie, if you'd listened to me in the first place, none of this would have happened. You wouldn't be pregnant with that scum's child, and you wouldn't need us to help you. You're just going to have to figure this out on your own. It's not our problem. It's yours!"

"Daddy, please," Nattie begged. "I am going to have your granddaughter in a few weeks. I need help. My baby needs help. I've got to leave. I need you guys. I was wrong, and I don't ever want to see him again. Don't you care?"

"We warned you about that man. Don't say we didn't. As a matter of fact, as far as I'm concerned, your baby is *not our grandchild*. If you can't take care of it, you need to have it aborted. I don't ever want to see a child of that guy you ran off with. When I know the baby is gone, then you may come home, and your mother and I will help you get a new start in life."

"Daddy, I can't believe what you're saying. This baby is alive and you want me to have it killed?" she screamed into the phone. "Never!"

She ended the call and handed the phone back to Joe, tears streaming down her face. Melia dropped to the cold concrete floor beside Nattie, put her arms around her shoulders, and cried with her. Joe was stunned. What he had just heard made his blood run cold. Nattie's dad was as bad as Lucas. He wondered what Nattie had gone through growing up. Maybe there was a reason she'd left home the first chance she got.

At least five minutes passed, and Melia was still comforting Nattie when Ron came out of the house using a cane, as he sometimes did, and approached the barn. He was not a healthy man, but he was a generous, kind, and loving person. "I see something is wrong," he said. "Would you guys like to tell me about it?"

Melia stood up and stepped back from Nattie and tried to answer her grandfather, but the words couldn't get past the tears. Joe stepped in and told Ron what had just occurred. He'd never seen Ron really angry before, but he did now. Ron was trembling with fury. "What a horrid thing for a father to say. Surely he didn't mean it."

"Oh, he meant it all right," Joe said. "We had the phone on speaker. He meant exactly what he said. He wants her to abort her baby."

Ron stepped over to Nattie, who was now standing, facing away from the others, and still sobbing softly, her face covered with her hands. Ron spoke gently to her as he walked around and faced her. "Nattie, you do not have to go back to your house. Melia and I have lots of room in this big old farmhouse of ours. You're welcome to stay here as long as you like."

She dropped her hands from her face. "What?"

Ron smiled as Melia joined them. "Grandpa wants you to live with us, and so do I. We will be your family. We'll keep you safe, and I'll help you with your baby when she's born."

Fresh tears poured from one who had already shed so many tears that there should not have been any more available. But there were, and they flowed freely.

Melia once again put her arms around Nattie. "Come on, Nattie. Let's go find you a room and get you settled in."

Joe had wiped tears from his eyes that the others had not seen. Then he stepped beside Ron and watched as the two girls walked slowly toward the house. "Ron, that is the most generous thing I've ever heard."

"Joe, she needs someone. We're here and can help her. It's the right thing to do. It is what the Savior would want me to do," he said as he watched the girls. "She needs things from her house. After she's had time to get her emotions under control and maybe take a shower, we'll take her there and get whatever she wants. I know it's getting late, but we need to do it."

"That sounds good, but I'll call Bo. If Lucas were to come while we were there, it would be dangerous for Nattie and for the rest of us," Joe said.

Bo's phone began to ring as he and Jim walked toward the sheriff's office. They had driven by Nattie's house earlier and saw that Lucas's truck was not there, so they hadn't stopped. The Price police had officers all over the area searching for both the truck and for Lucas.

Bo looked at his phone's screen, saw that it was Joe calling, and answered with, "Hey, Joe, is everything okay?"

He could feel the emotion in his cousin's voice as Joe responded. "No, it's not. Nattie can't go home. Her father said that unless she has an abortion, she's not welcome. He said her baby is not his grandchild. I can't believe any father would say something like that even if his daughter had not listened to them earlier. No one deserves to be treated like that, Bo," Joe said. "Whoever killed Emil did a terrible thing, but why would anyone want to kill an unborn baby? It's horrible, Bo. He could at least have suggested she release it for adoption, but he didn't."

"I agree with you. I don't know what this world is coming to. But that discussion is for another time. Right now we've got to think about Nattie and her baby. Her father has put Nattie in an impossible position."

"Ron asked her to live with him and Melia," Joe said. "So at least she doesn't have to go back to her home."

"Joe, she's in danger. Her being there could put Ron and Melia in danger as well," he said. "And you too, for that matter."

"I'm already in danger," Joe said. "I'm learning to live with it." He forced a chuckle but did not feel the humor.

Bo had stopped walking. As he held the phone away from his head, he said to Jim, "We've got to go back to the Brady farm," and turned back toward the parking lot. Then to Joe he said, "We're coming there. We'll talk to Ron. We've got to figure something else out."

"I don't think you can change Ron's mind," Joe said. "I know him pretty well. He's a stubborn man, and when he makes up his mind, he isn't likely to change it."

"We'll see about that. No one has been able to find Lucas, so you keep your eyes open. He could be near there for all we know," Bo warned. "Jim and I are on our way."

The killer was at his preferred hiding spot, spying on the Brady farm. He had arrived in time to see the two young women and the farmer walking toward the house. Joe was still standing near the large barn, talking on his cell phone. The killer did not like what he was seeing. Anger built in him.

Joe should be in jail. Clearly further action needed to be taken. Oh yes, Joe and his friends would pay dearly for their treachery. He wasn't a man who ever let anyone get in his way or go against what he wanted. Joe was going down for murder. He would do whatever it took to make that happen.

He continued to watch, and a few minutes later, his anger almost boiled over when he saw two deputies arrive, get out of the sheriff department SUV, then walk over to Joe, who was just coming out of the barn with a wheelbarrow. The farmer's dog ran from somewhere near the house and greeted the big ugly bulldog of Deputy Buckley's. Sometime, when he got a chance, he'd shoot that dog like he'd shot the collie.

The killer's anger and hatred had become so intense that killing anyone or anything didn't sear his conscience in the least. He'd seen enough for now, so he left. He'd be back, and when he came, no one would be expecting him. He had some ideas, and one of them involved that pregnant girl. He knew where she and her Hispanic boyfriend lived. He'd sneak into the house and do something that would get her attention. He'd do it just to make a point with Joe. Joe would see that he was going to have to admit to murder. Nothing else would do.

"Joe, we've got to change Ron's mind. Let's go in the house and talk to him. We can probably put Nattie in a safe house somewhere so she can have her baby and not have to worry about being in danger," Bo said.

"I'm sure you could do that, but Bo, you don't know Ron Brady like I do. He's a kind man and a generous one. He's sure been good to me. But there is no way he'll change his mind, and I don't think Nattie will either."

"I aim to try," Bo said firmly, and the three men started for the house.

"Bo, you guys go ahead. I still have a lot of work to do," Joe said as he stopped walking. "Thanks for coming out. I'll be here somewhere when you finish talking to Ron if you need me."

"Okay," Bo said. He walked with determination toward the house. Jim strode alongside him.

Bo knocked on the door, and Melia answered it. "Hey, Bo, Jim. Come on in. I guess Joe called you."

"He did. We'd like to speak with your grandfather," Bo said.

"He's upstairs with Nattie. He's getting her some bedding. I was helping until you guys knocked." Melia grinned. "Where's Joe?"

"He said he had to keep working," Bo said.

"I guess I should go help him. But first I'll go tell Grandpa that you want to see him," she said.

With that, she turned and ran up the stairs. A minute later, she reappeared and ran back down. "You guys can sit down. Grandpa will be down in a minute. I'll go help Joe now."

Bo watched Melia as she put on her coat, gloves, boots, and hat and then hurried out the door. "She's a good girl," Bo said. "She's not afraid to work. That's for sure. Ron's got to be proud of her."

"I can see that," Jim agreed.

The two officers talked about what they needed to do once they got Nattie and Ron convinced that she needed to be in a safe house and that it needed to be somewhere a long way from Price. "We'll need to get Family Services involved," Bo said. "They should be able to get her to where she needs to be."

Ron came slowly down the stairs a moment later. "Gentlemen," he greeted them as he headed for his recliner and sank wearily into it. "It's been a hard day. My old ticker isn't like it used to be. I'm exhausted."

"We need to talk to you about Nattie," Bo said, diving right into the matter he'd come for.

"What about her?" Ron asked. "She has a home here for as long as she needs it. She's upstairs resting right now."

"That's what we need to talk about," Bo said. "We believe she's in danger. And by you allowing her to stay here, you're putting yourself and your granddaughter in danger as well. Lucas Soto is a treacherous man. He may have already killed, and if so, he probably wouldn't hesitate to kill again."

"She'll be safe here," Ron protested weakly. "I'll make sure she's never alone."

Bo shook his head. "I don't think that's good enough, Ron. She needs to be in a safe house where she will have all the care she needs, both her and her baby when she's born. We'll contact Family Services and ask them to make sure she's where Lucas can't find her."

"What makes you think he can find her here?" Ron asked stubbornly. Bo could see that Joe was right; Ron was going to be hard to convince.

"Ron, just having someone with her only puts a second person in danger. You don't want to do that to Melia, do you?"

Ron smiled weakly. "Of course I don't, but you don't understand. I plan to keep the doors locked at all times. I'll keep a gun handy. I can shoot, you know. I'll teach Melia and Nattie to shoot as well. Joe will be here a lot, and I'll let him keep a gun close as well. He knows how to use guns."

"Please, Ron. Think about this. If you guys have to be armed, that means you realize that Lucas could come and that he could be armed too," Bo said.

"I suppose so," Ron responded. "But I really think you officers are overreacting. She needs to be taken care of, and we can do that here. She only has a few weeks until the baby is due, and I'll see to it that her medical bills are covered. I can afford that, you know. We will not leave her alone at the hospital when the time comes. Of that I can assure you."

"Ron," Bo began again.

Ron waved a hand at him. "She'll be fine. I'll make sure. Anyway, she wants to be here. Go up and talk to her if you'd like. You'll see."

"I think we'll do that," Bo said with a grim face.

"She's in the last room upstairs at the end of the hallway. I don't think I'll come with you. In case you're thinking that I look pretty weak, you have to admit it's been a rather tough day, and it's about my bedtime now. All I need is a little rest, and then I'll be able to take Nattie to her house and help her get her things. Joe and Melia will help too."

Bo shook his head. "We'll go talk to Nattie. I think she'll see that she needs to be in a safe house. Now, Ron, don't think that I think you are being too generous. You are a good man, but I just want to make sure everyone is safe." With that, he and Jim got to their feet and headed for the stairs.

Nattie was not asleep. In fact, she wasn't even lying down when Bo and Jim approached the door, which was wide open. But her eyes were red, evidence of a lot of crying, for which Bo couldn't blame her in the least. "Hi, Nattie. Can we visit for a minute?" Bo asked gently.

"Sure, come on in. Has anyone found Lucas?" she asked as she rose to her feet from the side of the bed.

"I'm afraid not, but a huge manhunt is on for both him and a man by the name of Bryan Bayle," Bo said. "Do you know who Bayle is?"

"I think I remember Lucas talking about meeting him when he was picking up some heroin from Emil," she said. "What's he wanted for?"

"He killed his wife this morning," Bo said.

Nattie went pale and sat back on the bed. "Oh no," she said as her hand flew to her mouth.

"Nattie, I'm only telling you that because I don't want the same thing to happen to you," Bo said. "I know that Mr. Brady is being generous by letting you stay here, but Deputy Grizzel and I think that you would be safer if you were in a secure safe house somewhere outside of this area. We will ask Family Services to arrange it for you."

Nattie sat silently for a moment. Tears began to flow again, but she wiped them away. "I don't want to be in a safe house. I don't want an abortion," she said. "Mr. Brady wants me to stay here, and I want to stay here if I can. He makes me feel like I matter and like my baby matters."

"It will be dangerous until we catch Lucas. And it could put Ron and Melia in danger too," Bo said sternly.

"I told Mr. Brady, Ron . . . he wants me to call him Ron. Anyway, I told him that, but he says that he thinks I should stay anyway, that he'd make sure I was safe."

Bo shook his head. "He does have guns, and he can lock his doors, but if Lucas is as dangerous as we think he could be, that might not be enough. You can stay here until Family Services comes to get you."

"Please. I feel like these people care about me, more than anyone in a safe house ever would. I know I barely met them, but they are such good people, and I could even go to church with them if I could get a nice dress," she said.

Bo could see that he was losing this fight. "Let's go down and talk to Ron again," he finally said. "He's got to understand how dangerous it could be for you to stay here."

Nattie slowly rose to her feet, walked past the two officers, and headed for the stairs. Over her shoulder, she said, "Maybe you're right."

Bo felt some hope at her words. They followed her down. Ron was asleep in his recliner, but he stirred when he heard them enter the room. "I guess I dozed for a minute," he said.

"You need the rest," Nattie said softly. "Ron, these officers think I should leave. I don't want to, but maybe they're right."

Ron came fully awake. "Nattie, I want you to stay. Please. I will make sure no one hurts you. I may not be in the best of health, but I'm not an invalid. I am a good shot with any kind of gun. I was an Army Ranger in my younger days before my father left this farm to me. I know how to fight, and I am still capable of fighting if I have to, but frankly, I don't think it will come to that."

"I don't want you or Melia to get hurt because of me. I deserve what's happening to me," she said. "I disobeyed my parents."

"No one deserves to be treated the way you've been treated, Nattie," Bo said, coming to her defense. "That's why all of us want to keep you safe."

For ten minutes, the pros and cons were batted back and forth, Bo feeling strongly one way and Ron just as strongly the other. Finally, Nattie said, "I think I should go."

"Please," Ron said.

"I appreciate what you've done for me and what you've offered to do, but I think I should go. I don't have any right to put you and Melia in danger."

"Will you come back as soon as they arrest Lucas?" Ron asked.

"Oh yes, for sure, if you want me to," she said with a catch in her voice.

"Thank you, Nattie. I will hold you to that," Ron said. Then to Bo and Jim, he suggested, "Why don't we help her get her things from her house. We can store what she doesn't need to take with her here in my house."

"I think that would be fine, but first give me a few minutes to see what I can work out with Family Services," Bo said. "I may not be able to reach them tonight, but I'll try. We'll be back in a little while. In the meantime, have your doors locked and a gun near you."

CHAPTER FOURTEEN

Joe and Melia worked hard. They soon saw Bo and his partner leave the farmyard. Bo hadn't come looking for him, so Joe guessed that whatever they had decided was firm.

"I hope they didn't change their minds," Melia said. Joe had explained to Melia that Bo wanted to send Nattie to a safe house. Melia had not liked that idea at all.

"I know Ron wouldn't have changed his mind," Joe said. "But I don't know about Nattie. She might prefer to not be a burden on you guys."

"Let's find out," Melia said. "She wasn't in the truck with them, was she?"

"No, but maybe they needed to work something out for her first," Joe suggested. "I'll keep at it here. I can finish up in a few minutes and come in. Then you can let me know what they've decided."

Melia was not gone very long. She came just as Joe was finishing up. She had a long face but a handful of cookies. "She's going, and Grandpa is not very happy about it. Bo just went to make arrangements for Family Services to find a place to take her. Grandpa's still growling, but it's Nattie's decision. She said when they catch Lucas she'll come back. So I hope they catch him soon. I would love to have someone so near my age to be friends with."

They finished up and went to the house.

"I wonder what time they are coming to get Nattie," Joe said as they shed their coats, hats, gloves, and boots.

"I don't know, but I'd be surprised if it's tonight," Melia said.

A few minutes later, Bo and Jim showed up at the door.

"When are they coming for Nattie?" Joe asked.

"They can't for a couple of days since they don't have any places available. I'm surprised by that, but it is what it is, so I guess she stays here for now," Bo said. “One of the people we talked to from Family Services made me really angry. He suggested we just give her a jail cell. I told the guy that was stupid and that we’d do the best we could until they could help her.”

“We’ll take good care of her,” Melia said. “Won’t we, Joe?”

“I won’t be staying here,” he said. “I’ll be okay at home. You guys just need to keep your doors locked.”

“Joe, you don’t even have Herc. I think you should stay with Ron and Melia. I would feel better about Nattie if you were here,” Bo said.

“I’ll come back early in the morning,” Joe said.

Bo shook his head. “You don’t even have your guns.”

“Yeah, and why not?” he asked with a bite to his voice. “I know my pistol was used to shoot Emil, but I should be able to have my shotgun and rifle.”

“You have a good point there,” Bo agreed. “I’ll try to get them back to you. In the meantime, let’s go get some of Nattie’s things.”

“I’ll go get Nattie,” Melia said, and she ran for the house. When she returned, Ron was with her as well as Nattie. “Grandpa insists on going.”

“That’s right,” Ron said. “We’ll take my truck, but I want Joe to drive.”

When they arrived at the Soto residence, Melia and Joe were both shocked. Melia didn’t know what to say, so she didn’t say anything. The place was in terrible shape.

“I’m sorry it’s so cold in there,” Nattie said. “I asked Lucas several times to please get us a new door, but no, he needed his *fix* instead.”

“How did you stay warm in there?” Melia asked.

“I wore a coat and often kept a blanket around me. I can’t believe I didn’t try to get away from Lucas a long time ago,” she said. “I wanted to, but I guess I was scared and stupid.”

Joe didn’t respond, but he could certainly relate to the stupid bit—on his part, not hers.

When they reached the sagging door, Bo said, “You guys wait out here. Jim and I will make sure there are no surprises inside.”

Both officers drew their guns and entered. A couple minutes later, they came back out with their pistols holstered.

“Nattie, I’m afraid someone’s been here,” Bo said. “But whoever it was is gone now.”

“It must have been Lucas. What did he do?” she asked weakly.

“It’s a mess in there. There’s not a lot for you to gather up,” Jim said as he and Bo again entered with Ron, Melia, Nattie, and Joe following.

No sooner had Nattie stepped inside than fresh tears began to flow. "I knew it. This is Lucas's doing," she said with a broken voice.

Joe and Melia looked at each other in horror. The house had been torn apart just like Joe's had been. The sofa was slashed, totally ruined. Lamps were busted up, and chairs were broken. They moved into the kitchen. Once again, the place was destroyed. The dishes were all broken, and anything that wasn't breakable in the kitchen was smashed. Kitchen chairs were in pieces. The table had been hacked apart with what could only have been an ax. But there was no ax to be seen.

"I wonder where Lucas got an ax," Nattie said. She had quit crying and was in control of her emotions. "He doesn't have one."

As they moved toward the main bedroom, Joe said to Melia, "This looks like my house after someone had been in it. It must be the same person. Lucas must have a terrible temper."

They entered the bedroom. The dresser drawers had been pulled out, and the items in it were ripped apart. Nattie looked toward her closet. She stood as if frozen in place. "My clothes," she said. "They're gone. I have nothing to wear. What am I going to do?"

"We'll take care of you," Ron said. He then looked pointedly at Bo. "And we'll take care of your baby."

"What about Lucas's clothes?" Bo asked. "I don't see any men's things."

"I'm sure Lucas took them," Nattie said. "I can't believe I let him do this to me. My parents are right. I wish I would have listened to them, but I was so unhappy at home that I jumped at the chance to leave with someone who acted like he cared. I guess Lucas is going to go somewhere a long way from here."

"Possibly, but then again, maybe he'll try hiding nearby," Bo said reasonably. "There is simply no way to know at this point. Nattie, do you and Lucas have any bank accounts?"

She shook her head. "He has a credit card, but he would never let me have one."

"Do you know what company issued the card? Also, what kind of card was it? Visa, MasterCard, or something else?" he asked.

"I have no idea. He mostly used cash. He'd get a welfare check and cash it."

Bo turned to Jim. "Make a note of that. If he uses a credit card, we can trace him. Of course, first we'll need to find out who issued it. Nattie, if he didn't have an account at a bank, how did he pay off his card, or do you know?"

“That I can tell you,” Nattie said. “He always bought a money order at the post office to pay it with when he actually made a payment. I would think that his card is about maxed out, although when I’d ask him about it, he’d remind me that it was none of my business.”

“Thanks, Nattie,” Bo said. “I’m sorry for what you’ve gone through.”

“Maybe we can figure this out by going to the post office in the morning,” Jim said.

They did salvage a few of Nattie’s belongings, which they took out to Ron’s truck. A trip to Deseret Industries was going to be necessary the next day as well.

Bo and Jim did not leave them until Nattie was secure in Ron’s house and Ron had gotten a couple of guns out, loaded them, and put them where he could easily get to them.

“I’ll bring your shotgun and rifle to you, Joe,” Bo said. “Don’t leave here until I come back with them. Although I would prefer that you sleep here for a few days.”

“I’ll be okay,” Joe said. “I’ll come early in the morning though.”

When the officers left, Melia said, “Please stay here with us.”

“That’s okay. I’ll be fine at home,” he said to Ron as he had earlier to Bo. “I’d like to fix things up a little more there.”

“You aren’t leaving until Bo has brought your guns back,” Ron said firmly. “You can’t be in your house with no way to defend yourself.”

“I’m really not too worried,” Joe said, even though, deep inside, he knew he wasn’t being honest with himself. But he didn’t want anyone to know it. He had to put on a brave face. He had brought his troubles on himself, and he would face them himself. Surely he’d be okay once he had his shotgun and rifle. Bo delivered the guns to him shortly after that. Joe felt more secure now. He’d be okay in his own home.

It was late by the time Bo and Jim quit for the night, but they met the next morning at the office, prepared to get back to work. Bo was on the phone and when he put the receiver down he frowned and said to Jim, “We need to follow up on what I’ve learned just now.”

Since coming into the office early that morning, Bo had been working on finding more about Bryan Bayle’s background while Jim was doing the same for Lucas Soto’s. “What have you learned?” Jim asked. “I have zip on my end.”

“Bryan has a brother. Or at least he had a brother. That brother has not been seen by anyone for a couple of years. I located a sister on Facebook. I found a phone number for her and called. She says that Bryan and the rest of the family have had nothing to do with each other for a long time."

"Did she say how long?" Jim asked.

"Long enough that she didn't even know he'd married Belle. But she did have contact with this other brother. His name is Jordan, and he is a couple years younger than Bryan, who, in turn, is three years younger than the sister," Bo explained.

"Where does she live?" Jim asked. "Is it around here?"

"No, she's in Phoenix, which is where the brother lived," Bo responded. "But get this: Jordan left Phoenix about two years ago. The last time she heard from him, he'd phoned and said he'd found where Bryan was living and was going to visit him. She told Jordan that she didn't want to know where Bryan was, that as far as she was concerned, she didn't ever want to hear from him again. So he didn't tell her, although surely she may have suspected that Bryan was living in their late mother's house."

"It sounds like she was pretty bitter," Jim said.

"That's for sure. The last time she saw Bryan was several years ago. She didn't remember how many, but at that time, they'd gotten into an argument, and he'd beaten her up badly. She ended up in the hospital, and Bryan left town. The cops looked for him but didn't ever find him. She says that was okay with her. She told me he has a hot temper and if she never saw him again it would be too soon."

"Wow! So where is Jordan, the brother? Is he someone we could talk to?" Jim asked.

"I don't know. Like I said, the last time the sister talked to Jordan on the phone was around two years ago. He never did call to tell her if he actually met up with Bryan. Now, knowing that Bryan has caused the death of a wife she didn't even know about, she's worried about Jordan more than ever. She says she tried locating him on social media, but he apparently hasn't been on it. He did have a Facebook page, but it's been idle for those two years. She said she gave up trying his phone when she couldn't reach him on it. She wondered about Price but didn't think he'd ever go back to the old family house."

"I wish Belle were alive so we could talk to her about the brother," Jim said, echoing Bo's thoughts.

"So do I, but since she isn't, I think we should go have another look at their house. Maybe we can find some sort of clue there," Bo suggested.

After Bo had let the Price City officers know what they planned to do and been told to go ahead, Bo and Jim began to search the dumpy little house. They worked for over an hour with no success while Two Face lounged on the dirty carpet in the living room. "Let's check the yard. I see a small shed back there," Jim said after they had exhausted their search inside.

"I doubt we'll find anything that will help us, but I guess it can't hurt," Bo said, and the two men and the bulldog went out the back door.

The yard was large, and there were bushes and some trees there, mostly dead ones. An old car and other junk littered the area. The shed had no door, and inside there were some old tools and implements that clearly had not been used for years, probably not since the previous generation. Bryan Bayle obviously had made no effort to do anything with his yard. There was a small porch on the back of the house, but there was no patio furniture of any kind on it.

"I don't think Belle ever spent any time on her porch," Jim observed.

"I guess there isn't anything else we can learn here," Bo said as he looked around for his bulldog.

At first he could not see Two Face, so the two men went through the tall weeds and shallow snow toward the back of the yard. There they found Two Face digging between some dead bushes. He was energetic about his work, and when Bo called his name, he looked up, barked, and then went back to digging.

"Did you see a shovel in that shed, Jim?" Bo asked as an ugly thought occurred to him. "I think I remember seeing one clear in the back hanging between a couple of nails. It's probably nothing, but I'd kind of like to poke around where Two Face is digging."

"Yeah, there was a shovel. I don't know what kind of shape it's in, but I'll get it," Jim said and hurried off. He came back carrying a rusty, dull shovel that had a flat nose and a short handle, not one good for digging. "I guess we can try this. If we need to, we can borrow a better one from somebody. The ground is probably still frozen."

"I'll try this," Bo said. He stepped near where his dog had been digging and tried to get the shovel to go into the ground. "It's pretty frozen, so I don't think I can accomplish much with this shovel. There must be something here or Two Face wouldn't be so determined. He's not making much progress though."

"Is it even worth our time to dig here?" Jim asked.

Bo put his foot on the shovel and tried getting it in deeper. "I don't know," he said, "but I can tell that the ground here, even though there's frost in it, is not packed as hard as I would have expected."

"What do you think's in there?" Jim asked.

Bo threw some dirt off to the side and looked up at his partner. "I'm probably way off base here, but just think. If Jordan Bayle is missing and his brother is not a good man . . ."

"You think Jordan's buried there?" Jim asked, stepping back and throwing his hands wide in surprise.

"Something is, or my dog wouldn't be working at this like he is. But I need something better than this shovel," Bo told him. He threw a little more icy dirt with the shovel. "What we need is a cadaver dog."

"I think that can be arranged," Jim said thoughtfully. "There's a lady by the name of Lottie Dawson who works with the search and rescue team sometimes. She has one."

"I'll keep chipping away at the ground here," Bo said. "You take my vehicle and see if you can locate her. If you can, see if she'll come. While you're at it, see if you can find a good shovel and a pick. If need be, we can go out to Ron Brady's place. He'd have good shovels for sure."

"Okay, I can do that," Jim said. He turned and started away.

Bo stopped him. "You know, I guess I don't really need to stay right here. I'm getting nowhere. Let's both go. We'll get a shovel and a pick, if Ron Brady has them, and then we'll see if we can find Lottie."

It was around ten by the time they got back to the Bayles' place with the tools and a promise of Lottie and her dog arriving soon. It was a nice day, and the sun was shining brightly. The officers worked with the pick and the shovel they'd borrowed from Ron Brady while they waited for Lottie to come with her dog. Two Face had been left in Bo's patrol vehicle so he wouldn't interfere with the cadaver dog when it arrived.

"It looks like I got the right place," Lottie said in an enthusiastic voice behind them.

Bo looked up and spotted her as she came around the house with a tri-colored beagle on a leash. The dog was walking sedately beside Lottie. He was a mixture of white, black, and brown and was clearly well cared for.

"Thanks for coming," Bo said as he put his shovel down and walked toward Lottie.

"What do you have here?" Lottie asked with a grin. She was a tall, slender woman in her mid-forties.

"We honestly don't know, but my dog was digging back here the best he could, considering the condition of the ground. The brother of the man who owns this place and who killed his wife this morning is missing. I'm probably way off base here, but I thought it would be a good idea to check things out with an expert. So if you don't mind, let's see what your dog can do."

"He's good. That's for sure. So some guy killed his wife?" Lottie said with wide eyes. "That doesn't sound good."

"It's not," Bo agreed.

CHAPTER FIFTEEN

"His name is Baxter, and he has a highly developed sense of smell. If there is a human body or even a small part of one in the ground, he'll tell me," she said.

"Even though the ground is still quite frozen?" Bo asked.

"Oh yes. Even if it's buried deep, Baxter can tell me." She knelt down and removed the leash from Baxter. Then, calling him by name, she told him to search.

Lottie did not take Baxter to the exact spot where Two Face had been trying to dig. Baxter scanned back and forth through the weed-infested yard, but when he went into the bushes and past them, he calmly sat on his haunches and looked at his owner.

"Well, boys, you have someone or part of someone in the ground there," Lottie said confidently.

She knelt beside Baxter, patted his head, and told him what a good boy he was and what a good job he'd done. "I always congratulate him like this as a reward when he is successful. And believe me, officers, he is telling me he found someone."

"I'll take your word for it," Jim said.

"As will I," Bo agreed. "Now I guess we've got to get whoever it is out of the ground."

Lottie stood up, reached in a pocket of her pants, and retrieved a small treat, which she gave to Baxter. "Another thank you," she told the men. "We've done our part, so it's up to you now. But if I might make a suggestion, you might need a backhoe."

"Yeah. I guess we'll get some help out here. The Price police will now come, I'm sure. If there's a body as Baxter says there is, then it becomes their case. I'll call them now," Bo said.

After the call and a promise that help was on the way, Bo said, "If we can't get to the body with a pick and shovel, we'll soon know it. Then if the Price officers agree, we'll follow your suggestion and see about locating someone with a backhoe."

Lottie patted her dog some more. "Detective, what kind of dog do you have? I saw him in your truck, but I didn't get a good look."

"He's a bulldog," Bo answered.

"He could be trained to search for cadavers if you wanted to go to the trouble," she said. "He knew he had something here. That's for sure," Lottie said. "I just don't know if he knew what he'd found."

"He's trained as a police dog. He protects me, but he also tracks very well," Bo said.

"Why did you keep him in your car?"

"I didn't want to take a chance on him messing up your dog's work by distracting him."

"He wouldn't have. Once my dog has a command, he is 100 percent focused on the task at hand. I'd like to meet your dog. Now that I think about it, I've heard about him. He's kind of unique for a police dog."

"Sure. Why not?" Bo said while Jim commenced swinging the pick again with a little bit of success.

After the introductions were made and Lottie, clearly a dog lover, had fussed over Two Face for a minute or so, she said, "It's good to meet you. Call anytime you need Baxter's services. I don't charge for my time or his. The only time I charge anything is if I have to travel. I do it as a service because I love doing it."

"I sure appreciate it," Bo said. "I hope I don't have too much need for him though." He smiled. "No offense."

"None taken," Lottie said and then she turned to her dog. "Let's go, Baxter. Your work is finished here."

As it turned out, a backhoe was not needed. With assistance from the officers from Price, the police chief, and the sheriff himself, they were able to get the body out of the ground. It had only been about a foot beneath the surface. Once they had broken through the frost level, the digging had been relatively easy.

The body was badly decayed, and special care had to be taken to keep it as intact as possible. A careful search of the clothing turned up a wallet in a back pocket of the corpse's blue jeans.

Bo opened it and found the driver's license for Jordan Bayle. "Well, it looks like Bryan Bayle must have killed his own brother."

"I wonder if Belle knew that," Jim said. "I mean, it was right here in the yard."

"My guess is that she didn't know," Bo said. "I think that would have been enough to cause her to leave him. Of course, we'll never know for sure. I'll be interested to see the autopsy results."

"It looks to me like he was shot in the forehead," Jim said as the city officers looked closely.

"If you're going to be able to charge Bryan with this murder, it would help if we knew that he was killed with one of Bryan's own guns," Bo said to the police chief, who agreed with him.

"We have Bryan's guns, so we can certainly get a ballistics test done," Jim suggested.

"It's looking more and more likely that Bayle was Emil's killer," Bo said. "We've got to find him before he kills again. That doesn't mean that I don't think Lucas is also dangerous. Ron has got to keep an eye out for him too."

What remained of Jordan Bayle's body was finally put into a body bag and sent to the state medical examiner's office late that afternoon.

Emil's killer, confident in his disguise, actually strolled up the street from where he'd parked his car and watched as a body bag was loaded into the hearse he'd seen arrive close to an hour ago.

So, another murder had been discovered. But he felt safe. He prided himself on being smarter than the cops. He also realized that the hunt for a killer or *killers* would be intensified, and he didn't want anyone getting the idea that he had killed anyone. It was time to do what he had to do, or perhaps what he wanted to do. No life but his was important. He totally believed that. He walked past a Price City officer as he left the area. Neither that cop nor anyone else paid attention to him as he walked back up the street and around the corner, where he climbed in his vehicle and drove off.

Yes, he told himself, he could do anything he wanted, and no one would ever find out it was him. He was above the law. The law was for other people. It didn't apply to him. He was untouchable.

It was late when Joe drove home, and he was lonely without his dog. In all honesty, he did not feel safe. He regretted not staying on the farm, but he would never let Ron or Melia know that. He worried about his own safety in addition to that of the girls and Ron. He moped around his house for a short while when he arrived and then decided that he should return to Ron's house and stay there—for their sake, not his. He was not about to admit he was frightened here at his place.

He called Melia, and when she answered, he said, "I'm worried about you guys. I think I'll come back and stay there."

"That's great," Melia said with relief in her voice. "We'll all be safer with you here, and that includes you."

Joe allowed himself a chuckle. "I'm fine. It's you guys I worry about. I'll see you in a few minutes."

"We have the doors all locked, so knock three quick times, then give a short push on the doorbell so I'll know it's you," Melia said.

Even as he responded that he would do that, he realized Melia was indeed frightened. He could hear it in her voice. It made him feel both sad and angry.

Before he left, he spent a few minutes attempting to secure his house. He taped a new piece of cardboard over the small square of broken glass, which had now been used twice to break into his home. Then he gathered up some clothes, including the ones he planned to wear to church on Sunday. It didn't take long since he didn't have a lot. He thought about taking his guns but then decided against it. Ron had plenty of guns in his house, and Joe knew how to use them.

The killer got around. He had seen Joe leave the farmhouse, late though it was. He'd first thought that Joe was going to stay there. But since he didn't, the killer had followed him back to his house, keeping a long distance between them. Joe was a fool for going home. After Joe had parked at his house, the killer waited outside. He'd been inside before, and he'd break inside again. But he'd give Joe time to get to sleep before he did.

Then he thought of a surprise for Joe. He was through waiting. Joe had to pay for Emil's death.

He watched as the lights finally went out in the house but was surprised when he heard the front door open. He was waiting beside Joe's truck, so he simply crouched down, holding his pistol in his right hand.

Finally feeling that his house was as secure as he could make it, Joe took his bag and left out the front door. He locked it behind himself and walked over to his truck. After putting his bag in the passenger side, he walked around the truck to get in. He failed to see someone crouched there until it was too late. He tried to dodge as something came at him. He had time to realize it was a large pistol, but that was all he saw. He felt a blinding strike on the side of his head, slumped to the ground, and then faded quickly into unconsciousness.

Melia and Nattie were sitting on the sofa chatting while Ron snoozed in his recliner with the TV on but the sound muted. The girls were waiting to hear Joe's truck crunch across the gravel in the yard. Melia kept looking at her watch. "He should be here any minute," she said to Nattie, talking softly so as not to awaken Ron.

"Maybe we didn't hear his tires on the gravel. He should be giving the knock-and-ring code you gave him anytime now," Nattie responded.

"Probably."

A couple of minutes passed before Melia said, "Nattie, he should have been here by now. I'm worried."

"He probably had to pack some things," Nattie reasoned. "Try not to worry so much. He'll be here soon."

Another five minutes passed, then ten. Melia's stomach was churning, and Nattie also had a worried look on her face.

"I'm going to call him," Melia said. She picked up her phone and called Joe's number, but it rang and rang before going to voice mail. "Nattie, something's wrong. Joe said he'd be right here, and he always does what he says he'll do. I'm scared."

"What's wrong, girls?" Ron asked as he stirred in his recliner.

"Joe called and said he was coming to stay, but he should have been here by now," Melia said, unable to mask the fear in her voice.

"If he said he'd come, he'll come," Ron said calmly.

"Maybe we should go check on him at his house," Melia said. "I don't know why, but I'm really worried. This isn't like Joe."

"I'll try calling Joe again, although I think he'll be along shortly," Ron said.

He had no better luck than Melia had when she'd tried. After putting his phone back in his pocket, he said, "Let's all get in my truck, and we'll drive to Joe's house. I'm sure there's a good reason why he hasn't come yet." Ron was already putting on his coat. "We'll soon find out," he said. "Hurry girls. We'll take this rifle and a pistol with us." He walked back over to his recliner and retrieved a small .38 caliber revolver from a drawer there and shoved it in his pocket. "Let's go."

The three of them piled into Ron's truck, and he drove faster than Melia had ever seen him drive. She was holding the rifle between her legs with shaking hands. The urgency of the situation was demonstrated by the way Ron was driving.

When they arrived at Joe's house a few minutes later, his truck was parked where he normally parked it in the narrow driveway beside his house. Melia, who was at the passenger door, started to open it as Ron pulled to a stop. "Wait!" Ron ordered sharply. "Hand me the rifle, Melia, and then you two stay in the truck while I take a look."

"But he must be in his house," Melia said.

"There are no lights on in there," Ron pointed out. "Just stay put, you two. I'll have a look around."

It was all Melia could do to keep from following her grandfather, but she and Nattie did what they were told and simply watched Ron as he approached Joe's truck, the headlights from his own truck lighting his way. He moved slowly, looking all around, which caused Melia's fear to escalate.

He finally reached the driver's door, peered in, and then opened it. The interior lights came on and Ron looked around inside the truck. He was shaking his head as he shut the door and slowly returned to speak with the waiting girls.

"His bag is in the truck," he said. "I can't imagine what Joe's thinking. I guess I need to check the house. Maybe he changed his mind and went inside. Although if he did that, why did he leave his bag in the truck?"

Ron retrieved a flashlight from a pocket of his door. "You guys stay here. Let me take a look."

"We don't have a key," Melia said logically. "What if he doesn't answer when you knock?" Ron hadn't even had time to respond before Melia went on, her voice quavering. "I'm scared, Grandpa. Let us come with you, please."

Ron hesitated briefly, and then he said, "Okay, but stay right behind me. You hang on to my .38, Melia, and keep it in your hand." He pulled it from his pocket, and she took it with cold, trembling fingers.

They approached Joe's house, walking close together. When they got to the door, Ron, who was wearing gloves, reached for the door handle. It was locked. He knocked hard, and they waited. Melia's heart was in her throat, and she was shaking with fear and cold. When there was no response, Ron said, "We'll try the back door."

"This was open earlier," Melia said when they reached the back door. She touched the cardboard with the tip of the .38. "He must have patched it again."

"Must have done," Ron grunted in agreement. He reached for the doorknob. It did not turn. He knocked on the back door, and when there was no response, he shouted, "Joe, if you're in there, open up. It's me, Ron."

No response.

"Grandpa, something's wrong. Joe would never do this to us," Melia said quietly.

"No, he wouldn't. Let's push that cardboard out and look inside," Ron said. The house was clearly empty and quite chilly. Joe's heat was turned very low. "I'll call Bo. Let's get in the truck and get warm. I don't want to wait in here while he comes."

He did that, and the three of them waited fearfully in the truck. Melia prayed that Joe was okay, and yet deep down, she feared the worst. But she kept her anguished thoughts to herself.

CHAPTER SIXTEEN

Bo HAD GONE TO BED earlier than he usually did, planning on an early day in the morning. So he'd been sound asleep when the sound of his ringing cell phone woke him. He grabbed it from beside his bed, unplugged it, and looked at the screen. What he saw brought him fully awake and set his heart pounding. The call was from Ron Brady.

"Joe's missing!" Ron practically shouted into the phone when Bo picked up.

"What do you mean?" Bo asked as he quickly began to dress.

"He's gone. He wouldn't stay at my house, but then he called and said he'd changed his mind," Ron said. He went on to explain how they'd tried calling him but got no answer. "Joe's overnight bag is in his truck, but we don't know where Joe is. We checked the house, but he's not in there."

"Are you at your place or at Joe's right now?"

"Joe's. I'm parked right behind his truck."

"Okay. Stay put and keep your eyes peeled. Where are Melia and Nattie?"

"They're with me," Ron responded.

"Okay. That's good. I'm on my way."

When Bo arrived at Joe's house, Ron and the girls piled out of his truck. "Hey, guys," Bo said in greeting. "I need to look around. How did you guys get inside the house?"

"The back door," Ron said.

"Okay, I'm going to have a look around outside, and then I'll go in," Bo said.

"We'll follow you," Melia said.

"No, it might be best if you waited in the truck," Bo countered. "I need to try to find some evidence."

"Like what?" Melia asked.

"I don't know right now, but I'll know it if I see it." He tried to grin at her but fell short.

He waited until they were all back in Ron's truck and then, with a very bright flashlight, slowly approached Joe's old pickup. He checked out the passenger side first. Joe's duffle bag was on the seat like Ron had told him. The little bit of snow from the previous night had pretty much melted, but he looked for tracks around the truck anyway. He found nothing obvious. He slowly circled around the front to the driver's side. What he saw there made his heart jump. He bent down and looked closer.

Blood! There was no question about it. It looked like it had pooled there. He took some pictures with his cell phone, and then, with gloved hands, he opened the door. There was no blood inside the truck. He stepped back and called for backup to help him process the scene.

When he rejoined Ron and the girls at Ron's truck, Ron rolled the window down. "What did you see on the ground there and in the truck?"

"We'll talk about it later. I have my partner coming to give me a hand here. I need to make sure I find and record everything that matters," Bo said as calmly as he could, although inside his gut was churning.

"Bo, please tell us what you saw," Melia said. Before he could respond, she continued, "Is it blood?"

Bo hesitated briefly, thinking that would upset them more, but then he realized they were already worried sick. They knew that what he found probably wouldn't make it any worse for them or not much worse at least. "It could be blood, but I hope not."

"It is blood," Melia said. "I know it is. How much is there?"

"Not a lot. Let's hope Joe's not hurt badly," he said. Then he addressed Nattie. "Tell me again what Lucas drives."

"It's a Nissan pickup," she said.

"Color?" he asked.

"Black. It has some scratches on it and some dents."

"Any other body damage?" Bo asked.

She was shaking—more with fear, Bo thought, than from the cold air coming in through Ron's open window.

"I'm trying to think," Nattie said, her voice breaking. "I'm pretty sure one of the taillights is broken."

"Which side of the truck?"

Nattie thought for a minute. "I think it's the left. Do you think he took Joe?"

"I have to consider it," Bo said. "You told me that you think he killed Emil, and if so, he might want to harm Joe in some way." He was thoughtful for a moment and then he added, "Whoever killed Emil wants Joe to go to prison for it."

"That would be something I can see Lucas doing," she said bitterly while rubbing her eyes.

"This is going to take us some time," Bo said. "Why don't you guys go back to the farm and stay inside with the doors locked. I'll come talk to you when Jim and I are finished here."

After arriving at the farmhouse, the three of them went inside. "Why don't you girls go to bed and I'll stay here in the recliner," Ron suggested. "I don't think we're in any danger now, but I'd like to stay where I can see the door. I can wake you when Bo comes."

"Nattie, I think I'll just lie on the sofa. You go to bed," Melia said.

"I want to stay with you guys. There are two recliners. I'll sit in the other one if that's okay," Nattie said.

Ron looked back and forth between the girls with concern. He forced a smile that he didn't feel. "That will be fine," he said as he sank into his recliner and set his pistol on the table next to it. "I'll honestly feel better knowing you two are close. But first, I think we need to have a prayer together. Do you mind if we do that, Nattie?"

"I'd like that," she said. "Joe needs God's help. So do we."

After their prayer and when all three were settled, Ron tried to relax, but his mind was going a mile a minute. He had grown to love Joe as if he were his own son. Yes, the boy had made mistakes, but he was essentially a fine young man. And he was intent on overcoming his faults, just like Ron was intent on overcoming his own. *No one is perfect*, he thought. *We could all do better.*

Tears wet his eyes as he thought of Joe. If he was alive, and deep down Ron could only hope that he was, Ron wanted him to come back. He needed him, not only because of the farm work that he could no longer do himself but simply because he and his granddaughter both liked having the young fellow around. He was good company for Melia, whose life had been hard with all the problems her mother had had, and those hardships had gotten worse after her mother's suicide. She seemed happy here with Ron and Joe. He knew she would be shattered if Joe did not return to them.

He rubbed the moisture from his eyes and closed them. He wished his heart were stronger. He'd like to be out there helping the police look for Joe, but he knew that was not possible. In fact, he'd overdone it already. He needed rest and plenty of it. He hoped he could go to sleep but knew it would take him a while.

He shuddered. What was Joe going through? Was he strong enough to make it through whatever was happening to him? Ron could only pray that Joe was alive and enduring whatever he had to endure.

Joe had no idea where he was. He'd been unconscious for who knew how long. He was tightly bound, blindfolded, and lying on something hard and cold. He couldn't see anything, and the blindfold was so tight it hurt his eyes. He ached all over, especially on the side of his head, and his face hurt from where his attacker had hit him, causing his nose to bleed. Who was this guy? Why was he so intent on causing Joe so much misery? Oh, how he wished he had never been as foolish as to get caught up in using marijuana. If he died, that would be the root cause of his death. It would have been his own fault.

Frankly, he feared that this person did not intend to let him live. That dark thought made him think of Ron and Melia. They cared about him. His disappearing like this would cause them a great deal of anguish. He even feared for Ron's life. How much stress could his weak heart take? If Ron died, what would happen to Melia?

He squirmed uncomfortably and tugged at the rope that held his hands behind his back. He tried to kick despite the ropes that held his feet bound. When he tried to get his feet beneath him, he couldn't do it despite not being tied to anything. For a moment, he would get partway up and then tumble back down, causing pain to jolt through his entire body.

He struggled in vain against his restraints. They were tied tightly, and he was beginning to feel his hands and feet go numb. How long could he endure the pain? He didn't even know how long he'd been here, wherever *here* was, or how long it had been since he'd been attacked while getting in his truck to go to Ron's.

He finally quit struggling and tried to think back to what he last remembered, to assemble the details in his mind the best he could. He'd driven home from Ron's. He remembered that, and he regretted not staying as Ron and Melia had asked him to. He'd thought he was tough and that he'd be okay. How stupid was that?

Instead of continuing to heap incriminations on himself, he put his mind to work on what had happened to him. He'd pulled into the driveway by his house. He remembered doing that. He also recalled going to his house and putting his guns away. Then he recalled his change of mind about staying by himself and how he'd packed a few things in his bag. All those things were clear in his mind . . . he continued to think.

After reviewing what he could remember, he wondered if that man was intent on him being accused again of Emil's death. He didn't know why he thought that, but after all that had happened with the notes, the assault in the jail, and so on, he had to think it was a possibility.

He felt very tired, but despite that, he still struggled against his bonds. It did him no good. After a few minutes, he quit and faded away again.

Bo was fairly certain that nothing inside Joe's house had been disturbed. "He was met with violence right here at his truck when he was ready to go to the farm," he told his partner, Deputy Jim Grizzel, who had arrived at Joe's place only a couple of minutes earlier.

"Look at this, Jim. There are spots of blood on the ground but none in the truck. What worries me is that some of the spots have been smeared. Was Joe knocked out somehow right outside his truck and then was he pulled through the bloody spots?"

The two officers studied the ground as other officers stood back and observed. "He was dragged this way," Bo said.

"The guy's car must have been somewhere where Joe hadn't been likely to see it," Jim reasoned. "Then he dragged Joe behind his truck. The kidnapper must have left him here on the ground while he got his car from wherever he parked it and brought it here. Then Joe was put in the guy's car and driven away," Jim concluded.

"The bottom line is Joe could be anywhere by now," Bo said bleakly.

"Either badly hurt or even dead," Jim said.

"Either is possible, I'm afraid," Bo responded. "I don't even know where to start looking for him. I guess since nothing else comes to mind, perhaps we should return to the homes of the suspects we've identified, not that I expect that will help us much."

"It's better than doing nothing," Jim agreed. "Should we start at Soto's house or Bayle's?"

"Whichever is closest. I don't think we can do much more here. I'll have a couple of the uniformed officers wait for the wrecker to pick up Joe's truck. I'm having it taken in so we can go over it with a fine-tooth comb," Bo explained. Then he remembered promising Ron and the girls that he'd come see them when he finished at the house. It was the middle of the night, but a promise was a promise. "We need to stop by Ron Brady's place first, Jim."

"And what do we tell them?" Jim asked.

"The truth, I guess. It doesn't look good for Joe," Bo said, rubbing his tired eyes with the back of a gloved hand.

A sound awoke Joe. It could have been a door opening. A cold breeze chilled his already freezing body. Then a door slammed, the cold breeze stopped, and footsteps approached. Was this going to be the end? The footsteps stopped, and the toe of a boot poked at his side. The same gruff voice he recalled when he'd been hit in the face said, "Wake up, you idiot. There's something you need to do."

What could that possibly be? In his current condition and state of bondage, there was not anything he could do. Joe said nothing for he had nothing to say. "Sit up," the voice commanded, accompanied by another not-so-gentle prod in his ribs.

He squirmed, but there was no way he could sit up, bound as he was.

"You can't do anything right, can you?" his tormenter said.

Joe finally managed to speak. "What did I ever do to you?" he asked, having a hard time getting the words out.

"You were born!" his tormenter growled. Then his growl turned to a low laugh, an evil sound if Joe had ever heard one. "And you just happened to be handy when I needed someone to put the blame on for Emil's untimely death."

"Why did you kill him?" Joe asked.

"You should just as well get it through your head right now, stupid. You killed him, and you are going to admit it."

"You know I didn't," Joe said.

The boot connected again, but this time, it wasn't a prod. Joe was kicked hard, and he felt some ribs crack. He cried out in pain.

"Shut up, you pansy! And sit up like I told you to."

"I . . . c-can't," Joe whimpered, ashamed that he wasn't able to speak boldly.

"Then I guess I'll have to sit you up," Emil's killer, and now Joe's mortal enemy, said. The man reached down, grabbed Joe by his bound arms, and lifted him clear off the floor. Then he kicked his feet forward and sat him back on the floor. The pain in his arms and shoulders was excruciating, and despite his best efforts not to, Joe screamed again.

"Shut up!" he was told by the angry voice. If only he wasn't blindfolded . . . Once again a boot connected—this time with his back—and it sent him sprawling on the floor. "I didn't say you could lie down again. Now I'll have to just lift you once more." He did, and it wasn't gently. The pain was almost more than Joe could stand, but somehow he managed to shut his scream off before it left his mouth.

He fought to stay conscious. His tormentor pulled him across the floor and propped him against a wall. Joe started to slip to one side only to get slapped soundly on his face. He fought back a whimper and put all his energy, what little was left, in avoiding toppling over.

Some time passed, and he began to feel marginally better. He was aware of the man standing next to him saying nothing for several more minutes. Finally, he spoke again. "I need you to write something, Joe."

Joe didn't respond. He didn't know what to say.

The man spoke again. "I have a pen and some paper. I am going to hand them to you, and you will write what I tell you to."

"I can't use my hands, and I can't see," Joe said, his whole body shuddering with the effort of speaking.

"I'll loosen your hands long enough for you to write the note. And I'll take off the blindfold. Don't even attempt to look at me, Joe, or I'll do more than bash you with my pistol; I'll shoot you in the leg."

"But I didn't do it," Joe protested again.

"Yes, you did, and your confession will clinch it."

"If I sign it, then what happens to me?" Joe asked, fearing the answer.

His abductor laughed. "That remains to be seen. But one thing is for sure; I'll be in the clear, and that's all that matters."

CHAPTER SEVENTEEN

Lucas Soto, like Emil's killer—whose identity Lucas still didn't know—used disguises to sneak around the area in an attempt to see what the cops were doing and was not happy to find that his girl, Nattie, had teamed up with Joe and Joe's employer. He had seen them at his house, which had been ransacked, but not by him. He'd taken his clothes and a few things he needed earlier. He did not know who had come later and trashed his house. He'd watched Nattie, the cops, and the others leave his house and go to the Brady farm. His hatred for Joe increased. Joe had interfered in Lucas and Nattie's relationship once before, and now he was doing it again in a much bigger way. That would not do.

The following night, Lucas had been watching Joe and had witnessed him being abducted. He didn't know what that was all about, but he made a decision at that point that he should be more careful than ever to not be seen by whoever that person was. He was afraid of the real killer. If Joe disappeared permanently, would Lucas be blamed for the murder? It was increasingly clear to Lucas that the killer was determined someone else would pay for killing Emil. But Lucas was more determined than ever that it would not be him.

Lucas began to scheme. One of his concerns was that Nattie might try to accuse him. She had never been totally loyal to him the way he'd wanted her to be. Perhaps he needed to do something to convince her that he was not the killer. He just wasn't sure how to go about it. He just needed to do some thinking. He'd figure something out.

He slunk away from his vantage point near Joe's house late that night after all the cops had left. He still hadn't figured out what to do about Nattie. He didn't want to hurt her, but he also didn't want her to blame him for something he did not do. So if he had to, he would do something to her, even if it pained him to do so.

Bo and Jim didn't learn anything new at either Bryan Bayle's house or Lucas Soto's. Not that they had expected much. Bo couldn't get Melia's sad face out of his head when he'd told her that they were stumped over Joe's abduction but hoped for the best. She broke down and cried, and finally, they had to leave while Ron and Nattie were both trying to comfort her. "He's dead, isn't he?" she'd kept saying over and over again.

"What now?" Jim asked as they sat in the Explorer outside of Lucas's house.

"It could be either Lucas or Bryan Bayle who has taken Joe," Bo said thoughtfully. "But perhaps we need to look elsewhere."

"Like where?" Jim asked.

"I'm thinking about Leonardo Augur. We need to find out where he lives and pay him a visit," Bo said. "I'm sure you're tired, Jim, and if you want to go home and get some rest, go ahead, but I'm going to keep at it until I drop. Joe's my cousin. I have to do everything I can to find him."

"I'm with you, Bo," Jim said.

Bo was touched by his loyalty. "Then let's see if we can find Leonardo."

"Here's what you'll write."

Some time had passed since Joe had, despite his best efforts, passed out and rolled onto his side again. His tormentor had splashed water in his face, waking him up, and then had pulled him to his bound feet and sat him at a small table. At that point, the blindfold came off, as did the ropes that bound his hands, but the threats continued as his abductor stood behind him.

Joe took the offered pencil in his hands, but they were numb and when he tried to place the point of the pencil on the paper, it dropped. "You are such a weakling," his captor complained.

"I can't feel my hands," Joe said weakly.

"Then I guess I'll have to give you a few minutes. But don't think that stalling will get you out of writing your admission to killing Emil in cold blood, *which is what you did*," the killer said.

Joe didn't have the energy to argue. So for the next few minutes, he sat there as Emil's killer paced behind him, muttering and cursing the entire time. It was all Joe could do to listen to the man's filthy language, but he kept quiet as he slowly felt the numbness leave his hands.

Eventually, his captor stopped pacing and cursing. "It's been long enough. I'm sure you can write now. So let's begin."

Joe picked up the pencil, and the killer slid the paper to where he could write on it. "Here's what you'll write. Write it exactly as I tell you or I'll bash your head in."

The guy was capable of that, as Joe had already learned. He couldn't figure out a way to avoid writing the confession without enduring serious injury, but at the same time, he was constantly trying to figure out a way to escape.

The evil man spoke slowly, and Joe wrote every word very carefully. He'd been thinking about how he might use some kind of code to make sure that not everyone would believe he meant what he wrote. The only thing he could think of would be to spell some of the words wrong, hoping that his captor wouldn't notice or would think the spelling errors were unintentional. If either Bo or Rosina or even Ron were to see the confession, they would know the spelling errors were intentional; they knew Joe was an excellent speller.

"Okay, read it back to me," the killer said from behind when Joe had finished.

Joe read it.

> *Dear Sheriff Hermock,*
>
> *I am riting this leter to you to cleer up the mater of the murdur of Emil Ifler. I'm sorry I lied to your oficers about it. I admit that I shot him with my own pistal and put his body in my trunk. He was making me get drugs from him when I didn't want two. Then when I codn't pay he was gong to take my stuf. I am not comng back to let you put me in prisan. But you can quit lokking for anybode else. I did it myself. But he had it comin.*
>
> *Joe Whalen*

As he read it, he worried that he might have made too many spelling errors. But his kidnapper took the letter from him, staying out of view, and then started to laugh. "You should have gone to school, you idiot," he said. "You can't even spell. What did you do, drop out of elementary?"

"I never could spell, but I did not drop out of elementary. I made it clear to the eighth grade," he lied, trying to sound ashamed.

"Well, you sure are a dumb guy. You shouldn't have killed Emil. They'll hunt you down and lock you up for the rest of your life," he said with an evil laugh. "Okay. I'm putting the blindfold back on you, and then I'll tie your hands up again."

"What are you going to do to me? They'll be looking for me."

"Let them look. They'll never find you. As for what happens to you, I still haven't decided for sure. But I'm kind of leaning toward suicide. That would clinch your confession, and it would save you from having to spend the rest of your miserable life in prison."

"How are you going to get my confession to the sheriff?" Joe asked.

"That's a good question. I guess I need a stamp and an envelope, and then I'll mail it," he said. "But I'll mail it from someplace a long way from Price. I'm not stupid like you are, you know." The killer put the blindfold on Joe, and then he put the ropes back on his wrists and tied his hands to his belt so Joe couldn't reach up to take off the blindfold.

Joe kept talking, hoping to distract the killer to the point that he wouldn't get the rope too tight. It wasn't just chitchat, though; he was begging for his life and for his freedom. "You can take me clear across the country if you want to," he said at one point. "I'll never come back, I promise. I don't want to die." On and on he went, blabbering and begging.

It worked, for when the killer finished, the ropes were not very tight, and Joe had some hope. It was a slim hope, but hope nonetheless.

"I gotta go get an envelope and a stamp and look up the sheriff's address," Joe's abductor said. "I'll need to drive pretty far to get this letter in the mail. Don't go anywhere until I get back." With that, the guy laughed loud and long. "As if you could," he concluded.

"Hey, I'm hungry, and I need to use the bathroom," Joe wailed. Both were true.

"Maybe I'll bring you a burger," the killer said. "And maybe I won't. Either way, you gotta hold it till I get back. You're a big boy. You can do that."

A minute later, Joe could hear a door open and then slam shut. He was sure it was locked, but he didn't waste any time before starting to work at the ropes that bound his wrists.

It took a while, but Bo and Jim found the place where Leonardo Augur was believed to be living. It was a nice home with a neatly kept yard in Castle Dale, a town to the south of Price in Emery County. "This is weird," Bo told Jim. "I can't see a drug pusher like him having a nice yard. It doesn't add up."

"Maybe we have the wrong place after all," Jim suggested. Bo rang the doorbell and knocked but got no response.

"It may be the wrong place, but I don't think so. Maybe we should check with some of the neighbors," Bo suggested. "But before we do, let me call the sheriff's office here and let them know we're in town and what we're doing." While Bo called, Jim looked around the front yard a little bit.

After the call, Bo told his partner, "We're fine to go ahead, but the officer I spoke with said they didn't have anything on Leonardo that he knew of. But he said he'd check with the drug task force—they might have heard of him."

"Maybe he does all of his distribution away from his hometown," Jim suggested.

"He must because we have definitely heard about him in Carbon County, although we don't have anything on him that we can arrest him for. Anyway, I was told that if we need help to call back. Hopefully we won't need to do that."

"I agree," Jim said.

"Let's split up. You hit a few houses across the street, and I'll knock on the ones near him on this side."

Bo knocked on the door of the next-door neighbor to the west of the house they believed belonged to Leonardo. A middle-aged lady with long dark hair and a pretty face answered the door.

"Hello. I'm Detective Bo Buckley with the Carbon County Sheriff's Department. Do you have a moment?"

"Sure. I'm Lucy Gibbons. What can I help you with?" she asked.

"I'm wondering how much you know about your next-door neighbor, Mr. Augur," Bo said.

"Is that his name?" she asked. "We really don't know him. We seldom see him. Sometimes he has visitors late at night, but most of the time he's gone. We do see his gardener quite often. I wish we could afford to hire him to help with our yard. He seems to be good at what he does. Of course, there's no gardening going on this time of year, but the fellow comes by if there's even the smallest amount of new snowfall and shovels and sweeps until there's not a single flake left on the walks in either the front or rear. And you should see the flowers in the summertime. The guy's a genius."

"That's nice to know, but are you saying you don't know your neighbor's name?" Bo asked.

"No, I've never heard it. I guess we aren't very good neighbors," Lucy said.

"Or he isn't," Bo suggested.

"Well, yes, he does keep to himself. We've left notes for him, inviting him to a couple of block parties, but he's never showed up to one. He's lived there two or three years. You'd think we'd have had a chance to get to know him, but he is very reclusive."

"What does he drive?" Bo asked.

"Seriously? You're here asking about him, but you don't know what he drives?" she asked with raised eyebrows. "Is he wanted for something?"

"We're just checking," Bo said. "We've heard some things and wanted to make sure they either are or are not true."

"Could I ask what kind of things?" she asked. "Now I'm getting nervous."

"No need for that, Lucy. Again, what does he drive?" Bo asked.

"It's a tan Nissan pickup, very new. He drove a Toyota pickup, a small one, until just a few months ago."

"So it has Utah plates?" Bo asked.

"Oh yeah. The other pickup had been wrecked the last time we saw it here. It was drivable but pretty bashed up on the entire passenger side. I guess he'd been in a wreck. At any rate, it was gone and replaced with this new one within a couple days," Lucy said.

"Do you know if any of the other folks in the neighborhood are friendly with him at all?" Bo asked.

"Not that I'm aware of."

"What's the gardener's name?"

"Hank. I only know that because my husband managed to strike up a conversation one day, but usually, Hank just comes, does his work, and leaves."

"What does he drive?" Bo asked.

"He has an older white pickup. I honestly don't know the make. It's full of snow shovels and brooms this time of year and shovels and rakes and such as that in the spring, summer, and fall. He works hard when he's here. Like I said, my husband talked to him that one time, and when he did, he asked if he was interested in helping out with our yard."

"I take it he wasn't."

"He said he had all the customers he could handle," Lucy said.

"Is he here every day?"

"Oh no. He only comes once or twice a week except for winter. Then he comes when it snows and takes care of things. Why are you asking about him?"

"We'd like to locate the gardener and speak with him. We're just trying to figure Mr. Augur out. Does he have a wife or girlfriend?"

"I've never seen a woman around his place except for a cleaning lady who comes once a week or so, so no, I don't think he does. At least if he does, she lives somewhere else."

"Thanks for your time, Lucy," Bo said, and she stepped back into her house.

Bo checked several more houses, but he didn't learn anything more. It appeared that Leonardo was very reclusive, lived alone, was gone much of the time, and had occasional late-night visitors.

When Jim rejoined him, he reported the same type of information from the few people he was able to talk to. Leonardo Augur, it seemed, was a man of mystery. "Jim, I think we should try to find out who the gardener is and have a chat with him."

"How do we do that?" Jim asked.

"Let's drive around town for a little while to see if we can spot an older white pickup with snow shovels in the back," Bo suggested.

"I can't seem to reach Joe on his cell phone," Dr. Scanlon said. "His dog is doing much better and is recovering faster that I would have ever expected. He's a strong dog if I've ever seen one. So I see no reason he can't go home today. He'll just need to be watched closely. Could you get the word to Joe for me?"

"I wish I could," Ron said. "Joe vanished last night, and the sheriff's department suspects foul play, as do I."

"Oh no!" the veterinarian exclaimed. "First the dog and now the young man! What is this world coming to?"

"There are lots of problems in the world. That's for sure, Dr. Scanlon. Listen, if it's okay with you, I'll come out, get Herc, and keep him here at my place until we locate Joe," Ron said.

"I could keep him longer if need be, but I hate to run up the expense on Joe," the vet said.

"I understand. I'll come for him. Thanks for saving the dog's life," Ron told him. "I'll be there in a few minutes, and I'll bring my checkbook to cover the costs for Joe." Ron was thinking—and he didn't like his thoughts—that Herc may need to make a permanent home on his farm with Ace.

Ron pulled on his warm coat and gloves, stuck a hat on his head, and pulled on his boots. Then he headed outside. He walked past his truck in the garage and went to the barn. He found Melia and Nattie hard at work there. He'd tried to talk the girls into staying in the house all day, but they had insisted on working. He'd gone out with them for a while, but he was soon exhausted. Melia had asked him to let her keep the pistol until they finished what needed to be done, and he'd agreed. If she hadn't asked, he'd have insisted.

"Hey, Grandpa. We're okay," Melia said when Ron walked into the barn where they were cleaning stalls again. "You didn't need to check up on us."

"Actually, I came out to ask you girls to help me," he said.

"With what?" Melia asked.

"Help me drive to the vet's and pick up Herc. Dr. Scanlon said he's doing so well that there's no point in running up Joe's bill by keeping him there any longer."

"That's great," Melia said. Then her eyes began to water up. "I wish Joe were here to go get him."

"But he's not, and we need to take good care of Herc until Joe gets back," Ron said, having a difficult time keeping his voice from breaking with emotion.

"I can stay here and keep working," Nattie said. "You two go."

Ron shook his head. "I'm not leaving you here alone, Nattie. We'll all go."

Nattie started to protest, but Melia interrupted. "You've been telling me how afraid you are of Lucas now."

"He's probably glad to be rid of me," Nattie replied bitterly.

Ron shook his head. "I doubt that. I promised to keep an eye on you, and I haven't done a very good job today, but there is no way I'm leaving you here alone. Let's go get that beautiful dog."

Lucas had debated with himself all day. The longer he thought about Nattie running off with his unborn baby, the angrier it made him. He hadn't wanted a girl, but she had no right to run off. It was, after all, his baby girl, not just hers. He knew that he needed to get away from Price, but there was no way he was going without Nattie. If she didn't want to come, he'd make her anyway. He'd even thought charitably that he would promise her he wouldn't use drugs anymore. That was always their biggest problem—as if he could manage such a thing. He was already feeling the withdrawals coming on. He desperately needed a fix.

He was watching from his usual secluded spot through his binoculars. He knew the two girls were alone in the barn. With Joe gone and the farmer in the house, it should be easy enough to grab Nattie and leave.

Or at least that was the thought that had been on his mind when he'd seen the old farmer leave the house and go to the barn. The old guy had his rifle with him. Lucas swore. He didn't like that at all. The longer he stuck around, the more dangerous it was for him. But now he would be forced to wait a little longer. Still, he would get his girl, and they would leave whether she liked it or not.

CHAPTER EIGHTEEN

As Ron and the girls walked toward his garage to get his truck, he saw a reflection from the sun off of something some distance away. He stopped and looked for a minute. It did not go away. His gut churned.

"What is it, Grandpa? Are you feeling worse?" Melia asked with concern on her face. "If you aren't up to going now to get Herc, I'm sure we can go later. Or maybe we could call Rosina and see if she'd pick Herc up and bring him out here."

Ron shook his head. "No, I'm okay. Let's go get him."

He had no intention of mentioning to the girls what he'd seen. He knew very well that there was nothing that could possibly send that distinct glint of the sun reflecting off glass from those distant trees besides a small mirror or a pair of binoculars, and it was the thought of binoculars that made him nervous. After getting in the truck, he drove to the road but turned the opposite direction he needed to go to drive to Price.

"Grandpa," Melia said, "you turned the wrong way. Are you sure you're okay?"

"I'm sure. I just want to check something out, and then we'll turn around. Don't worry. It's nothing."

A moment later, he glanced at the girls. Nattie was seated next to him with Melia at the passenger side by the window. Nattie was frowning, and her eyebrows were drawn together. He was afraid she knew that he was worried about something, but he said nothing and just drove toward where the reflection had come from. He drove faster than he normally would have because of his concern over what he'd seen.

The grove of trees was on his property, a hundred yards or so south of the road. He slowed as he passed the area. He caught a glimpse of someone or something moving deeper into the trees. He didn't need anyone to explain to him what was happening; they were being watched. Ron was not normally a fearful man, but a wave of alarm shot through him now.

"Grandpa, I saw someone in those trees," Melia said. "What would someone be doing there? We need to get out of here."

Nattie's face had turned the color of paste. "I saw it too. Someone is out there. Is that not normal?"

"It's not. Melia, call Bo. I think someone is watching our place. From those trees, you can see the house, the yard, and the barn. I'll keep driving while you call."

Melia already had her phone out. She dialed Bo's number and put her phone on speaker so they could all hear. It rang several times before Bo finally answered.

"Someone is watching our place from a thicket of trees," she said, hardly able to control the fear in her voice. "Grandpa, whoever it is just ran back that way from the trees."

"I see him," Ron said.

"Whoa, you guys, what exactly is going on, and where are you?"

"We're in the truck," Melia said. "We were going to get Herc from the vet, but Grandpa saw something and drove the opposite way. Someone was hiding in the trees. He's running now."

"Nattie, are you there?" Bo asked.

"Yes," she said in a whimper.

"Keep talking," Bo said. "Jim and I are in Castle Dale, but we're heading back now as fast as we can. Ron, be careful. Don't confront anyone."

"There's a vehicle," Melia said. "It just drove out from behind the trees."

Nattie moaned. "It's Lucas," she said. "He wants to kill me." She slumped over, falling into Melia.

"What's happening?" Bo asked.

"Nattie just passed out," Ron said. "A small black truck just drove out of the trees. It's going dangerously fast now. It's almost certainly Lucas."

"Ron, listen to me," Bo said. "Turn around. Go back to Price and get the dog. Make sure Nattie is okay. My partner is on his phone speaking to our dispatcher. Every officer in the area will be looking for Lucas now. Leave it to the police. Do you understand?" Bo asked, his voice full of authority.

"Yes, I do. I'm turning around," Ron said.

"Okay. Call me when you get to the vet. You are to remain there until we get there. You are not going home without us escorting you. Does Nattie need to go to the hospital?"

She stirred and pulled herself upright. Then she spoke, her voice very soft and anguished. "I'm okay now. I'm just afraid of Lucas. That was him."

"Okay. Go to the vet clinic and wait there. We're coming your way," Bo said.

"Why can't he just let me go?" Nattie said through sobs that now racked her body.

"The police will catch him now," Ron said, trying to sound a lot more positive than he was feeling.

"You don't know him," Nattie said, her voice stronger now as she took control of her emotions. "He's slick. He'll hide and come back for me later. I know he will. I'm putting you guys in danger. I just need to go with him."

"Nattie, listen to yourself," Melia said. "A minute ago, you said he would kill you."

"Maybe, but it's not fair for me to put you guys in danger. Maybe if I promise to go away with him, he'll take me somewhere far away and not kill me."

"Is that what you want?" Ron asked sternly.

"No, but I can't let you guys get hurt because of me. Maybe if I go with him, he'll let Joe go," she said.

"We don't know that he took Joe," Melia said.

"He killed that horrible drug pusher. I know he did! I know he took Joe. I just hope he hasn't hurt him yet . . . or worse."

"Nattie, you need to calm down," Ron said sternly. "The cops are working on this. You are not going anywhere but with me and Melia. When we get home, we'll barricade ourselves in my house. I promised to take care of you, and that is exactly what I intend to do. I am not going to let you and Melia go out to the barn without me again. Maybe we can get Rosina and Bo's girlfriend to finish the chores, those that have to be done. The stall cleaning can wait. You guys cleaned them good yesterday. Another day won't hurt the horses."

He glanced at Nattie, who nodded. "Okay. I know you're right. But I'm so sorry I got you guys into this mess."

"You didn't," Melia said. "Now let's talk about how we'll take care of Herc when we get him home."

"He's an outside dog. I think he would be okay in my enclosed back porch," Ron said, grateful to his granddaughter for shifting the conversation away from Lucas. "We can put a pan of water there and some food. He can't hurt that floor out there, and he can't get out. I'll just have to clean up any messes he makes."

"I can do that," Melia said. "You don't have to."

"I can help," Nattie chipped in, her voice getting stronger now. "You guys are amazing. I don't deserve you."

"We're only doing what the Savior would have us do," Ron said as he glanced at her red eyes. He was glad to see color returning to her face. "We care about you . . . and your unborn baby."

"Thank you," she said.

For the next little while, they let comfortable silence stretch between them.

When they arrived at the veterinary clinic, Ron got out first, looked carefully around, and then he said, "Let me take the pistol, Melia. I'll shove it in my coat pocket when we go in. We'll lock my rifle in the truck."

Dr. Scanlon met them inside. He looked worried. "I got a call a little bit ago from Detective Buckley. He said that when you got here I was to lock the doors and keep you in a back room until he and his partner get here. What in the world is going on?"

"It's a long story," Ron said.

"Does it have anything to do with Joe being gone?" the vet asked.

"It may," Ron said. "We're not taking any chances. Maybe we can go back and see the dog now, and I can settle the bill while we wait for the officers."

Dr. Scanlon looked at them. When one of his assistants came out, he told her, "We are to keep the doors locked until some officers arrive. Don't ask why—just don't let anyone in until I tell you to."

A wave of fear passed over the lady's eyes, but she agreed without asking any questions.

"I prepared a bill for Joe Whalen's dog. It's on the computer. Print it out and bring it to us. We're going to be back with the dog," the vet said. "And keep an eye out for a small black pickup. The driver is dangerous and may be looking for these folks." The lady looked more shocked than she had a moment before but said nothing. The vet ushered them all out of the reception area.

He opened the pen where Herc was waiting. Herc moved slowly when he came out and went straight to Melia and began to lick her hand. She knelt on the floor, took the dog's head in her hands, and spoke softly to him. He licked her face.

"That dog loves you," Nattie said as she joined Melia on the floor. She looked up at the vet. "Is he going to be okay?"

"He'll be fine. He'll be weak for a while, but he's healing faster than I would ever have imagined." Dr. Scanlon looked at Ron. "He has quite a few stitches, but they will dissolve. Just keep an eye on him, and if he develops any redness, let me know. That could mean infection, although I don't expect that since I've given him a lot of antibiotics. I'll send some pills home with you. You'll need to give him one a day for the next week, starting in the morning."

"Will he swallow pills?" Melia asked doubtfully, looking up from the big collie for a moment.

The vet chuckled. "He will if he doesn't know he's getting them. You'll just need to put them in a little patty of hamburger or a hot dog, and he will scarf them right down."

The vet's assistant stepped in, handed the bill to Dr. Scanlon, and started to step back out, but Ron stopped her. "If you see a small black pickup out of your windows, the one your boss mentioned, get back in here with us and I'll go up front with my pistol and take a look."

Fear shone on her face, but she promised to do what she was told.

Ron pulled out his checkbook, looked at the bill, and said, "This is too low."

"It is what I'm charging," Dr. Scanlon said, "so don't argue with me." He smiled.

Ron's phone rang. He handed the check to the doctor and then answered the call. "Are you almost here, Detective?"

"We're right outside," Bo told him. "Have you seen Lucas's truck?"

"No, but we've been watching."

"Okay. We'll let you out now."

Twenty minutes later, the entire party pulled into the farmyard. Bo and Jim got out of their Explorer first and looked around. Finally, Bo signaled that the rest of them could get out. Ron parked in his garage, which was a short way from the house, and led the way inside, carrying his rifle and pistol.

Bo and Jim only stayed for a few minutes, and then Melia took Herc out to the enclosed porch in the back. She gave him some dog food and a pan with water, and then she spent a few minutes with him. Ron's dog, Ace, was just outside the porch door, which was securely locked. He whined and begged for Herc to come outside and join him.

Melia had barely come in from the porch when there was a knock on the door.

"That will be Rosina and Karmen," Ron said, but he peeked out of the drapes before opening it, his pistol in one hand just to make sure. He looked beyond the young women before he allowed them to come in. He locked the door behind him and shoved his pistol in a holster he now had on his belt.

"Sorry that we resemble Fort Knox, ladies, but we can't be too careful," Ron said.

"We understand," Rosina said, and then she stepped past him and held out her arms to Melia, who fell into them. Both girls sobbed for a couple minutes before Rosina finally pulled back and said, "We'll get through this, Melia. I don't know how, but we've got to. Now, Ron, tell us what needs to be done, and we'll go do it."

When the young women were ready to go out a few minutes later, Ron gave each of them a gun—one a shotgun, the other a pistol. "You do know how to use these, don't you?" he asked.They both replied that they did.

"Okay. Keep your eyes open. I don't expect you to have to use those, but I want you to have them just in case. If anyone, and I mean anyone, but the officers drives into the yard, you call me and then go into the saddle room and stay there until I tell you it's okay to come out."

Melia watched the girls' faces, and she could see that Ron was doing the same thing.

"Hey," Ron continued, "we can let things go for now if you want. I know I'm putting you in a bad situation."

"That's okay. I can shoot if I have to," Rosina said confidently.

"So can I," Karmen echoed. "We don't want your animals to suffer. We'll get them fed. It's doubtful that anyone will come."

Melia wasn't so sure of that, but she sure hoped no one would. But it was growing dark outside, and that was when someone would most likely come if they came at all.

Lucas knew a couple guys who used drugs. He'd been friends with them for some time. He drove slowly past one of their houses. When he was sure no one was home, he parked and broke in through the back door. He rummaged around for a minute and finally found what he was after; they had a stash of heroin in their bathroom. He took it, used a hefty dose, stuck more in his pocket, and left. Now he would be okay. He could get Nattie and leave Price.

Joe was desperate. He had managed to loosen the rope on his hands but not enough to free them. It had been very difficult, and his need for the restroom made it ten times harder. As time passed, he needed a restroom more and more until it was so bad it was all he could do to keep from having an accident. It was actually a relief when he heard the door open and his captor come in. "Please," he begged instantly. "I need a bathroom really badly."

"Okay. I hate to have you be embarrassed," the killer said with a harsh chuckle. "As soon as you're done, you will need to address this envelope to the sheriff so I can mail it. To show you that I'm really a pretty good guy, not a killer like you are, I brought you a burger and a couple bottles of water. I still haven't decided for sure how I'm going to handle this."

A few minutes later, Joe was again seated at the table. A gloved hand reached around him and laid the pencil and envelope on the table followed by the confession note. One of his hopes was dashed: there would be no fingerprints on the paper or the envelope but his. On the other hand, if his captor intended to kill him, why did he care if Joe saw him or not? That thought gave Joe some hope.

The fact that Joe was allowed to eat and drink added to his optimism. He dug right in, and his captor didn't attempt to stop him. When he was done, he felt some strength in his limbs, and he was told to go ahead and address the envelope.

"I don't know the address," Joe said as he picked up the pencil and scooted the envelope closer to him.

"I do," the killer said with a haughty note in his voice. He then gave the address slowly to Joe as he, in turn, wrote it down. He intentionally misspelled *sheriff*, writing *sherrif* instead. "I see your spelling hasn't improved in the past few hours." Another harsh chuckle. "It must be really miserable being so stupid. I've never had that problem, so I wouldn't know."

Joe gave no reaction to the taunting. He just wrote the address as dictated. "What address do I use for the return address?"

"Your address of course. How could anyone be so dumb?"

Joe wrote his address. Then the killer instructed him to put the note in the envelope and seal it. As soon as that was done, the killer handed him a stamp from behind him with his gloved hand. Joe affixed it in its proper place. "Now what?" Joe asked.

"Hand me the letter over your shoulder," was the instruction. "I will mail this as soon as I put the blindfold back on you and tie your hands again."

As before, Joe talked and asked questions as the rope was being tied on his hands in an attempt to distract his captor and possibly make the rope looser than the first time. "Where are you going to mail the letter from?" Joe asked.

"What difference does that make to you?" the killer asked with a touch of anger. "I'll mail it somewhere out of town so it will appear to the sheriff that you're fleeing and in hiding somewhere."

"What town?" Joe persisted.

His captor swore. "It doesn't matter where. Now shut up. I'm done, and I'm leaving. I hope you don't have to do your thing again, because I'll be gone a long time."

"How long?" Joe asked.

His captor swore again and left Joe sitting at the table. A moment later, the door opened and closed. Joe was alone again, and it worried him how long that might be this time. He immediately began to work at the ropes on his hands. They were not too tight. Maybe he could get them off this time. It was a gymnastic effort, for he had to bend his head as low as he could and work with his teeth. But he was determined. So he kept at it until he got a knot in his neck and had to straighten up and take a break.

CHAPTER NINETEEN

Lucas was getting high and feeling good. Now was the time to get Nattie. He'd been forced to choose a different spot to watch the Brady house since his earlier one had been compromised. He hadn't been able to find a place that was quite as good, but it was okay. Even though it was now dark, he could see what was going on in the farmyard because of a bright yard light. He could not quite see the door to the house. His hope was that Nattie and the Brady girl would go back to the barn to finish whatever it was they'd been doing when they'd left earlier. He had every intention of grabbing Nattie when that happened and leaving the other girl tied up so that she couldn't immediately tell her grandpa what he'd done.

Once again, however, his plan was foiled. Two other young ladies drove up and went into the house. A short while later, the two headed to the barn, and they both carried guns and flashlights. Those who stayed in the house probably had guns too. He tromped about for a few minutes as he tried to decide what to do. He didn't want to stick around the Carbon County area too much longer. He'd already had one really close call. But he had to grab Nattie and take her with him.

Perhaps, he finally decided, he would need to make an assault on the house. He didn't want to kill anyone, but if he had to, he would. He figured he was smart enough to find a way into the house and then pull his gun on Ron and the two girls. From there, he would simply take Nattie and leave, making sure Ron and his granddaughter couldn't call for help. He would have to accomplish all this before the two girls at the barn went back inside. It was either that or he would have to wait until the middle of the night, and he was getting antsy. He wanted to get this over with and have the night to make good on his exit from Carbon County.

This was a desperate move he was considering, but in the altered mood he was in from the drugs, he was no longer thinking too clearly. At any rate, he felt compelled to proceed. He worked his way closer to the house.

Then he was confronted by a dog!

He had learned one thing by watching Emil break into Joe's house; he'd seen Emil spray something in Joe's dog's face that took the fight right out of him. The only thing he'd been able to figure out was that Emil had used Mace, so Lucas had bought some for an occasion such as this. He dug in his pocket for it but not before the little beast bit him in the calf. He sprayed before he got bit again, and he sprayed a lot. The dog, a mostly black-and-white one, went yipping toward the barn. Lucas smiled to himself. Now he could proceed.

Lucas crept closer to the house, becoming angrier by the minute that Nattie was making him do this. He recognized that the heroin was fueling his anger, but it didn't deter him; it only made him more determined.

The house was an older two-story model. He crept around it, looking at the windows as he went. It seemed to him that it would be best not to try to get through any of the windows to the living room or kitchen. A bedroom window, he thought, would be best. He noticed some vines growing up a trellis at the back of the house, leading right past one of the upper floor windows. That was the way he would go.

There was an enclosed porch right beside the vines. He stepped next to it and tested the strength of the lattice. It was very strong, so he began to climb. He was almost to the window when a dog started barking inside that porch. He remembered seeing them take Joe's dog, which seemed to have been injured, into the house. They must have put him in the porch. What should he do?

For a moment, Lucas froze in place. His leg was hurting where the dog had bitten him, but he couldn't imagine that it could be too serious. He chose to ignore it. He was so close to the window that he hated to go back down.

The dog inside the porch continued to bark, but it couldn't hurt him. In fact, it might help distract Ron Brady. He climbed the last couple of feet until he was able to touch the window.

Lucas held tightly to the vines with one hand and reached for the window with the other one.

"Something has upset Herc," Melia said, sitting upright on the couch. "I'd better go check on him."

"No, let me do that. You two stay right here. It's probably just Ace outside the porch that has gotten him all excited," Ron said calmly.

Melia looked at Nattie where she was sitting in the second recliner. Her eyes were wide with fright. "It might be someone trying to get in the house," Nattie reasoned, her voice trembling.

Ron had just reached the door to the porch when his cell phone rang. Herc quit barking. Ron grabbed the phone from his pocket and looked at it. Melia watched him closely. Could it be Bo saying they had caught Lucas or found Joe or had some other good news?

"What is it, Rosina?" Ron said. Ah, so not Bo. Ron listened for a moment, not yet opening the door to the back porch. After a moment he said, "Are you sure?"

Melia stood and approached Ron but backtracked when he signaled for her to return to the couch. Then into the phone, he said, "Listen to me, Rosina. You and Karmen go into the saddle room like I said earlier. Take Ace with you if he will go. Wait there until you hear from me."

"Is someone out there by the barn, Grandpa?" Melia asked, her voice trembling. Before he answered, she looked at Nattie, whose face was white.

"It kind of looks that way," Ron answered, his voice much calmer than Melia thought the circumstances called for. "Rosina is pretty sure that something has been sprayed in Ace's eyes."

"It's Lucas," Nattie said weakly. "He had some Mace the other day. I saw it when he emptied his pockets so I could wash his jeans. He's out there. What are we going to do? Maybe I should go out there and go with him before he hurts one of you guys."

"We've already been over this. You are staying right here," Ron said firmly but kindly.

Melia was already on the phone dialing Bo's number.

Bo answered and asked, "Is there a problem out there?"

"Someone Maced our dog, and Herc is all upset out on the back porch where we put him," she said.

"Are Rosina and Karmen outside finishing the feeding?" he asked.

"Yes. Grandpa told them to get in the saddle room in the barn with Ace and to stay there. They have guns," she said, her voice wavering. "Nattie says Lucas bought some Mace recently."

"Okay, so it could be him. We are on our way," Bo said. "You guys stay put but be alert."

"I should go," Nattie said again, getting to her feet.

"Nattie wants to go," Melia said as her voice began to crack. "She thinks that if she goes with Lucas it'll be safer for the rest of us."

"We don't know if it's Lucas," Bo said. "Hand your phone to Nattie. Let me talk to her."

Nattie was on her feet now. Ron hurried over and grabbed her by the arm. "Don't go anywhere," he commanded, his voice that of the Army Ranger he used to be, not the loving farmer he was now.

"Bo wants to talk to you, Nattie," Melia said, holding her phone out to her.

Nattie shook her head. Tears were streaming down her face, but she held out her hand and took the phone.

"That was Melia," Bo said to Jim. "Someone's there at the farm. Ron Brady's dog has been sprayed with something. Sounds like it could be Mace. Call for some more officers. This may be a dangerous situation. I'm going to talk to Nattie now. She thinks that if she leaves, Lucas will take her and leave the others alone."

"Hello," he heard Nattie's voice say on the phone.

"Nattie, think about your baby as well as yourself. You can't go outside. We don't even know if it's Lucas or if it's someone else," he reasoned.

"It's Lucas. I just know it," she said, sobbing so hard it was difficult for him to understand her.

"Calm down, please. If it is Lucas, he may have Joe somewhere. If you go to Lucas, and he takes you with him, we may never find Joe. I am coming right now, and my partner is with me. Wait there with Ron and Melia. Ron's a smart man. Do whatever he says to do."

"I don't want anyone hurt because of me," she said, her voice becoming stronger. That worried Bo. "I'm going out. I have to."

"Nattie, don't do that!" he shouted into the phone. There was no response for a moment.

Then Melia's voice came across the line. "It's Melia. Nattie ran outside. She doesn't even have a coat on."

"Oh my!" Bo exclaimed. "Let me talk to Ron."

Lucas was listening at the top of the stairs and heard Nattie say she was going out. But he'd just reached the inside of the house. He had to get back out there . . . but he was torn. He could shoot his way past Ron Brady. A quick peek revealed that Ron had taken hold of Melia and pulled her to the edge of the room while still holding his phone. Lucas ducked back out of sight before they spotted him.

"Okay," he heard Ron say. "We'll stay right here."

Lucas turned back and headed for the window. The heroin was fueling his anger. He'd find Nattie outside, and they would get away in the dark. That was the safest bet. He didn't want Ron Brady to shoot him, and the old man might just be upset enough to do that. Lucas was certainly upset enough that if the old man tried, Lucas would shoot him back. In his drug-frenzied mind, his judgment was becoming increasingly impaired.

Ron thought he heard steps upstairs. That alarmed him. He motioned for Melia to sit beside his chair, and he watched the top of the stairs very carefully. He had a shotgun on his lap, loaded and ready to fire if the intruder appeared. He listened but didn't hear any more steps, but he was fearful that the intruder was up there.

"What is it, Grandpa?" Melia asked in a frightened whisper. "Is someone up there?" She nodded toward the head of the stairs.

"I don't know, but we have to assume that could be the case."

Bo stopped his sheriff vehicle just beyond the area lit by the Brady's yard light. He'd approached the last mile with his headlights off, no siren, and no flashing red-and-blue lights but driving at breakneck speed.

"The intruder may have left already, but we need to treat this situation as if he hasn't. Ask dispatch to instruct any other responding officers to approach silently and without lights. There's enough moonlight to drive okay. They should only use their headlights if they see other traffic. We don't need to cause a wreck. Make sure everyone knows that the girl is out there now. I don't want anyone taking any stupid shots."

Jim did as instructed as Bo got his dog out and put a leash on him.

Then Bo spoke softly into his cell phone. "Ron, we're out here. We made a silent approach. I have my dog on a leash. We'll circle the house first."

"Herc is on the enclosed back porch," Ron responded. "There are some vines that grow up beside the porch that go clear to the roof. They are strong enough for a man to climb. And there is a bedroom window right beside the trellis. I'm pretty sure I heard footsteps up there. He may be inside already."

That made Bo worry even more. "Keep Melia safe. I'm coming. I assume you have your guns."

"I've got them. I don't hear anyone up there now, but he's probably just standing still. I'm sure he came in," Ron responded in a whisper. "I'm watching the top of the stairs. If I see someone, I will probably shoot."

"I'm almost to your house. Can you unlock the door for me and then hide?" Bo asked. "Make sure Melia stays out of sight while you do." Without waiting for a response from Ron, he spoke to his partner, who was jogging alongside him. "Jim, you make a dash to the barn and make sure the girls are okay there. Ron thinks the guy is inside the house, but we have to make sure he isn't in the barn. When you get there, keep your eyes peeled and listen carefully. Whoever sprayed the dog could be anywhere."

Jim took off, running and dodging swiftly. Bo prayed that he hadn't just sent him on an errand that could get him shot. He kept moving even as he listened to Jim's retreating footsteps. A quick glance to his right a moment later was all that was needed to assure himself that Jim had reached the barn. Bo needed to get in the house now.

To his surprise, Ron and Melia were waiting for him on the front porch. "We heard him again upstairs, so we came out," Ron explained, his breathing sounding labored.

"Where in the house?" Bo asked.

"It sounded like he was in the room that has the window by the vines," Ron explained, still keeping his voice very soft. "I need to sit down."

Melia helped him to a deck chair, which he sank into with a groan. Melia squatted down beside him. Bo turned back and ran around the house. He spotted the vines, and sure enough, a figure dressed all in black was partway out of the window, one hand already gripping the vines.

Bo drew his gun and aimed it at the black figure. He almost shouted for the man to stop, but then he hesitated. Once he was on the vines, Bo could then order him to stop. The guy would be more or less helpless.

Melia suddenly screamed for help. Her scream sent the burglar scurrying back inside.

Bo had to go to her. He ran back around the house and onto the porch just as another patrol car slipped from the darkness into the illumination of the yard light.

"Bo, hurry!" Melia said. "Grandpa just passed out."

At that same moment, Jim ran toward them. “He’s in the house,” he shouted.

“I know,” Bo responded. “Get these other officers to surround the house and call for a SWAT team. I’m calling 911. Ron needs an ambulance. Have you seen Nattie?” Bo leaped onto the porch and handed the phone to Melia. “I’ve dialed 911. Have them send an ambulance. I’ll check your grandpa out.”

Ron didn’t look good, nor was he safe here on the front porch with a dangerous man inside. He had to move him away from the house. Bo picked Ron up and kept his eyes and ears alert for any sound inside the house as he heard Melia quietly give instructions to the 911 dispatcher. She had calmed down now, and she was talking in a reasonable manner.

Two more patrol cars arrived. Officers scrambled from the cars as Bo carried Ron from the porch to the garage, the nearest unattached building. Melia stayed right beside them. An officer shouted to him for directions and Jim moved forward to organize the officers. Bo laid Ron on the floor of the garage beside his pickup and began to check his vital signs. His breathing was shallow, his heartbeat irregular. Melia followed him in and knelt beside her grandpa.

“Is he dying?” she asked, once again emotional after so calmly calling for the ambulance.

“He’s not in good shape, but if that ambulance gets here in time, they can save his life. You did good shouting for me,” he said. “I hated to move him, but with someone in the house, I felt I needed to get him here where we would be safer.”

“I’m sorry. This is my fault,” a voice said from just outside the garage.

Melia sprang to her feet and rushed out, grabbing Nattie and pulling her into the garage and then hugging her tightly. “None of it is your fault.”

“Lucas is in the house. I saw him as he was climbing out the window, but he went back inside again. He was dressed in black, but I know it was him. I hope it’s not too late to save Joe.”

“They’ll find Joe,” Melia said, fearing that she had just told a lie but not knowing what else to say.

The two young women held each other as Bo attempted to give care to Ron and officers surrounded the house. The sheriff himself arrived as SWAT members assembled. Sheriff Hermock knelt beside Bo. “An ambulance will be here soon. After they take Mr. Brady, you can explain to me what exactly has occurred so far and then help me decide what action we need to take next.”

“Okay,” Bo said.

Once the ambulance had arrived and Ron had been stabilized, they loaded him in.

"May I go with him?" Melia asked. "I'm his granddaughter."

It was allowed. She climbed in, and the ambulance roared out of the yard. Bo prayed for Ron as he turned his attention to the sheriff. "Okay, Sheriff," he said. "Here's what's happening."

Bo glanced at Nattie standing a few feet away. She looked so forlorn that it broke his heart. "Just a second, Sheriff," he said. "I need to make sure this girl is taken care of." He dialed Rosina's phone, and as soon as she answered, he asked, "Where are you and Karmen?"

"We're still in the barn like you asked."

"Okay. I'm going to escort Nattie over there, and you guys will need to keep an eye on her. She's pretty shook up," he said. He looked at the sheriff then. "Sheriff, walk with us while I fill you in."

They were halfway to the barn when Nattie stopped walking. She looked up at Bo and said, "Lucas is in the house. I will go with him if you will let him go. This is all about me. I can't let any of you get hurt because of me."

"You know we can't do that," Bo said.

"He's right," the sheriff added. "If he knows where Joe is, we need him to tell us. I'm afraid that if you go with him that will never happen."

"Maybe he will tell me after we get away, and then I can call and tell you," she said in a soft, emotional voice.

The sheriff shook his head. "We can't take that chance," he said. "I cannot allow you to go into a dangerous situation."

For a moment, Bo thought she was going to beg, but instead she said, "Okay, if you guys say so." A minute later, she was with Rosina and Karmen in the barn.

CHAPTER TWENTY

Joe's neck was killing him, but he persisted, and finally, he pulled one end of the rope out. He straightened up for a minute, attempting to let his neck muscles relax. Then he bent over again, and within another minute or so, his arms were free. He pulled the blindfold off to discover that it was totally dark in the room now. Apparently the killer had shut the light off before he left.

He would deal with that later. First, he had to untie his feet. That took what seemed to him like an hour, but in reality, it had probably been only about fifteen or twenty minutes. It took him more time to get feeling back into his feet and then to get his legs to work. Finally, he was able to stumble to a wall and then feel his way around it until he found a light switch. When light filled the room, hope filled his heart. The room was not too large, and there was only one door. Other than the table and a couple of hard-backed chairs, there was no furniture. The floor was covered with badly worn green linoleum. There were no windows. He had to figure out how to get through the door and escape from this room.

Every effort was being made to get Lucas to leave the house and surrender to the officers. They used a bullhorn to give instructions, but no sound came from within the house.

"Let me talk to Nattie," Bo suggested to Sheriff Hermock. "Maybe she can tell us if Lucas might have his cell phone on him and, if so, what the number is."

As they made their way toward the barn, they passed a couple of the SWAT officers. "You should have let me handle this case, Sheriff," one of them said. "Joe killed Emil, and Bo has only put suspicion on a lot of innocent people."

Bo recognized Will Merianos's voice. He'd forgotten that he was part of the SWAT team. He wasn't happy to learn that he was here.

"You were on the wrong track, Deputy. You still are. Now pay attention to what's going on here," Sheriff Hermock said, and he and Bo walked to the barn.

"You'll see, Sheriff," Will called after them. "Bo has messed up big time."

The sheriff made no further response to Will, but to Bo, he said in a low voice, "I should have fired him."

Bo didn't say anything, but he agreed with the sheriff.

Nattie was standing at the barn door with Rosina and Karmen. Bo told her what he wanted, and Nattie said, "He has a cell phone, but I don't know if he has it with him now. He took it when he left the last time I saw him."

"Do you know the number?" Bo asked.

"Yes," she said.

"Sheriff," Bo said. "I know you have a hostage negotiator here, but would you mind if I try to get him to surrender—if he answers his phone?"

"That would be okay," Sheriff Hermock said.

"Okay, Nattie, would you punch the number into my phone?" Bo asked.

She took it from his hand, pushed some numbers, and handed the phone back to Bo. It began to ring. It rang several times, and Bo was ready to end the call when a slurred voice said, "What do you need, pig?"

"Lucas, my name is Detective Bo Buckley," he said even as he wondered if Lucas was high on something.

"I know who you are, but what makes you think I'm some Lucas guy?"

Although Bo had not put the phone on speaker, he'd held it so that Nattie, who was leaning close, could hear. He glanced at her.

"It's him," she whispered. "But he's on heroin. That's how he sounds when he's high. I don't know where he could have gotten it."

Bo nodded to Nattie. "I rang your number, and you picked up. Lucas, it's time you gave up. Come out on the porch with your hands in the air, and this will go a lot easier for you."

"I ain't coming out," he insisted. "You come in and get me if you think you dare try."

"It doesn't work that way. You come out, and we can end this thing."

"I just told you that I ain't coming out. Why don't you have Nattie come in? I'll come out with her, and we'll leave. I didn't kill Emil, so it ain't me you want anyway."

"Maybe you did, and maybe you didn't," Bo said. "Come on out, and we'll talk. If you are innocent of murder, we'll figure it out."

"Ain't coming without my girl," he said.

"Give it some thought, Lucas, and I'll call you back," Bo said, and with that, he ended the call.

"He won't come out, Bo," Nattie said. "I know him. If I go in, maybe he will come out with me."

Bo and the sheriff both shook their heads. "We can't let you do that," Bo said. "You would be risking both yourself and your baby. Anyway, seriously, I don't think you really want to, do you?"

Nattie ducked her head, and as tears started to trickle down her cheeks, she said, "No, but I don't want any of you officers getting hurt. It's bad enough that Ron collapsed. That would never have happened if—"

She was cut off by Rosina's hand covering her mouth. "It's time you quit blaming yourself, Nattie. None of this is your fault. Here, why don't you sit down again with Karmen and me?"

Nattie looked up at Bo, then at the sheriff, and finally at Rosina. "Okay."

Further calls to Lucas by the negotiator did no better than Bo's call had. The standoff continued. Eventually, Bo sent Nattie away with Rosina and Karmen.

"Is it okay if we go to the hospital before we go to Rosina's apartment?" she asked. "Melia needs support right now."

"Yeah, she does, doesn't she? Yes, that would be great," Bo said.

"We'll take care of her, Bo," Rosina promised.

At that moment, a thought slammed into Bo. "Wait, you ladies can't go without police protection."

"But the danger is in there," Karmen reasoned, pointing toward the house.

"Lucas is in there, but we don't know that he killed Emil. If he didn't, then someone else is out there, somewhere, who did it, and that person is dangerous."

"But he's probably with Joe," Rosina said.

"Maybe. Let me see if the sheriff will send someone with you to the hospital. I don't like the thought of Melia being there without protection, now that I think of it," Bo said.

Bo spoke to the sheriff a moment later and explained the situation.

"I agree," the sheriff said. "Where's Deputy Grizzel?"

"He's over there by the garage," Bo said.

"Send him," the sheriff instructed. "Next to you, Bo, he knows more about this case than anyone and how many other men could potentially be the killer." As soon as Jim and the girls had left, the sheriff said, "I hate to break Ron's window, but I think it's time to use some tear gas."

"Just a minute, Sheriff," Bo said. "Joe's dog is in there. As badly as he was injured, tear gas could kill him. He can't just come out like Lucas can."

"So what do you suggest we do, Bo?"

"I can go around the back, open the door, and let him out. We can lock him in the barn with Ron's dog," Bo suggested.

"Could be dangerous," the sheriff said.

"Yes, it could, but for Herc, it's more than just *could*."

"How would you get him out?"

"I'd quietly unlock the door, and he'll come to me. Then I'll carry him to the barn," Bo said.

"But how would you unlock the door? We don't have any keys," Sheriff Hermock said.

Bo reached in his pocket and pulled out a set of keys. "I took these from Ron before the ambulance came," he said. "I figured we might need them."

"Okay. Do it then, but we need to let these other officers know what you're doing."

As soon as that was done, Bo walked all the way around the backyard and then made his way, hunched low and moving slowly, to the back door.

He unlocked it, whispered, "Herc," and waited. The dog came to him, and Bo carried him back the same way he'd just come.

All four young women and Deputy Jim Grizzel were in the waiting room when a doctor came out.

"I'm Doctor Cummings. Are any of you ladies Ron Brady's next of kin?"

Melia stood up. "I'm Melia Brady. He's my grandfather."

"Are you his closest next of kin?" the doctor asked with a cocked eyebrow.

"I am," she said tearfully. "Is Grandpa going to make it? I can't lose him."

"He needs open heart surgery. We'll need to fly him by helicopter to the University of Utah Hospital. Surgeons are standing by there to operate on him as soon as he arrives. Is that okay with you?" the doctor asked.

"If it will save his life, then of course it is," she responded.

"Will you sign a consent form for surgery so we can fax it to the university hospital?"

"Yes," she said.

"I'll be right back with the form," he told her.

After the consent was signed, Melia said, "I need to go to the bus station. I need to go to Salt Lake to be with Grandpa."

"You don't need a bus ticket," Karmen said. "I'll take you. Rosina, will you help Nattie—you and Deputy Grizzel—and keep her safe?"

They agreed, but then Melia had a thought, a difficult one. "I want to be with Grandpa, at least when he comes out of surgery, but there are still animals to feed on the farm."

"You go," Rosina said. "I'll take care of the animals after the standoff is over."

"And I'll help," Nattie volunteered.

"Thanks, guys. Then I'll go. Please let me know what happens at my house."

"We'll let you know," Deputy Grizzel promised. "You don't have to worry about anything here. You go be there for your grandpa."

They did not go to Rosina's apartment as they had planned. After a quick call to Bo, the decision was made to find a hotel room for the two of them with Jim keeping watch outside their door.

Sheriff Hermock gave the order, and two canisters of tear gas were fired into the house from two different directions. Then they waited. "When Lucas comes out, hold your fire," he ordered the officers. "If a shot needs to be fired, I will give the order."

They waited some more, and a second round of tear gas was fired into the house. Finally, the front door opened, and Lucas Soto stumbled out onto the porch, coughing and rubbing his eyes fiercely with one hand. In his other hand was a pistol, but it was hanging at his side. A single shot rang out.

Lucas grabbed his chest as he fell over backward.

"Who did that?" the sheriff shouted as Bo rushed forward to the downed man.

No one spoke up. Finally, after the sheriff asked a second time, one of the SWAT officers pointed at Deputy Will Merianos.

"Will, what were you thinking?" the sheriff demanded.

"Are you blind, Sheriff? He had a gun. Am I the only one smart enough to recognize a threat?" Will asked.

"It was hanging at his side, and he couldn't even see because of the tear gas. Deputy, you are suspended. Turn your weapons over to the SWAT commander. Then I'll see you in my office at noon tomorrow."

"You can't do that, Sheriff. I might have just saved your life," Will argued, angry and unrepentant. "This guy's taken care off. Now you need to find and arrest Joe Whalen for murder. I'm sure he's just faking a kidnapping."

"That's all, Deputy. You do as I just told you and do it now." With that, the sheriff joined Bo and two other deputies on the porch.

Bo looked up. "We've called for an ambulance. He's been shot in the chest, but he's still alive."

"Deputy Merianos had better hope he lives," Sheriff Hermock mumbled.

"Was that who shot him?" Bo asked.

"He's been suspended," was the sheriff's answer.

It had been several hours, and Joe's captor still hadn't come back. Maybe Joe was going to be left here to die. That thought spurred him to action. He was going to get out of here if he had to tear the door down with his bare hands.

He looked around the room, as he had been doing for several minutes, while he got his arms and legs loosened up. His bare hands were not such a good idea, but surely he could break some of the furniture and beat on the door with the pieces until it broke too. If the killer came back before he had accomplished that, then he'd try to bash him on the head with whatever he used on the door.

Table legs were his first choice. Joe worked for several minutes to get a table leg loose. Then he took hold of the small end of the leg and began to swing the thick end at the door. It only took a couple swings before he figured out the wooden door was a solid-core one. He beat the door handle off, but that didn't help as it appeared that it was locked further from the far side. He smashed for all he was worth at the middle of the door, hoping it wasn't too thick. Unfortunately, he didn't have a lot of strength. The hours he'd been tied up coupled with newly broken ribs and the injures he'd received in the jail still hurting him left him doubled over after just three or four minutes.

He rested for a bit, and then started on the door again. Once more, he had to rest, but he did it beside the door so that if his captor opened it, he could use the table leg on him.

To Joe's dismay, the door did open as he rested. The killer stepped in, and Joe let him have it with the table leg. The man dodged, and the club only hit him on the shoulder, but it was enough to slow him down. Joe hit him again, this time striking the killer's left arm.

He wished it would have broken the killer's arm, but the guy did not go down. Instead, he leaped with a loud yell and tackled Joe's feet. Joe went down, smashing his head on the floor. He was dazed for a moment, and the killer started kicking him.

Fighting for his life, Joe scrambled unsteadily to his feet and threw a punch that caught the killer in the face. Blood spurted from his nose. Joe again tried for the door, but once more, the killer stopped his bid for freedom by grabbing the back of his shirt.

Joe spun and kicked the killer's right knee. That brought a yell and curses. Joe kicked the other knee, and this time, the killer went down. Joe finally managed to dash through the door, took a quick look around to orient himself, and then headed for what appeared to be the front door of the house. It was locked. He tried to unlock it but realized he needed a key.

He bolted for the back door, finding it similarly locked. Finally, in desperation, he kicked out the front window. Glass shattered and spread all around him. He readied himself to leap for his freedom when he felt a strong tug at his shoulder. At that exact moment, he heard a gunshot. It knocked him to his knees. He tried desperately to get up, but before he could, the killer fired a second shot, which struck Joe in the back. This time, he fell forward on his face in the glass. He had only enough time to realize he'd failed before the world went black.

The same ambulance that had hauled Ron to the hospital earlier came roaring into the farmyard again and slid to a stop in front of the house. The ambulance attendants bolted through the gate to the yard and joined Bo and a couple other officers who were attending to Lucas. Bo was relieved that he could step back now and leave Lucas's life in other hands.

Lucas was injured badly, and Bo was not at all sure that he would live long enough to get to the hospital. He walked over to the spigot on the side of Ron's house and turned on the water. He washed the blood from his hands and face as best he could. Then he rejoined the sheriff and a handful of officers who were in a heated discussion just beyond the fence to the yard.

"You should just fire him, Sheriff," Bo said with a touch of venom when he realized they were talking about Will Merianos. Two other officers voiced their agreement.

"I'll deal with him later," the sheriff said. "Right now, we have a large crime scene to process." With that, he barked out orders to several officers and told the rest that they could leave. The entire SWAT team was no longer needed here.

Bo turned away, having received no orders himself, and walked wearily to the barn. He found Herc and Ace in the stall where he'd put them before the shooting. Herc seemed none the worse for wear, but now Bo wondered what to do about them. They were outdoor dogs, unlike Two Face.

"I'll get you some food and water," he said. Then he left them in a stall that had no horses in it and was fairly clean.

He let Two Face out of the Explorer, then he walked to the house and explained to the sheriff that he needed to get some dog food for Ace and Herc. "Sure. Go ahead, Bo," he said. "Where is it?"

"It's on the back porch where Herc had been until I got him out," he replied. He and Two Face walked back there. Bo went in, found what he was looking for, and then he and the bulldog exited out the back door and started toward the barn with a sack of dog food in Bo's arms. As they rounded the house, the ambulance was just leaving with Lucas. He shook his head sadly and proceeded on to the barn, his faithful bulldog right at his heels.

CHAPTER TWENTY-ONE

"Bo, we'll finish up here and lock the house when we're done," Sheriff Hermock told him after Bo had finished caring for the dogs. "I'd like you to go to the hospital, and if Lucas wakes up, question him. Maybe he knows where Joe is and will tell you."

"I'll do that, Sheriff," he said. Exhaustion was dragging him down, but he didn't have time to rest.

"I'll send another officer to relieve Deputy Grizzel of his watch at the hotel, and he can join you at the hospital in a while," the sheriff concluded. "I will need to know where he and the ladies are."

"I'll find out and let you know," Bo said. Bo and Two Face headed for the hospital, but as soon as he was on the road, he called Rosina. "Are you and Nattie okay?"

"We're at a hotel. Nattie is resting on one of the beds, and Deputy Grizzel is on a chair just outside the door," she said.

"Have you heard from Karmen and Melia?"

"They just got to the hospital in Salt Lake. They aren't even inside yet, so I don't know anything about Ron Brady's condition," she reported. "I'm worried about the animals that didn't get fed."

"They won't die without one meal," Bo said. "They can wait until tomorrow." Then he told her where Ace and Herc were. "They'll be fine until morning as well. You and Nattie need to get some sleep."

"I'm worried about Deputy Grizzel," she said. "He's got to be tired. So have you for that matter. What are you doing now?"

"I'm heading for the hospital to check on Lucas. Does Nattie know he's been shot?"

"She knows. She's both sad and relieved, if that makes any sense," Rosina said.

"It makes a lot of sense. What hotel are you at? I need to let the sheriff know so he can send someone to relieve Jim. I'm going to need his help," he said.

Once the sheriff knew where to send a replacement for Jim, Bo continued in silence toward the hospital, his mind working overtime. Where were his other suspects? Lucas, in his mind, could still be the killer. If so, he would know where Joe was at, for Emil's killer was most likely to know.

Bryan Bayle? He had not been seen, and he was being watched for by officers all over the state and beyond. He was a murder suspect because of his wife and his brother, both of whom he had almost certainly murdered. He was also a suspect in Emil's murder, and right now, in Bo's mind, he was the most likely of them all, even more so than Lucas. His wife, when she wrote that desperate note that never got finished, seemed to have been pointing to Bryan as Emil's killer.

Then there was Leonardo Augur. He was a drug pusher. He'd sold once to Joe and was angry when Joe refused to buy from him a second time, instead going back to Emil. Leonardo's motive was more than just anger over one customer, namely Joe, but it could be that he simply wanted Emil's customers—all of them. With Emil dead, that would likely be accomplished.

After he talked to Lucas, if Lucas even survived and could talk, he needed to get back to Castle Dale. Leonardo had to be around somewhere. If so, Bo felt it was urgent that he find him. He and Jim had never been able to finish their search for Leonardo's gardener, and that also needed to be done. That gardener could very likely give them some good information on Leonardo, possibly even his location.

Finally, the one person whose name he didn't know came to mind. That man was a suspect simply because Joe said he'd threatened Emil if he didn't pay him what was owed. Very little was known about him. Much more needed to be learned about that man, including his identity.

Lucas could be the key to learning more about each of these other men if he turned out not to be Emil's killer, something that was up in the air at the moment. Bo's thoughts turned to his young cousin Joe Whalen. Where was he? Was he hurt badly? Was he even alive? An interview with Lucas was critical. But he could only be interviewed if he lived and if he became conscious and lucid enough to talk.

Bo wanted to wring Will Merianos's neck. There had been no need to shoot Lucas like he had. What he'd done had been against the sheriff's specific orders. Will's action was inexcusable. Yes, Bo admitted to himself, Lucas had had a gun in his hand. But he was not pointing it at any officers. In fact, as he recalled, Lucas had been rubbing his eyes with one hand, coughing, and holding the gun with the other hand as he'd emerged from the house. Bo parked his Explorer at the hospital and then shut his eyes, trying to bring back the memory in clearer form.

There was no question that the tear gas had severely affected Lucas. If Nattie was right, he was also high, and that made him even more messed up. Rubbing his eyes told Bo that he couldn't have seen well enough to aim his pistol if he'd wanted to. He was coughing so hard that he would not have been able to hold the gun steady, high on drugs or not. Then into Bo's mind came a clearer picture. The pistol, the one Will had used as an excuse to fire at Lucas, had been hanging in his free hand at his side. No, Lucas had not been a threat in that moment. Will, as the sheriff had said, had better hope Lucas survived, for there was no way it could be ruled as a justified shooting.

Bo got out of his Explorer and walked slowly toward the hospital. Inside, he identified himself and inquired about Lucas. He was told that Lucas was in surgery and no one knew how long it would be before the surgery was finished. No one could tell him what chance Lucas had of survival either. No one he talked to seemed to know, or if they did, they wouldn't tell him.

Bo sat down in the main waiting room and leaned his head back against the wall.

"Hey, partner, wake up," he heard suddenly, and he jumped in his chair. Jim was standing there grinning. "Sorry, but we need to find out how Lucas is doing."

Bo looked at his watch. He must have fallen asleep as soon as he'd laid his head back. That had been over a half hour ago. "Sorry, but when I checked last, he was still in surgery."

"Let's check again," Jim suggested.

Bo forced himself to his feet, and the two tired officers made the inquiry. Lucas was still in surgery. There was no estimate as to when he would be out. Bo called Sheriff Hermock. "Are you still at the Brady farm?" he asked him.

"Yes, and we will be for a while yet. Although I'm not sure there's a whole lot more to be learned here. How is Lucas?" the sheriff asked.

"He's still in surgery. Should Jim and I wait here?"

"No, go get some sleep for at least three or four hours, and then head back to the hospital. It'll be daylight by then. Unless, of course, there's something else you can do tonight that will be productive."

"I can't think of anything," Bo admitted. "I have other suspects, but they still need to be found. As to where Joe is, I don't think we'll learn anything until we can talk to Lucas—if we can talk to him at all."

Both deputies left the hospital. Bo told Jim to meet him at the sheriff's office in four hours. Then after he was back in his car, he called Melia. She sounded very groggy when she answered her phone. "Hi, Melia. It's Bo," he said. "How's your grandfather?"

"He's still in surgery," she said. "We got a report from one doctor who says it's touch-and-go right now. He may or may not live. I don't know what I'll do."

"We'll work that out together, Melia, but let's pray he lives. Are you and Karmen holding up okay?"

"We're fine. So what about Lucas? Did he surrender?"

"Not exactly," Bo said. "But he is in custody."

"Did he tell you where Joe's at?" she asked, her voice choked with emotion.

"Not yet. I haven't been able to talk to him," he said.

"Why not? Won't he talk to you?" she asked.

Bo debated with himself and then decided she had a right to know. "Lucas got shot. He was trying to surrender, but one of the officers didn't give him a chance."

"Oh no. Is he dead? How can he tell us where Joe is if he's dead?" she moaned.

"He's not dead, but he's hurt badly. He's in surgery, and when they're through with the operation and he wakes up, then I'll see what he knows or what he will tell us."

"If he was giving up, why did someone shoot him, Bo?"

"That's for Sheriff Hermock to find out," Bo said. "Listen. I've got to go, but I'll call you back later and check on your grandfather."

"Will you call me if Lucas tells you where Joe is?" she asked.

"You know I will. Let me talk to Karmen for a minute," he said then.

He talked with his girlfriend the rest of the way home, filling in some of the details of the culmination of the standoff.

Joe woke up in extreme pain. It took him a few tortured minutes to remember what had happened to him. He'd almost gotten away, but then he got shot. So where was he now? And where was the man who shot him?

He strained himself but was unable to look up from the floor where he was lying. He tried to move so he could look around but discovered that his feet were tied. To his horror, so were his hands. His head flopped down again. He guessed that the killer had left him here to die, and there was nothing he could do about it.

Joe thought of Melia, Rosina, Ron, and Bo. What were they thinking, and was anyone looking for him? If they were, how would they even know where to look? Once again, he chided himself for smoking pot. He was going to die for that mistake, and he guessed that was fair. But his loved ones, his friends, didn't deserve the sadness he'd brought into their lives. Not one of those four had ever been anything but good to him. Now he'd caused them to go through so much pain.

When Bo and Jim got back to the hospital, they were told that Lucas had survived the operation but that he was sleeping now. If they could wait an hour or two, it might be possible to speak to him. While they waited, they both got on their phones. Jim was trying to find out if anything had turned up on Bryan Bayle or Leonardo Augur and seeing if he could learn anything more about the elusive dealer whose name they did not know.

Bo was talking to Melia. She was very positive about Ron. "He survived the surgery and the doctor told me that they were able to make some repairs to his heart that should make him feel better than he has for a long time," she said.

"Have you been able to talk to him yet?" Bo asked.

"He's still in recovery, but he should be in a room in the next few minutes. Then Karmen and I will get to see him," she reported.

"Did you and Karmen get any sleep?" he asked.

"A little, if you call dozing with your head back in a chair sleeping. Karmen is sure a nice person, Bo. She likes you a lot. You are lucky."

"I am at that," he agreed.

"She's getting us a hotel room so we can sleep after we've seen Grandpa." With barely a pause, Melia asked, "Do you know anything about Joe yet? Have you talked to Lucas?"

"Lucas also survived his surgery, and no, nothing more on Joe, but dozens of officers are searching for other men who may have taken him. Lucas is not our only suspect," he reminded her. After finishing his call with Melia, he spoke with Karmen for a little while, and then he called Rosina. "Did I wake you?"

"No, Nattie and I are sitting on our beds talking. We didn't get much sleep last night. I talked to the officer who's outside our door, and he said that it had been quiet all night," she told him.

"After I talk with Lucas, which should be in the next hour or so, then we can decide what you guys need to do," Bo said.

"We already know," Rosina said. "We need to get out to Ron Brady's farm and feed his hungry animals. The officer at our door said he would go with us."

"Not until Sheriff Hermock and I say it's okay," Bo warned.

"I figured that," she said. "I just hope Lucas can and will help you find Joe. Have you talked to Karmen or Melia yet this morning?"

"Yes," he said.

"So have I. It sounds like Ron's going to be okay."

"It sure does. Let me say hi to Nattie, Rosina," Bo said.

"Hello, Detective Buckley," Nattie said a moment later.

"You can call me Bo. How are you feeling this morning?"

"I'm okay. I'm just tired and worried like you guys are. But I'm glad Lucas didn't die. I don't ever want to see him again, but I'm still glad he's alive. Will you tell him that for me when you talk to him?" she asked.

"If you would like me to," he said.

"I would, please. Also tell him not to ever try to contact me again." She paused. "I'm glad Ron is okay. He is such a wonderful man." They talked for another minute or so, and then Bo ended the call.

A few minutes later, his phone rang. It was the sheriff. "Bo, I assume you are familiar with Joe Whalen's handwriting."

"I am. Why?"

"I have a letter here. I think you should come read it."

"What's it about?" Bo asked as he glanced at Jim with narrowed eyes.

"Just come. Are you at the hospital?"

"We are."

"Have you been able to talk to Lucas yet?"

"No. He survived the surgery. They told us a few minutes ago that we may be able to talk to him in about an hour," Bo said.

"Okay, good. Come here, look at what I have, and then you can go back and work on Lucas. Bring Deputy Grizzel with you." The sheriff ended the call on that note.

As the two officers rode toward the sheriff's office, they reported to each other on what they had learned. Bo's report was fairly straightforward. Jim's was a little more complicated: "No sign of Bryan Bayle or Leonardo Augur. An officer in Castle Dale drove by his house a short while ago and said it didn't look like anyone was there. They checked several times during the night as well, but he hasn't been seen."

"That figures," Bo said. "He may know we're looking for him. For all we know, he may have seen us there yesterday. Anything on the identity of the other drug dealer?"

"Yes. I talked to a guy who used to be on drugs. He thinks the guy's name is Devonte Grillo. I checked, and that name doesn't show up anywhere that I can find. I checked the databases he should show up on. He has no driver's license, at least not in Utah. There are no vehicles registered to him in the state. I guess we can check for both those things in other states. I checked with the Bureau of Criminal Identification. There's nothing on him there. He's never been in prison. There's nothing on him on NCIC. It's like the guy doesn't exist."

"I think you just hit on it. He doesn't exist, at least not with that name. We know he is a real person, and a bad one at that. Maybe he's used Grillo as an alias. If we just had some fingerprints to run . . . but we don't," Bo said.

"We don't even know where to go to check for some," Jim said.

"Wait, Jim. What about the jail?" Bo said with a sudden flash of brilliance. "If he was the one who went and had Joe beat up, maybe he left prints on the roster he signed."

"If he's the killer, that is," Jim said. "And if there haven't been so many other people sign the roster that his prints are indistinguishable."

"Let's see what we can learn at the jail when we get a free minute. Also, I think we should try to find out Bayle's, Lucas's, and Devonte's blood types. I collected blood from Joe's door and floor that was left there by whoever busted that square of glass out of Joe's back door. That was probably Emil, but we should make sure. Someone may have been in there waiting when Emil came in. I don't know why I didn't think of that sooner. Some detective I am."

"Hey, partner. Give yourself some slack. You're new at this," Jim said.

"Yeah, but I still should have thought about it," he lamented. "Another thing we should do is check for utilities, rent, home ownership, and so on for the elusive Mr. Grillo or whatever his name is. For now, we'll refer to him as Grillo."

They arrived at the sheriff's department. Bo's mind had turned to the matter he was coming in for. The two of them went straight to the sheriff's office. His door was open, and he waved them in. "Good morning, guys," he said without so much as a hint at a smile. "I wasn't going to come in so early after such a late night, but my secretary called and said I had a letter that she thought I might want to see."

He slipped a pair of latex gloves on and threw another pair to Bo, who began to pull them on.

"This letter is supposedly from Joe Whalen," the sheriff said as he reached in a drawer and pulled out an envelope. "It's addressed to me here, handwritten, and Joe's address is in the return address location. It seems to have been mailed in Spanish Fork." He pulled out the letter and handed the envelope to Bo.

Bo felt a twist in his stomach as he took the envelope and looked at it. "Yeah, this looks like Joe's writing," he said. He handed the envelope back, and the sheriff handed him the single sheet of paper that had been in the envelope. Reading the statement written there was almost more than he could handle. But he finished and handed it back to Sheriff Hermock. "It's Joe's handwriting. I'm certain of it. But the spelling is horrible. I'm confused about that."

"What does he say, Bo?" Jim asked.

"It's a confession," Bo said, fighting hard not to let his emotions show. "Joe claims that he killed Emil Eifler, but what it's really saying is that he *didn't* kill him."

"What are you talking about?" the sheriff said. "You just said that it was his handwriting."

Bo stood up and stepped over to the sheriff's desk. "Put the note here, and let's all three read it together. I want to see if you guys notice what I noticed."

They all leaned over the letter, and Bo read out loud.

> *Dear Sheriff Hermock,*
>
> *I am riting this leter to you to cleer up the mater of the murdur of Emil Ifler. I'm sorry I lied to your oficers about it. I admit that I shot him with my own pistal and put his body in my trunk. He was making me get drugs from him when I didn't want two. Then when I codn't pay he was gong to take my stuf. I am not comng back to let you put me in prisan. But you can quit lokking for anybode else. I did it myself. But he had it comin.*
>
> *Joe Whalen*

When Bo had finished, he looked up.

"Joe is a terrible speller," Jim noted.

"I noticed that too," the sheriff agreed. "He even misspelled *sheriff* on the envelope. Is he trying tell us something?"

"You just made my point, Sheriff. Joe is an excellent speller. He reads a lot and had excellent grades in high school. The person who isn't smart is the one who killed Emil and kidnapped Joe. Joe was *forced* to write this letter. By making those intentional errors, he was telling me that he was not writing it because he *wanted* to but because he *had* to. So we know now that the killer either is a bad speller himself or else assumed as you did, Sheriff, that Joe is a bad speller."

"You're sure of this?" Sheriff Hermock asked.

"Positive. Let's get his sister down here. I'll bet she has letters from him. If she does, we'll see minimal spelling errors."

"I believe you, Bo. Will she come down if you call her?"

"I know she would. But remember, Nattie is with her and one of your deputies," Bo said.

"Call her. Have the deputy bring the two of them here in his patrol car."

While they were waiting for Rosina to arrive, Bo asked the sheriff what he was going to do about Will Merianos shooting Lucas.

"I've turned it over to the county attorney to see if charges can be filed, but based on what we witnessed, Will can no longer work for me. I will be firing him at noon. I wish I'd fired him before."

"I'm not sure what he was thinking," Bo said, "but I have my suspicions. I think he was afraid Lucas might say something that would cinch Joe's innocence, and he wasn't about to let that happen. He accused Joe, and to save face, he wants the murderer to be Joe."

"That's my take as well," the sheriff agreed. "And if the county attorney agrees, Will could be facing attempted murder charges."

The men discussed the situation for some time before Rosina, Nattie, and the officer who'd been with them arrived.

Rosina soon confirmed what Bo had stated. "Joe is a good speller. He was forced to write that."

"I'd like you to give a written statement to Bo and Jim stating what you just told me," the sheriff said. "Bo can pick it up anytime. Right now, he and Jim have an interview to do at the hospital."

CHAPTER TWENTY-TWO

LUCAS WAS CONSCIOUS AND AGREED to talk when Bo and Jim entered his room. He said, "I know you guys think I shot Emil Eifler. I was mad at him—that's for sure—but I am not a killer."

"Let me read you your rights," Bo said. "You are not under arrest at this time, but I want to make sure you understand what your rights are in case it becomes necessary. And I will need to record our interview."

"Read them," Lucas said almost flippantly for a man who had undergone surgery to remove a bullet from his chest the previous night. "I guess I should be relieved that this is an *interview*, not an *interrogation*."

Bo made no comment to that but turned on the recorder, read Lucas his rights, and asked him if he understood them. Lucas said he did and that he would tell them whatever he could.

"Okay. So where were you on the night Emil Eifler was killed?" Bo looked at his notes and stated the date.

"I was sort of hiding behind a tree watching Joe Whalen's house," he said.

"Why in the world were you doing that?" Bo asked, taken aback by the answer. "Did you have something against Joe?"

"Well, yes, but that wasn't why I was there. My beef that night was with Emil. I followed him there and then hid a short distance away and watched. I figured Emil was probably going to do the same thing to Joe that he had to Nattie and me."

"And what was that, Lucas?"

"Steal from him, of course."

"Did you go in Joe's house?" Bo asked.

"Not until the other guy left," he said. "But I didn't have to break in; Emil had already done that. Before going in, I waited and thought Emil would be leaving too, but I thought I'd heard a gunshot in or near the house before that other guy had left. So when Emil didn't come out after a while, I went in. I didn't stay long. Something didn't feel right in there. I wanted to be gone before Joe came home."

"Okay, Lucas, let's back up a minute. First, did you see someone do something to Joe's dog?" Bo asked.

"Emil sprayed him with something. I figured it must have been Mace, so I got me some. I had to use it on that dog of Brady's right after it bit me," he said. "Do you want to see where it bit me?"

"No, that's okay. So after Emil sprayed the dog, then what happened?" Bo asked.

"He went inside. He busted that little square of glass out to get in, but you probably know that," Lucas said. "Anyway, pretty soon this other guy comes along. He must have been watching like I was because he headed right to the back door and went in. He'd been in there for several minutes before I heard that shot. When he left, he went back the same way he'd come."

"Can you describe him?" Bo asked.

"Not much, Detective. He was a big man, a lot bigger than me. He was dressed in black just like I was. That's about all I can tell you about him."

"So you believe that man, the big one, shot and killed Emil?"

"Yeah, no doubt about it."

"So Joe didn't?" Bo asked.

"He couldn't have done. He wasn't even home then. He was with you."

"You didn't see Emil in the house?"

"Nope, but I saw a little blood. I was looking for it, you know, because of the shot and all. I couldn't figure out what had happened to Emil. I sort of wondered if he hadn't been hurt bad and had left after the other guy because I had started to leave and then came back, so he could have left then without me seeing him."

"Lucas, when did you learn that Emil had died in Joe's house that night?"

"The next morning. I was curious then, and I went back and watched again. I saw you come, and that made me wonder what was going on. Then more cops came, and then there was that hearse, and a body was carried out. 'Course I knew then it was Emil. I just can't figure why I didn't see his body when I was in there. But I didn't look in any closets or anything like that, so I guess that was how I missed it."

Bo intentionally threw a question at Lucas that he didn't think he was expecting. "Lucas, where is Joe now?"

"What do you mean? I don't know. I just know he wasn't at the farm last night or I would have seen him," Lucas said.

"You didn't kidnap him and take him somewhere?" Bo asked.

Lucas's eyes popped open wide. "No! No! Why would I do that?"

"Somebody took him, Lucas. Would you have any idea who that might be?"

"Well, I suppose it might be the man who killed Emil, the big guy."

Lucas started tiring, so Bo said, "How about we come back later and talk some more, Lucas."

"That's fine. But there's one more thing I think you should know. I knew Joe hadn't killed Emil, but since I'd been in his house, I got to worrying that you might figure that out and arrest me for the murder. But I didn't do it. I didn't like Joe, and I sort of figured that if someone was going to get arrested for that murder, I wasn't going to let it be me. That's why I didn't say anything about this earlier."

"Thanks for explaining that, Lucas. There is one more question before we go. Did you see the vehicle that the other guy, the big man, might have driven there?"

Lucas said he hadn't, and Bo and Jim left a minute later. They then returned to the sheriff and reported their conversation with Lucas.

Rosina had cut class to work at the Brady farm. Her best friend, Karmen, was doing the same in order to be with Melia at the hospital in Salt Lake. Both girls had agreed on the phone earlier that they were missing for a good cause and that they'd just have to find a way to make it up later.

She and Nattie were busy trying to catch up on the chores that had not been done the day before. The deputy sheriff who was supposed to be guarding them pitched in and helped. But he came to attention when a couple of pickup trucks drove into the yard. He sent the girls into the barn and then approached the trucks. Three men in work clothes and heavy coats got out of each of the trucks and stood looking around.

They informed the deputy that they were there to do Ron Brady's chores. Rosina, upon hearing them, came running out. Within a couple of minutes, there was a crew of knowledgeable and hard-working men at work. Rosina only had to show them what still needed to be done.

"I can't believe people will do something like this, Rosina," Nattie said. "They must really like Ron."

As Bo and Jim were leaving the office, they met Will Merianos coming in. One look at his face was all it took for Bo to steer around him. Will looked like he was mad enough to chew nails. After they had passed him without a word, Jim said with a grin, "I think he's upset."

"If you think he's upset now, can you imagine what he'll be like when the sheriff delivers the bad news? Can you imagine how he's going to react when he finds out he's fired and that the county attorney is considering charges against him?" Bo asked.

"I don't want to be around him after that," Jim said. "So are we going to Castle Dale now to see if we can find the gardener?"

"Seems like a good idea to me," Bo responded.

Once they reached Castle Dale, they drove directly to Leonardo's home. Jim let the local sheriff's department know they were there just as they were pulling onto his street. They parked, got out, and approached the house. There was no answer to the doorbell or to their repeated knocks.

They went to the house next door and rang the bell. Lucy Gibbons answered after a short wait. "If you fellows are looking for my neighbor, I'm afraid you won't find him at home. We haven't seen him since you were here before."

"I guess you wouldn't know if he's gone away somewhere, would you?" Bo asked.

"I couldn't tell you that. It's like I told you before—he isn't very neighborly. If you could catch his gardener or his cleaning lady, they might know."

"It's hard to believe he has both a cleaning lady and a gardener," Bo said. "He must have a good-paying job."

"I guess, but no one knows what he does. My husband and I can't afford a cleaning lady or a gardener, and my husband has a pretty good job," she said.

"Do you know the cleaning lady's name?" Jim asked.

"I've seen her before in the post office and the store. I don't know her name, but someone will. She's probably fifty years old or maybe even younger and is slightly heavyset with short brown hair. She wears glasses and walks with a slight limp," Lucy said. "Oh, and she drives an older car. I think it's a Buick, and it has a lot of rust on it and a few dings. It was blue at one time, I'd say."

"You've been a big help. If either of them comes around, would you give us a call?" Bo said. "It is very important that we locate Mr. Augur."

She agreed, and they gave her both of their cell phone numbers. Then they proceeded to drive around the city, looking for the white pickup with snow removal shovels and large brooms in the back and the older, rusted Buick. About thirty minutes later, when they were about to give up, they spotted the truck they believed could belong to the gardener.

It was parked in front of a white frame house with a yard and lawn that looked like they would be gorgeous come spring. Empty flowerpots were lined neatly below the windows, waiting for flowers to be planted. "I think this is where the gardener lives," Bo said. "I wasn't sure it would be a nice place. You know, like he uses his skills on other people's yards but not his own. Still, I suspect that this is his home just because the house is so old, and I can't imagine he would make all that much money gardening."

They stepped up to the front door and waited after ringing the doorbell.

"You fellows looking for me?" a short, stocky fellow of around fifty asked as he came around the side of the house.

"If you are the man who takes care of Leonardo Augur's yard and shovels his snow, then yes, we are," Bo said.

The fellow beamed. He was wearing a floppy, soiled brown hat with earflaps pulled down over his ears. He took off a pair of leather gloves and stuffed them in the back pocket of his striped coveralls. "I'm Tom Lensky, and I'm the man you're looking for. I ain't done nothing wrong, have I?"

"No. We're just looking for information about Mr. Augur," Bo said.

"I don't think I'm a lot of help. The guy is reclusive. He hired me, and he pays me, but he doesn't talk too much," Tom said. "You fellas want to come inside so I can warm up?"

They followed him inside where he took off his light winter jacket and hung it on a peg beside the door. The inside of his house was as clean and neat as the outside. He offered them a seat on a sofa and sat near them on a large recliner.

"Okay, fellas. What do you want to know? I'll see if I can help or not," Tom said. "I don't have a lot to do today, but when it snows, I shovel walks, clean out driveways, and even shovel off roofs if it snows too much. Those days, I'm way too busy, but it keeps me in groceries."

"Sounds like you have a good job," Jim said.

"I like what I do. I just worry about when I get too old to do this kind of work. But I'm putting money away for when that day comes. Now about Leonardo, I suppose you've been by his place already and discovered that he isn't home."

"That's why we came looking for you," Bo said. "Neighbors mentioned you."

"That's nice," he said. "Well, you won't find Mr. Augur for a while. He told me he was going on a trip and asked if I'd keep a close watch on his place. So I drive by at least once a day, more often twice."

"How long has he been gone?" Jim asked.

"I'm not sure. Just three or four days. He didn't say where he was going," Tom told them.

"What does he do for a living?" Bo asked.

Tom shook his head. "I don't mean to start a rumor, so please don't pass this on, but I think he's into something illegal. Whatever it is, he seems to make good money at it, and yet he drives that small Nissan pickup. I'd think he could afford any car he wanted."

Bo grinned. "Maybe he likes small pickups."

"He must."

"What kind of illegal stuff do you think he does?" Bo asked.

"Again, fellas, I don't want no trouble with the guy. He's a good customer, but . . . I kind of think he might deal in illegal drugs, stolen goods, or something like that. I asked him once what he did for a living, and he told me it was none of my business. That's when I got to wondering. I'm just guessing. I could be way off track."

"He has a cleaning lady too," Bo said. "Do you know her?"

Tom's face went red, and he grinned. "Yeah, I guess I do at that. She's sort of my gal, if you know what I mean. Look how good my house looks in here. Sarah helps me, but she don't charge nothing, and I help her with her snow and her yards. We sort of have an arrangement that works well for both of us."

"You called her Sarah. What's her last name, and where can we find her?" Bo asked.

"Her last name is Lerner. She's a nice woman and not bad to look at either. I tell you what I'll do, fellas; I'll let you follow me to her house. It gives me a good excuse to see her, you know," Tom said with a grin.

Sarah Lerner was in her late forties, and she was short and round with a pretty face and big smile. Although the smile, Bo thought, was mostly for Tom. They asked her much the same questions they'd asked Tom, and her answers were about the same.

"Are you sure Leonardo didn't mention to you where he was going for this trip he claimed to be going on?" Bo asked her.

"He didn't. He took a fair amount of luggage. I know that because I was there cleaning when he carried it out to his pickup," she said.

"Could he still be in the general area?" Bo asked.

"I guess it's possible. But it looked like he wasn't planning to come back anytime soon."

"So you're saying that he packed like he was leaving the area?"

"Looked like it to me," she said. "I don't expect he'll be back very soon."

"Do you ever see the people who come to see him?" Bo asked.

"Well now, that's a good question. Some of them don't look like people that someone with his kind of money would hang out with. Some of them are . . . well . . . not the kind of people I'd want to be around," she responded. "I wouldn't want them in my home. That's for sure."

"Do any of them transact business with him when you're there?" Bo asked.

"I wouldn't know that. He has a nice office in his home. When people come, they go in there, and he shuts the door. I know I'm not supposed to interrupt when he has *guests*, as he calls them."

"Sarah, would you be willing to venture a guess as to what kind of business he might be transacting in his office?" Bo asked.

She looked at Tom, who said, "I already told them what I think. You and I think alike on this."

"Okay, so we do," she responded and turned back to Bo. "I think it's something illegal. I told Tom that sometimes I think I can smell marijuana on the people who come in. I do know that smell."

Tom was nodding. "Most of the people must come at night. At least that's what a couple of neighbors have told me. Sarah sees them more than me because even in the summer when I'm there quite a bit, I may not see them because I'm working in the backyard. It's very big and requires a lot of my time to keep it to the standard that Leonardo likes."

"I just thought of something," Sarah said, her eyes growing slightly wider. "A couple of times I've been there when a guy in a fancy car came to see Leonardo."

"What kind of car?" Bo asked.

"I don't know. You tell him, Tom. You saw the car once. You told me what it was," she said.

"It was a Mercedes," Tom said. "A silver one."

Bo exchanged a glance with Jim, who nodded and gave a tiny smile.

"I don't suppose you heard the man's name?" Bo asked.

She slowly nodded her head, and a mischievous smile appeared. "I wasn't supposed to hear this, but I did. They were just going into the office, and I heard Leonardo call him Mr. Bundra. The other guy spoke rather sharply just as the door shut, but I heard him say, 'My name is Grillo. Don't you ever call me by anything else.' After that, the door was shut, but even though their voices were raised for a minute or two, I couldn't tell what was being said."

CHAPTER TWENTY-THREE

As soon as Bo and Jim were back in the Explorer, Jim said, "Do you want me to see if I can find anyone with the last name of Bundra in any of the databases?"

"Absolutely," Bo said. "Too bad we don't have a first name, but we could try Devonte. Who knows, maybe he only uses a different last name. And while we're at it, I think we should check to see if Leonardo has flown out of any of the major airports in the state or surrounding states."

"Are you thinking what I am?" Jim asked. "Are you wondering if he's still around but just doesn't want his employees to know that? He's looking more like he could be our killer. He was attempting to take over Emil's territory—if what Lucas and Joe said is true."

"Yep. Let's go back to the office and see what we can learn. Who knows. We might find out that Grillo-Bundra may have a record somewhere," Bo said.

The sheriff, in an abundance of caution, had a female deputy move into Ron's house to stay with Nattie while Melia was in the city and Ron in the hospital. Rosina, of her own volition, volunteered to stay there as well. Social services did not offer any reasonable alternatives, and when Ron spoke to Rosina on the phone, he still insisted that his home was Nattie's home as well. With Lucas out of the picture, Nattie was safe now, or at least, that was the hope. It was possible that there could be others who might be a danger to her, but it was not likely.

Melia stayed with her grandfather at the hospital, and Karmen returned home with the promise to come get both of them once Ron was released.

The men who had come to help with Ron's chores turned out to be from his church—The Church of Jesus Christ of Latter-day Saints. And the elders quorum president in the ward assured Rosina that someone would come every day for as long as needed to keep the farm running. Nattie still couldn't believe people could be that nice.

Joe did not try to fool himself. He was going to die, and there was nothing he could do about it. He had not seen his captor since he'd regained consciousness. He was helpless, weak, choking with thirst, and in agonizing pain. Since he was going to die, he wished it would come quickly. What he was going through was unbearable.

The hours ticked by so slowly it seemed like he'd been here in this helpless position for days. In reality, he'd lost track of time. He tried to think of happy things to pass the time. He thought of his dog, Melia, Ron, the farm, and the animals on the farm. Those were all things that had made him content with his life in the past. He also thought of fishing with Bo. But with thoughts of Bo, depression deepened. Bo would be trying to figure out where he was, but that would be useless. No one could find him, at least not before it was too late for him.

Joe tried something he was not any good at; he tried praying. The words that came to his mind were jumbled, but he believed that God would get the gist of it. If nothing else, He would read Joe's mind. God could do that. What Joe was trying to tell his Father in Heaven was that he was sorry for smoking pot, terribly, terribly sorry. And he was begging for forgiveness and asked that since he was to die, to please let it happen soon.

Then he forced his prayer from his own needs. He prayed that Melia and Ron would be okay and that the farm and animals would be taken care of. He asked God to help Bo understand the message he'd tried to send by misspelling words. If Emil's killer was never caught, he prayed that at least his so-called confession would not be believed and that he would not die with people believing he was a murderer.

Eventually, his prayer faded away, and he fell into a deep sleep. In that state, he felt no pain, and his worries vanished.

The killer, disguised and in yet another stolen vehicle, drove slowly past Joe's house and then past the Brady farm as he had done a couple times before. As he'd expected, it was dark at Joe's, but there were vehicles in the yard at the farm. He'd been playing with an idea in his head, and as he drove on down the road past the farm, the idea became firmer.

He laughed out loud at the justice of it all. At least in his mind, it was justice. He knew the cops wouldn't think it was justice, but that didn't bother him. He was untouchable. Joe had confessed to the crime, and there would be no reason not to believe his confession. He—the real killer—was in the clear. He had killed Emil, and he'd killed before too. No one had ever suspected him before, and they wouldn't now.

Later he went back to the old house where Joe was lying bound and wounded on the floor. Maybe he was dead by now. He hoped not. Joe had become a toy to him, a toy to be played with and then slowly allowed to die. He couldn't let him die yet, he decided, if it was not already too late.

Bo and Jim were exhausted, but they'd made some progress. Unfortunately, they had not made progress in figuring out where either Bryan Bayle or Leonardo Augur was hiding out or had fled to. Nor did it involve any progress in the search for Joe, a search that now involved officers in several counties going to abandoned houses and outbuildings. The thought that Joe could be in one was the only thing any of the officers could come up with. It was taking countless hours and tons of manpower, but it was the only course of action anyone in law enforcement could think of.

No, the progress had to do with another, though lesser, suspect. Devonte Grillo's true identity had been discovered through some diligent database searching, both on the computer and through phone calls to many people.

"I think we've got it," Bo said to Jim. "This mystery man who was putting pressure on Emil has to be Devonte Bundra. Apparently he must have felt some attachment to his first name. But that made it easy for us since Bundra is such an uncommon name."

The silver Mercedes was registered under the name Devonte Bundra, as was an address in West Valley City and its utilities. Another vehicle, a pickup truck, was listed under Bundra.

"So now do we go to West Valley City and check out Bundra's house?" Jim asked with a yawn.

"I guess we should," Bo responded. "If he happens to be our killer, we might find Joe there, but I don't think so. We might find the other vehicle, his Dodge Ram, at that location, but I'm not sure how that would help us."

"His arrest record under the name Bundra is rather extensive, but there's nothing recent. I was hoping we would find out he's on parole since we could more easily have him brought in to question him. I'm afraid we struck out there," Jim lamented and not for the first time.

"We'll keep looking and contacting people who may have known him. Who knows. We might get lucky."

"I think the two of us need some sleep so we can think clearer," Jim suggested.

"I'm afraid you're right, although I sure hate to quit working. Joe is out there somewhere. I will never quit looking until we find him, even if he's dead," Bo said. "Let's give ourselves six hours, and then we can decide what our next move will be."

Joe awoke to someone prodding him in the side. He forced his eyes open. They were not covered, and he moved his head enough to see. The killer was wearing cowboy boots. Maybe his suffering was about to end.

"Hey, Joe. Are you awake now?" his tormentor asked.

"Yes," Joe managed to say through his parched throat and dry mouth.

"I'm taking pity on you. I got some water and a sandwich for you. Do you think you can eat?"

Joe was stunned. He'd expected to die at any moment. "I'll . . . try," he managed to choke out.

"Then sit up," the killer ordered.

He couldn't do that. "I . . . can't."

"Oh, Joe, you are such a wimp. I guess I'll have to sit you at the table because you *are* going to eat."

The killer was a big man, and after untying Joe's legs, he managed to get him to his feet and to the table, though it was not the same table Joe had broken the leg off of. It wasn't even the same room. For all Joe knew, it wasn't even the same house.

The hope he'd felt when told he was going to get food and water vanished when, for the first time, his abductor let him see his face. Why would he feed him if he was letting Joe see his face? It made no sense. He knew then that he was going to die because if he didn't, he'd be able to describe this man to the police.

Once at the table, the killer freed Joe's hands as well. He was chuckling when he handed a bottle of water to Joe. Joe was so weak that he couldn't even get the cap off. The killer helped him but said, "If you want a drink, you'll have to do it yourself. I won't hold the bottle to your mouth and feed you like a baby."

It hurt, but Joe forced himself to hold the bottle, and even though he spilled a little, he managed to get some of it in his mouth, and he swallowed it. The relief was wonderful. He drank some more and began to feel a little strength return to him. He finished half the bottle before the killer took it and placed it on the table.

"That's all for now. You need to eat. I brought you a grilled cheese sandwich. Eat it."

Fifteen minutes later, the sandwich was gone and so was the rest of the water. Joe was in terrible pain, but at least he felt stronger. Although, he wasn't strong enough to even think about trying to fight his captor.

"I need medical help," he managed to say as he sat with his hands on the table, his head bent over.

"That won't happen. Just be glad you got to eat and drink some water. I have to leave again. When I come back, maybe you'll feel a little better," the killer said. "Now, let's get those ropes back on you."

Joe didn't have the strength to resist, so he soon found himself once more bound and lying on the floor. The killer left without another word to him. Joe wanted to have hope that he was going to be allowed to live, but he couldn't manage it. Why he'd been given food and water was beyond his comprehension. He feared that he had no future. He once more drifted into an uneasy sleep—the only relief he could get from the excruciating pain.

At her grandfather's insistence, Melia returned home to be with Nattie and to keep an eye on the farm. "I'm going to be okay now," Ron had told her. "I'll be home soon myself, but I want you to go as soon as you can. You're needed more there than you are here with me."

She had argued, but he was insistent, so she obeyed his wishes. Karmen gave her a ride home, and Bo and Jim had both met her at the farmhouse upon her return. Bo explained that they were going to West Valley City. They would have left earlier but decided to wait when Karmen told Bo that she was headed back to Price from Salt Lake with Melia.

"You need to know about a false confession that was mailed to the sheriff with Joe's return address on it," Bo said. He explained how he knew it was something Joe had been forced to write. As he was explaining, Nattie, Karmen, and the female deputy listened in.

"At least it shows that he's alive," Melia said as she rubbed tears from her eyes.

"Yes, it does," Bo agreed. "We're going to let the press know about the letter but not that it's bogus," Bo told them. "If the killer hears that the confession is believed and that new charges are being brought against Joe, he may relax and slip up in a way that helps us find him and Joe."

"Are you really going to charge him with murder again?" Melia asked.

"No, but the press won't know that, so neither will the killer," Bo explained. "You guys keep your eyes open, and don't take any chances. We still don't know for sure that the killer doesn't present a danger to you, Melia, and to you, Nattie, for that matter."

Melia was not comforted by that, but she put on a brave face.

Bo and Jim left for West Valley City shortly before noon. They found the home of Devonte Bundra, and accompanied by a couple of West Valley City officers, they approached the house. No one answered the door, so they canvased the neighborhood to see if anyone had seen him.

They learned that no one had seen him or his car for a couple of days. None of them knew him by the name of Bundra; he was Devonte Grillo to them. That made sense to Bo because Grillo had plenty of reasons not to be known by his real name. That was what had kept them from realizing he was more than just a suspected drug pusher. Once his real past had been uncovered, they knew he was a very dangerous person.

They wanted to go into Devonte's house but did not have enough probable cause to get a search warrant. The only thing they gained from the time spent there was a promise from several neighbors that they would call Bo if they saw Bundra, or Grillo as they knew him, or even his car or his pickup. Disappointed, the two officers headed back to Price.

As they were driving down the freeway toward Spanish Fork, Bo got a call from Sheriff Hermock. "We just got a break," he told the officers. "Bryan Bayle was just picked up in Salt Lake. He got in an argument with someone at a gas station. Someone else called it in, and officers went there. By then, Bayle had assaulted the other customer and was arrested. He's at the Salt Lake County jail now."

"We'll turn and head back that way," Bo said. "What have they done with his vehicle?"

"He was driving a stolen car, one taken from a parking lot right here in Price this morning," Sheriff Hermock said. "Apparently, he's changed his look, but there's no question it's him. Let me know what you learn. The Price police are working to get him brought back here to face murder charges, but they agreed that since you two were in the area, they would like you to bring him back."

"We'd love to," Bo told him as he took an exit so he could head north again. "If he'll talk to us, we'll question him before we head that way. If he's our killer, and there's a good chance he is, then he should know where Joe is."

"The police in Price are okay with you doing that, but they don't want you to question him about the murders of his brother or wife or the stolen car. Of course, if he offers some information without you asking about it, that will be okay," the sheriff said.

Bryan spoke with a lisp, leaving no doubt about who he was, although he'd had no ID on him when he was arrested. He certainly didn't look like the photos the Price police had obtained that showed him with long, dirty-brown hair and a long, scruffy beard. He was now clean-shaven and had a shaved head. Still, the shape of his round face and his heavy body and that distinct lisp left no doubt as to his identity.

His fingerprints had been taken at the jail, and when they were run through the system, they matched Bryan Bayle. Once he realized his identity had been established, he began to blab.

All Bryan Bayle wanted to talk about was his wife. He didn't mention his brother at all. He apparently did not realize that his brother's body had been found buried in his backyard. He was under the mistaken impression that the only reason he had been arrested was the stolen car, which he admitted to without a single question being asked. As for his wife, he blurted out—without the officers even asking—that someone had killed his wife, but it wasn't him.

"We are here to talk to you about a separate matter," Bo told him, ignoring what Bryan had just said about his wife. "We are investigating the murder of Emil Eifler, your drug supplier. And don't tell us he wasn't your supplier, because we know he was. If you will recall, you told us he took your stuff at gunpoint."

"Oh yeah, he was a nasty character. But if you're gonna say I killed him, you'll be wrong. I didn't like the guy, but I never killed anybody ever."

That was a lie, but Bo let it go. The officers from Price City could deal with that. "Tell us where you took Joe Whalen," Bo said, attempting to catch him off balance.

"Oh, him? Wasn't he the one who killed Emil? If he was, why are you pestering me about it?" he asked.

Bo pursued a few more questions about Joe's location, but he got nowhere, and outside of Bryan's presence, he and Jim discussed what they'd learned. "I don't think he took Joe," Jim said.

"I think you're right. But if not, then he's probably not Emil's killer either. Despite that, I don't feel comfortable in ruling him out just yet. Maybe when the officers in Price speak with him about his brother, he'll realize he's in pretty deep trouble and confess to killing Emil."

"Maybe," Jim agreed, but Bo could tell that they were both skeptical about that happening.

"Let's load him up and head home," Bo said.

CHAPTER TWENTY-FOUR

Several more hours had passed, and the relief Joe had felt from the single bottle of water and one grilled cheese sandwich had worn off. He was getting more dehydrated by the hour, and his pain level, which he had thought earlier was unbearable, constantly crept upward. It was especially bad where the bullets had struck him in the back and in one shoulder. He was quite sure that the bullet that had entered his back had not come out and that it was responsible for much of the internal pain he was experiencing. He wondered what kind of damage had been done inside his body, not that it mattered at this point. Without medical attention, he was doomed to die. He accepted that fact, looking forward to it as a relief from his intense suffering.

Joe's mind remained active despite the pain, and he kept thinking back over what had happened to him since his fishing trip with Bo. Over and over again he blamed himself for all of his troubles, including his impending death. He was sure there was infection in both his back and shoulder, and that would only make things worse. He honestly did not know how he could possibly stand any more pain.

He heard a door open. The killer came in, making no effort to keep his face from Joe's view when he looked up from the floor. If ever given the chance, Joe could easily describe his abductor, but he didn't expect that chance.

His abductor came slowly across the floor to where Joe lay helpless and in agony. "Okay, Joe. It's dark outside and quite late, in fact. It's time for me to take you for a ride. Get up and let's go."

Joe said nothing. He couldn't have spoken now even if he wanted to, at least not clearly enough to be understood. His throat was so sore that he could barely suck air through it, let alone talk coherently. If his abductor was going to take him someplace else to die, there was really nothing he could do about it, but he wasn't going to make it easier for the guy if he could help it.

"So you aren't going to cooperate, Joe?" the wicked man said with a deep chuckle. "Very well then, I guess I'll have to carry you."

Rough hands grabbed him beneath his arms, and despite his sore, swollen throat, Joe managed a weak scream. He couldn't help it. The pain was appalling.

"Shut up!"

He tried, but for a minute or two, he simply could not stop. If he could only die, it would be such a relief.

"I said shut up!" his abductor shouted. "You are only going to make this worse on yourself."

Joe wasn't sure how it could be worse, but he really didn't want to know, so he managed out of sheer desperation to stop the flow of painful screams.

"That's better. Now we're going for a ride, Joe. And if you make an attempt to scream once you're in my car, I will give you more reason to scream. The sheriff knows now that you killed Emil, and charges for murder have been brought against you. So your future is set. If I were to let you go, you would spend the rest of your worthless life in prison," the killer said with a chuckle.

The guy hoisted Joe onto his shoulders and lugged him toward the door. Joe wished if he couldn't die right then, that at least he could pass out. But that didn't happen.

The killer kept talking as they went out the door. "It's all over the papers, on the radio, and on TV about how you confessed by sending a note to the sheriff. The law is searching for you all over the state and all the neighboring states. A warrant for your arrest has been issued. Trust me, the police and the prosecutors believe what you wrote." He chuckled again and then said nothing more until he'd packed Joe into a vehicle of some kind. Joe's eyes were stinging now, and he couldn't open them, so he couldn't see what model of car he was being put into. But he was pretty sure it was the back seat of whatever the killer was driving.

His abductor covered him with something, perhaps a blanket or a tarp, and then spoke again. "We have a bit of a drive ahead of us, Joe, so relax. I don't expect to get stopped by a cop, but just in case, I don't want anyone to look back there and see you. That's why I covered you. Now enjoy the ride the best you can, for I have decided that this will be your last one. I am going to deliver you to the fate that awaits you."

As the killer slammed the door shut, he was laughing. A moment later, Joe felt the vehicle rock slightly as the killer got in the front. Then the engine started, and Joe's last ride began. He had no idea what the fate that awaited him was. Probably death, although the killer was an arrogant person. Perhaps he would actually deliver Joe to the sheriff in some way, hoping that he would stand trial for Emil's murder and he could be free and satisfied with his work while the press had a heyday over Joe's demise.

Joe didn't think he could hang on much longer, and he was right. As the vehicle jostled on what had to be a rough road, it was more than Joe could take. Blessed darkness finally took over.

He had no idea how much time had passed when he awoke to the pain and the motion of the car. He felt it slow and turn. There was the crunch of gravel beneath the tires. The car stopped, and the killer stepped out. He was gone for what could have been two or three minutes, then he got back in, chuckling. "That was fun," he said, but he did not say what he'd done. "Now we are going to take you to where I plan to leave you, Joe, if you can hear me. It will be someplace that you may never be found. I hadn't originally planned to let you die, but since you tried to bash me and hurt both my knees so that I had to shoot you to keep you from getting away, you made me rethink things. One thing is for sure; they know you killed Emil, and so I will never be suspected. Oh, but life can be good." He laughed again as the car pulled back onto the road. "You should never have tried to get away from me."

Joe knew his death was close, but he would welcome it. The pain that he'd thought to be unbearable before was worse than ever now. He simply didn't see how he could take much more. Perhaps, when they got to wherever the guy was going to leave him, he'd shoot Joe and take him out of his misery.

The next time the car stopped, the killer dragged Joe out, and when he hit the ground, he blacked out once again.

Melia tossed and turned that night in her own bed at her grandfather's house. She had watched the news with Nattie while Deputy Reingold, a really nice lady, kept watch both inside and outside of the house. The lead story was the extensive manhunt that had been launched for the cunning young killer, Joe Whalen. The story hurt even though Bo had assured her that the confession was not believed by him or the sheriff or the prosecutors.

She and Nattie had both been warned not to say anything to anyone that might reveal the deception that was being played in an attempt to lure out the real killer. Apparently, Bo and the others believed that once the killer was satisfied that Joe was the only one being focused on, he would let his guard down.

Bo had even said, "Whoever it is will want to see his handiwork carried out by the large manhunt."

His partner, Jim Grizzel, had added, "Arsonists start fires but often stick around to see them burn. It's part of their mental makeup. We believe that the same may be true of this person, whoever he is. He may even want to see Joe captured and put on trial."

"What if it's that Bayle guy?" Melia said. "He's in jail and charged with other murders. If he was the one that kidnapped Joe, then Joe is probably dead and will never be found."

Both officers had agreed, but she got the feeling that they didn't think it was Bryan Bayle who had murdered Emil and kidnapped Joe. They didn't say who else they thought it might be though. As she tossed and turned, she kept praying that Joe would be found alive and that he would be okay. She had come to care for him quite deeply, and she couldn't imagine going on with the work at the farm without him. She also prayed for her wonderful grandfather's full recovery. She didn't want to lose him, but he seemed to be doing okay now. It had been a close call. The doctors had told her that.

Melia wanted to go to sleep, but her active mind wouldn't allow it. She finally gave up, got out of bed, and wandered downstairs. The deputy currently assigned to keep an eye on the Brady household was standing near the living room window, peering out. She turned as Melia reached the bottom of the stairs. "Can't you sleep?" Deputy Reingold asked, her voice full of sympathy.

"No, so I thought I'd get a glass of warm milk and see if that would help. That's what my grandpa does," Melia said.

"That sounds like a good idea," the deputy said.

"Is there something outside? Did you hear something?" Melia asked, concerned by the fact that the deputy had been looking through parted drapes.

"It was probably just someone who was lost. A car drove in a while ago, turned around, and then left. That's all."

Melia couldn't have been more wide awake after that bit of news. It alarmed her. "What did the car look like?" she asked as she approached the window and parted the drapes herself.

"It's gone now," Deputy Reingold said. "There's nothing more to see. I did get a good look at it under the yard light. It was sort of a gold color, not too new, but in good shape from what I could see."

"What make was it?" Melia asked.

"I don't know. I didn't get that good of a look at it."

"How long was it out there?" Melia persisted, unable to mask the concern in her voice. The sweet deputy put an arm around Melia's shoulders. "Did you see it come into the yard?"

"No, I heard it, then it was quiet for a minute or two, and I thought I'd imagined it. But then your dogs started barking, and a moment later, I heard the car again, so I decided I should look out through the window. It was just leaving the yard," Deputy Reingold said. "I don't think it's anything to worry about. As soon as it was gone, the dogs stopped barking."

"Probably not," Melia said, but she worried anyway.

"You need to go warm up some milk and go back to bed," the deputy told her. "I'll keep watching here at the window."

"Okay, thanks," Melia said, but her unrest had only gotten worse. There was no way that she would be able to sleep now, warm milk or not.

A minute later, as the milk warmed in the microwave, Karmen and Nattie both entered the kitchen as well. "I heard you and Deputy Reingold talking. I was wide awake, so I thought I'd come down and see what was going on," Karmen said.

"I was awake too," Nattie said. "For some reason, my baby seems restless tonight. It keeps kicking in here." She patted her large abdomen. "When I heard Karmen's door open, I decided to join her. Now all of us are down here."

"I guess we could have a party," Melia said, trying to lighten her own mood as she pulled her milk from the microwave.

"Or we could watch a movie," Karmen suggested, "since none of us is in the mood to party." She smiled at Melia as she spoke.

Melia smiled back. "Actually, that might be a good idea. Maybe if we pick a boring one, it will put us all to sleep."

"What's the warm milk for?" Nattie asked.

Melia explained and then added, "But I don't think it'll help. I just wish I knew who drove into the yard a little while ago and then left. That's what Deputy Reingold and I were talking about."

"Do people often just drive in here and turn around like that?" Karmen asked.

"Not really. I mean, we are close to the road, and it's clearly not another road coming in here, just a short lane, and you can see that it ends right here easily enough," Melia answered.

"I think I'll talk to Deputy Reingold," Karmen said.

When the three of them went into the living room, the deputy was once again peering through the drapes. "Did it come back?" Melia asked.

"No, but I've been thinking. This isn't a place people would likely drive into and out again as close to the main road as it is," she said.

"That's what we were just talking about in the kitchen," Karmen said. "Maybe we should go out and have a look around."

"I don't know if I like that idea very much," the deputy said.

"I don't either," Nattie agreed.

"Well I do," Melia said. "Maybe you and I could go out while these guys wait in the house."

"If you guys go, we all go," Karmen declared. "And we'll go carrying guns."

They discussed the idea briefly but finally decided they should do it. "I don't know what we would be looking for," Deputy Reingold said.

"I don't either," Karmen agreed. "But like Bo tells me, sometimes you don't know what you're looking for until you see it."

So they went out, each with a firearm and a flashlight. Ace ran right to them. Herc, limping badly, followed. "You still hurting?" Melia asked as she patted him fondly on the head.

Herc whined and looked toward the road, then walked a few steps in that direction. "I think he wonders what the car was doing in here just like we were," Melia suggested.

The four ladies walked over to the barn, looked inside, walked around the corrals and barns, and then returned to the yard. They even looked in the garage. They found nothing, but Herc's strange behavior worried all of them. "I don't like the way Herc is acting," Melia said. "Something about that car bothered him. He keeps walking toward the road."

"I'll tell you what I'll do," Deputy Reingold said. "It may be possible to see fresh tracks in the road past where the gravel ends. If we can see something, I'll take a picture or two with my phone. We could let Detective Buckley look at them in the morning if we even find something. I'm not sure what good it would do, but it can't hurt."

They did find some that were in a spot at the edge of the road where there was still a skiff of snow remaining. The deputy took some pictures, and they looked some more, but there was nothing more that could be identified. "There have been a lot of vehicles in and out of here lately, but maybe whoever made these was drunk and nearly ran off the road," Deputy Reingold said.

"Maybe," Karmen agreed. Melia said nothing as a thought she'd had an hour ago while lying in her bed came to her mind. She'd dismissed it then, but now it made her think.

They started walking the hundred yards back to the yard with Ron's dog, Ace, trotting alongside them. Herc, who had barely made it to where they were, stepped in front of Melia and whined. She reached down and petted him. "You're hurting pretty badly still, aren't you, Herc?" she said. She shined her flashlight on him, and he looked up at her, then he turned and faced the road and barked.

"For some reason, he seems upset by that car coming in here," the deputy said. "That's the only thing I can think of that's making him act like this."

"Maybe it's just because he remembers a strange car coming to his place and hauling him off and shooting him," Melia said. "Or maybe he just wants to go home, thinking Joe's there. I mean, who knows what's in a dog's mind."

They walked the rest of the way back to the yard.

"While we're out here, I want to get something from my car," Karmen said. She didn't say what it was, but the others waited while she walked to where she'd parked beside Ron's garage, alongside Deputy Reingold's patrol car. She suddenly screamed, and the deputy led a fast charge toward her.

"What's wrong?" Deputy Reingold asked.

"My tires. Two of them are flat, and it was done on purpose," Karmen said in frustration as she shined her light to show the rest of them.

Deputy Reingold looked closer. "Someone put a knife in them," she said. She then turned her light onto her car and found that it also had two flat tires.

"We'd better look at Grandpa's truck," Melia suggested as a shiver of fear shook her.

It was in the garage, but the door had been left open, and two tires had also been flattened on it. "Let's get back in the house," the deputy said. "I don't like the feel of this."

They hurried back, and the dogs, with Herc limping, followed clear to the door. Back inside, they locked the door again, and out of an abundance of caution, they checked the other doors and windows. The living room window was new, as was the one on the kitchen side of the house that had been shattered when the tear gas had been fired inside to end the standoff with Lucas. They were a newer type of window, but they were locked.

"I think we should call Detective Buckley," Deputy Reingold said. "He'll want to come see what's happened."

CHAPTER TWENTY-FIVE

Bo awoke to the ringing of his cell phone, something that happened too much since his promotion to detective. His heart jumped when he saw it was Karmen calling. He knew she was at the Brady farm, and for her to call at this time of night was not a good omen. He sprang from his bed as he put the phone to his ear.

"Hi, Karmen," he said, trying to keep the concern from his voice.

"Bo, we need you out here. Someone drove in the yard and cut the tires on all of the cars. We're really worried," she said.

Her voice carried a tone of something more than worry. Fear, maybe? "I'll come right out. Are you all okay other than the worry?" he asked.

"Yes. We are all in the living room. Deputy Reingold is checking all the windows regularly," she answered.

Bo was getting dressed as he talked on the phone. "So you went outside?"

"Yeah, the dogs were kind of excited, especially Herc. We were concerned that something had been done, but we didn't expect slashed tires! Deputy Reingold got some pictures of some tracks you will want to look at."

"Okay, I'm coming. Call me back if anything else happens." Bo ended the call, and in another minute, he and his bulldog were on their way. He pulled in close to the yard gate and hurried up the walk. Deputy Reingold had the door open by the time he reached it. She locked it after he'd entered the house. "Okay, ladies. Tell me all about it," he said calmly. He listened, they talked, and he looked at the pictures of the car tracks. "This is all really strange," he said. "Clearly, you guys can't drive anywhere until some tires are brought out. But why would someone do that?" he asked as he tried to wrap his mind around such a strange thing. "We'll take care of the tires as soon as some tire shops are open. For now, you'll need to stay here, and I mean in the house. Don't go out again. I want to look at the tire tracks for myself. You guys don't need to come. I'll find them." Then he noticed that Melia was strangely quiet. "Melia, are you okay?"

"I just keep thinking about a bad dream I had," she said. "I'm okay though."

Bo looked at her for a moment. She didn't sound okay, but she was probably just very scared, and that was understandable. "All right, I'll be back. I'm going to take a look around out there myself."

Karmen had mentioned Herc's strange behavior, and as he walked toward the road, the injured dog tried to keep up with him, whining the whole time. He picked the dog up.

"Hey, old boy. Are you having a rough night?"

Herc whined some more. Bo put him down when he reached the road. He found the tracks Deputy Reingold had told him about and took his own pictures, although he couldn't imagine how they might help. When he started back toward the farmyard, Herc barked and started limping up the road. "Hey, Herc. Come back here," he said. But the collie kept going until he caught up with Herc and picked him up again.

As Bo carried him back to the yard, he was trying to figure out what Herc was trying to tell him. It was only when Melia told him a few minutes later that she wanted to go to Joe's house that an idea formed in his mind.

"Joe's truck is at his house. I know this sounds lame, but I think we should see if his tires are flattened too," she said. "I don't know why, but I really want to go there." She had a strange look on her face, something he could not define.

That made up Bo's mind. "Deputy," he said to Deputy Reingold, "I'm taking Melia with me. The rest of you stay here. Let me know if you see or hear anything, and I'll come right back."

When he and Melia reached his truck, where Two Face was still in the back seat, Herc barked and looked toward the road, limping in that direction again. "Can we take Herc?" Melia asked.

"I think that's a good idea," Bo agreed. He lifted Herc into the back seat with the bulldog, and they headed for Joe's house.

Joe woke again. He couldn't believe he wasn't dead. He was curled in a fetal position. He could feel the ropes binding him. When he tried to move, he simply couldn't. He had no idea where he was, but the stench was bad. He assumed it was from his infected wounds. Surely he wouldn't live much longer.

He recalled hearing the killer's voice sometime earlier. He was pretty sure the man had said that he was taking Joe to a place that they'd never find him. The last thing he remembered was the killer pulling him out of the car and his head thumping on the ground. And then he'd passed out again. There was no way of knowing how long ago that was. It could have been a few minutes or a few hours. But it didn't matter. He just craved for this pain and misery to end. Surely it wouldn't be long now.

Joe's truck was still parked in his driveway, and all of the tires were inflated. "Well, now we know his tires are okay. Let's get back to the farm," Bo said.

"No, I want to go in. I don't know why, but I do," Melia said stubbornly.

"Okay, but I don't see what good that will do," Bo told her.

"It's that dream I had," she said, again feeling that it wasn't a dream but something else.

Herc began to bark. "He misses Joe, and bringing him here only makes it worse for him," Bo said. "Maybe this wasn't such a good idea."

"Please, can't we go inside for a minute or two? Maybe when Herc sees that Joe isn't here, he'll settle down," Melia said in a pleading voice.

"You may have a point there," Bo said. "Let's go around back. And we'll let both dogs come with us."

Herc limped right to the front door and barked frantically. "Come on, Herc," Bo said. "Let's go around back. This door is locked."

Herc ignored him, and to Bo's surprise, Two Face joined him at the front door, and he too barked. "What's with these dogs?" Bo asked as he and Melia walked up to the front door.

Melia grabbed the door handle. To her surprise, it turned, and the door opened. Both dogs rushed past her, barking loudly, and began to run around the living room, their noses to the floor. "Someone's been here," Bo said as he flipped the light switch on. "I know that door was locked."

Melia watched the dogs, and her dream, or whatever it was, came back to her. She felt a lurch in her stomach. Something was wrong here. She was sure of it. And she had been meant to come. The dream wasn't a dream, she decided. It was a prompting. She knew that now. What she didn't know was why.

The dogs were sniffing the floor. Then they both entered the hallway. She and Bo followed them. Melia expected them to go to Joe's bedroom, but they didn't. They went to the closed door of the spare bedroom. Both dogs barked loudly, and they scratched at the door.

Melia looked at Bo. His brow was wrinkled in concern. "Melia, I'll open the door. You stand back."

She did that, and both dogs rushed in. They went straight to the large trunk, where they went crazy, barking and lunging at the chest.

"Open it, Bo," Melia said as the prompting she'd felt became clearer to her.

Joe was conscious of dogs barking, and his tortured mind went to his beloved Herc. As the barking drew closer, a strange feeling of euphoria came over his riddled body. That sounded like Herc, and the deeper bark resembled Two Face. It couldn't be, but maybe it was just his imagination helping him to have a pleasant death. He thought he heard voices too, but that was just too much. Suddenly, light flooded over him, and for a moment, he thought he was finally dying.

Someone screamed. At first, he thought it was him that was screaming. The screams stopped as a voice that was very familiar said, "Joe's alive, Melia. Call 911 and get an ambulance on the way. I'll see if I can get him out of here and onto the bed."

It was then that Joe realized he was not dead, that despite what the killer had said, he'd been found. He was in some kind of large box. Where was it that Bo and Melia had been able to find it? He tried to wriggle, but a firm hand touched his injured shoulder.

"Joe, it's Bo. Just relax and let me do the work. I'll get you out of here. This is a tighter fit for you than it was for Emil."

That statement made no sense to Joe, and he gave it no real thought. As Bo began to lift him, the pain was so bad that blackness once again overcame him.

Melia had stepped out of the room to make her call, her heart pounding unmercifully in her chest. She stepped back in as Bo was lifting Joe from the trunk. Tears stained her cheeks. She cried harder when Bo got him stretched out on the bare mattress of the single bed. Joe smelled awful, but she forced herself to endure it. He looked even worse. "What happened to him, Bo?" she asked, her heart aching for her friend.

"He's been shot. I need to roll him onto his good shoulder because I think he's been shot in the back as well as his shoulder."

Bo was right. Melia knelt beside the bed and touched the pale face of her best friend. His skin was cool but not cold. "An ambulance is on the way," she mumbled as Herc forced his way beside her and began to lick Joe's face.

"I need to see if there's anything I can do for him before it gets here," Bo said. "These wounds are old, and infection has set in. I hope that ambulance hurries."

Melia continued to touch Joe's face as Bo carefully removed the cloth from around the wound on his shoulder. "Herc knew, didn't he?" she asked.

"Knew what?" Bo asked.

"He knew that Joe had been in that car that came into the yard. And he knew it had come this way," she said.

"I think you're right," Bo said. "He's a smart dog."

"I think I knew too," she said with a lump in her throat.

Bo glanced at her. "I think you really did."

"Is he going to live?" Melia asked in a hoarse voice.

Bo glanced at her. "Your face is white, but cheer up. I think that he'll live. Why else would you and Herc have been inspired to come here?" he said. "He wouldn't have lived much longer in that trunk, though. What was the killer thinking?"

When Joe woke next, there was still pain, but nothing like what he'd been enduring. It didn't take him long to realize he was in a hospital. He was propped on one side. After thinking for a little while, he realized why. He was lying on the side opposite his injured shoulder to stay off that bullet wound and the one in his back.

"Joe," a sweet voice said, "are you awake?" Melia stepped up to the head of his bed and came into view.

"Hi," he said, his voice raspy but usable again.

"It's good to see you, Joe. You gave us all a scare."

"It wasn't intentional," he said with a weak smile. "How long have I been here?"

"A day and a half," she said. "How are you feeling?"

"Not great but a lot better than when I thought I was going to die. I actually wanted to because it hurt so badly, but now I'm glad I'm still alive," he said.

"Hi, big brother," Rosina said as she too stepped to the head of the bed. "I just called Bo. He wanted to know as soon as you woke up. I think he has some questions for you."

"I hope I have some answers," Joe responded with a hint of a grin.

When Bo got there, he got right down to business. "We got your confession, Joe," he said. "That was smart what you did. We knew right away that you'd been forced to write it."

"I figured you'd know," Joe said.

"Just for your information, we have not released the fact that you were found and are alive. I'm hoping you can give me enough information to figure out who did this to you," Bo said.

"It was the guy who killed Emil," Joe told him.

"I figured it must have been. Did he admit it to you?"

"Yes, he laughed about it."

"Did you see him?"

"Not at first, but I guess when he decided that he wanted me to die, he let me see his face. He said that I would die someplace where no one would ever find me. How *did* you find me?"

"Thank your two best friends, Herc and Melia," Bo said with a grin. Then he, with Melia's help, explained what had happened.

"I guess that man underestimated the power of strong friendships," Joe said. "He's probably someone who has no friends."

"Tell me about him, and describe him the best you can," Bo said.

"He wears cowboy boots," Joe said. "He's maybe four inches taller than me. He's not fat, but I think he weighs at least two hundred pounds. He's very strong and has a stocky build. He has black hair, which he wears combed straight back from his forehead. His eyes looked black to me, and he has a narrow face and bushy eyebrows."

"That's a good description," Bo said as he met his partner's eyes. Jim had joined them there in the hospital room only moments before. "What about a beard?"

"Yeah. It's not very long, and he has a moustache. I think he keeps them trimmed pretty well. When I saw him, he was wearing blue jeans and a western shirt," Joe added.

"I have some pictures here. If I show them to you, can you tell us if any of them are this guy?" Bo asked.

"I'm pretty sure I can," Joe said. "Oh, and he may have a bruise on his face and be limping. Before he shot me, I hit him pretty hard in the face, and I kicked both knees."

Bo searched on his phone for a moment. "I'm going to show you several pictures. I'll go slow, and you look at each one carefully. Tell me if one of them looks like him."

Bo had only shown him one picture when his phone rang. "It's not that guy," Joe said as Bo stepped back and answered his phone.

Bo listened for a moment, and then he said, "Is that for sure, Sheriff?" he listened a little more, and then he told Sheriff Hermock, "Joe is just looking at pictures of the suspects. I'll get back to you as soon as we think we know who it is."

Joe looked at the second picture when Bo showed him his phone screen again. "Not him, but I've met him. He was one of Emil's customers." He then looked at a third picture. "Not him either, but I can tell you about him." As soon as the fourth picture was shown to Joe, he said, "That's the guy."

"Are you sure?" Bo pressed.

"Positive," Joe answered. "But I don't know his name or anything about him."

"We do, don't we, Jim?" Bo said as he showed that last picture to his partner.

"Never had the pleasure of meeting him," Jim said with an exaggerated drawl. "But we know who he is all right."

They told Joe his name, and he knew then who the guy was and why he had killed Emil Eifler. Devonte Grillo-Bundra was almost undoubtedly Emil's supplier.

As soon as Bo and Jim left the hospital, which was very quickly after Joe had identified the killer, Jim asked Bo, "What was the call from the sheriff about?"

Bo chuckled. "One of our suspects was arrested in LA this morning."

"Tell me it was Devonte Bundra," Jim said.

"I wish. No, it was Leonardo Augur. I have no idea what he was doing there, but he apparently got in a scuffle in the airport and ended up seriously injuring a man. He's in jail now."

Jim chuckled. "That's the kind of behavior that got Bryan Bayle arrested. Crooks can be so stupid sometimes. I'm glad they got him, but we still don't know where Devonte is," Jim said. "When he finds out that Joe is alive and that we're not really charging him with murder, he may come after Joe again, and that's very concerning, Bo. We know he's good at disguising himself, like he did when he visited Gus Hammond at the jail to order him to beat Joe up."

"I think we need to figure out a way to bring him out of the shadows. That might best be done by revealing that we have found Joe and that he can identify his abductor," Bo suggested.

"It goes without saying that if we do that, we need to keep Joe safe," Jim said.

"Of course. And where better to keep him safe than in jail?" Bo said with a grin.

"You're kidding. Hammond's been charged with assault on a prisoner since his attack on Joe," Jim said. "I'm sure he'd love to get another whack at him."

Bo nodded. "We won't really keep him there, but we can let it be known that he is patched up from some wounds and is there awaiting court dates for the murder charges."

"And you believe that will get Devonte to come to the jail," Jim said. "But how will we know him? Remember, he is good at disguises."

"He is, but I think we can figure him out anyway. We know what he looked like the day he visited Hammond from the video at the jail. Who knows. Maybe he will try the same disguise. And if not, we know his size and build. I think we can figure him out. If he goes there," Bo reasoned, "he will be trying to get Joe killed. I would say that it's very likely he will think that he can see Gus Hammond again. We'll get him when he, whatever he looks likes, comes to visit Hammond."

"It's worth a try," Jim said, "as long as Joe is safe."

"Hey, Joe's my cousin. I would never take a chance on letting him get hurt again."

CHAPTER TWENTY-SIX

THEY NEVER HAD TO REVEAL that Joe had been found and was in jail because an hour after leaving the hospital, as Bo and Jim were briefing the sheriff, Bo got a call. The caller, who did not identify herself, simply told Bo that Devonte Grillo was home. She agreed to keep an eye on the house and to let Bo know if he left. She also stated that he had driven right into his garage in his silver Mercedes.

As soon as Bo told the sheriff and Jim what the call was about, Jim said, "He's pretty sure of himself."

"If Joe had died, we wouldn't have had a thing to go on. We could have picked him up for questioning, but he would have had no reason to cooperate or admit anything," Bo said.

"I'll go with you two," the sheriff said as he grabbed his hat. "But first, let's call the West Valley police and have them keep an eye on the place and let us know if Devonte tries to leave and ask them to detain him if he does."

As soon as that was done, they headed for West Valley City in Bo's Explorer. "Will they have someone stake his house out?" Bo asked as soon as they were on the road.

"I talked to the police chief. He said they would do better than that. He's putting a SWAT team on standby, ready to move at a moment's notice. He'll have several officers watch the house in addition to that."

The three officers made good time, and they let the police chief know as soon as they were in Devonte's neighborhood in West Valley City. The SWAT team assembled out of sight a block away, and then Bo, Jim, and the sheriff approached the door. There was no response to either the doorbell or their knocks.

Bo's phone rang, and the same anonymous caller told him that Devonte was still in the house. The police chief, when they joined his officers a block away, made the same assurance. They discussed their options and decided to go ahead and use the SWAT team. They would have them surround the house, and they would use a bullhorn to order Devonte to surrender if he didn't answer the doorbell after another attempt.

They all moved very quickly, and when everyone was set, Bo and a West Valley officer approached the front door. Bo rang the bell. He and the other officer held their weapons ready and stood back at either side of the door. To Bo's surprise, Devonte opened the door a few inches and said, "What do you guys want?"

"Devonte Bundra, we need to talk to you," Bo said.

"I don't know anyone by that name. My name's Grillo, and I haven't done anything wrong," he said, his dark eyes looking as belligerent as his voice sounded. "So you can tell those officers out there to get lost."

"Come on out, and we'll talk about it, or we can come in if you prefer," Bo offered.

"You tell me what it's about, and then I'll decide," he said. "But you got the wrong guy."

"Not according to Joe Whalen, we don't," Bo said.

Devonte's face went white, and he slammed the door shut. "I guess he wants to do this the hard way," Bo said, and the two officers retreated behind the SWAT line. He then used a bullhorn and called out Devonte's name. "Come out, Devonte. You are wanted for the murder of Emil Eifler and the kidnapping and attempted murder of Joe Whalen. Surrender now."

Nothing happened for a full minute. Bo was just ready to speak through the bullhorn again when suddenly, the garage door flew apart, and a silver Mercedes backed out so fast that it was all some of the SWAT officers directly in its path could do to scramble to safety. Devonte actually hit two of them, knocking them to the ground. Then the car smashed into a parked police vehicle.

The suspect was trying to drive forward, but another police vehicle, an armored truck, pulled in front of his car, blocking his path. He shoved a gun out of his window but was hit with a Taser before he could fire a shot at anyone. From there it was easy. Emil's killer was in custody.

Joe and Ron recovered together in Ron's farmhouse, attended to by Melia and Nattie. Before their recovery was complete, they were joined by a little girl that Nattie named Josephine and who she nicknamed Joey. Joe was strong enough to resume the work before summer arrived, and Ron, his heart in the best shape it had been for years after his surgery, was able to do some of the work.

Nattie, after a couple of months, was approached by her parents and told that she could come home and bring their little granddaughter. Her father didn't seem terribly excited about the idea, but her mother had taken control, and she was not about to let that grandbaby grow up without her loving grandmother. Nattie agreed to visit regularly, but she was content for the time being to stay in the big farmhouse in Carbon County where she had felt more welcome than anywhere else at any time in her life.

After he was strong enough, Joe proudly wore his DI Sunday best to church every week. Melia, who turned twenty in April, always sat beside him, and no young men in the ward dared make the attempt to ask her out.

She was present with a big smile on her face when Joe was baptized. She hugged him, and he hugged her back tightly. "I'd have never done this if it hadn't been for you. I didn't realize how badly I needed the Church. Thank you for introducing me to the gospel. It has changed my life. I love you, Melia," he said.

She grinned. "And I love you."

Later, in the hallway as people were drifting out, he said to Melia, "I spoke with your grandfather."

"About what?" she asked.

"I asked his permission for something, and he told me that it would be okay with him."

"Permission for what?" she asked, her eyes bright with anticipation.

"I'll tell you later," Joe said with a grin. "This isn't the time or the place. But I think you'll like it. I hope you will."

That was all he was going to tell her for now, for he hadn't yet bought a ring.

ABOUT THE AUTHOR

Clair M. Poulson was born and raised in Duchesne, Utah. His father was a rancher and farmer, his mother a librarian. Clair has always been an avid reader, having found his love for books as a very young boy.

He has served for more than forty years in the criminal justice system. He spent twenty years in law enforcement, ending his police career with eight years as the Duchesne County Sheriff. For the past twenty-plus years, Clair has worked as a justice court judge for Duchesne County. He is also a veteran of the U.S. Army, where he was a military policeman. In law enforcement, he has been personally involved in the investigation of murders and other violent crimes. Clair has also served on various boards and councils during his professional career, including the Justice Court Board of Judges, the Utah Commission on Criminal and Juvenile Justice, the Utah Judicial Council, the Utah Peace Officer Standards and Training Council, an FBI advisory board, and others.

In addition to his criminal justice work, Clair has farmed and ranched all his life. He has raised many kinds of animals, but his greatest interests are horses and cattle. He's also involved in the grocery store business with his oldest son and other family members.

Clair has served in many capacities in The Church of Jesus Christ of Latter-day Saints, including full-time missionary (California Mission), bishop, counselor to two bishops, Young Men president, high councilor, stake mission president, Scoutmaster, high priest group leader, and Gospel Doctrine teacher. He currently serves as a ward missionary.

Clair is married to Ruth, and they have five children, all of whom are married: Alan (Vicena) Poulson, Kelly Ann (Wade) Hatch, Amanda (Ben) Semadeni, Wade (Brooke) Poulson, and Mary (Tyler) Hicken.

They also have twenty-six wonderful grandchildren and three great-grandchildren.

Clair and Ruth met while both were students at Snow College and were married in the Manti Utah Temple.

Clair has always loved telling his children, and later his grandchildren, made-up stories. His vast experience in life and his love of literature have contributed to both his telling stories to his children and his writing of adventure and suspense novels.

Clair has published over forty novels. He would love to hear from his fans, who can contact him by going to his website, clairmpoulson.com.